# IN PLAIN SIGHT

## TONYA SHARP HYCHE

## Novels by Tonya

*Trick Play*
*Data Bank*
*Faded Memories*
*Glass Shadow*
*Intersection of Lies*
*Swept Away*
*Breathless* (Sequel to follow in 2024)
*In Plain Sight*

Just For You Trilogy
*Just For You*
*Fearless*
*Painted Fear*

All titles available on Kindle & Amazon
Follow me on Facebook: Tonya Sharp Hyche

# PROLOGUE

Maria Hawks sat in the front passenger seat of the SUV and listened as the three young girls aged fourteen to sixteen chatted about their new dresses, hair, and makeup in their native language. They playfully held out their hands and admired their new diamonds, all giggling as they touched each one. The diamonds were fake, but the girls never questioned their true value.

Maria turned to the girls in the back seat. "English. You girls need to keep practicing."

The older blonde obeyed, "Yes, ma'am. We are excited. We just forgot."

Maria turned back around and watched as Jayden Hart, the driver, took an exit off the interstate. She glanced at his mounted phone and saw that they were a little over three miles from their destination. If all went well, these two weeklong operations would soon come to an end. These three girls were the last of a shipment of eighteen. They had been too many for her to handle, and she had told her husband. He had listened and promised to reduce the next shipment. She had had her doubts but had said nothing more, as that would have caused an argument. Arguments were not wise to have. The more she pleased her husband, the better her life.

Over the last few months, she had been dropping subtle hints about her concerns over getting caught. She secretly hoped the shipments would stop. More Americans were waking up about the horrors of human trafficking and demanding change from their government. But when there was a demand for something, it continued—drugs, for instance. Gazing at the rare blue diamond on her right hand, she wondered how much money her husband, Sebastian, needed to stop. The rare diamond was another one of his gifts. It was larger than her wedding ring.

Maria thought back to the day she had met him at the age of sixteen. She had been meant to be one of the girls in the back seat, a package to be delivered for money. There had been ten other girls with her, all from Eastern Europe. Some had even been from her native country of Hungary. They had arrived at an island in the Caribbean during the night. None of the girls had had a clue where they were.

The boat ride had been horrific sitting in a small, confined space for days with one girl after the other getting seasick. They were to remain out of sight during the day and were allowed some fresh air only at night. Maria had no idea how long she was on the boat; she had lost count after day three. They all sat huddled together in the hull of a boat when a man appeared. His eyes scanned over them all and then landed on her. He told her to stand. Then he neared and touched her face. She was so scared, she shook.

He spoke Russian in a gentle voice, saying, "Don't be afraid. I have great plans for you." Then he walked away.

Three more days passed before she saw him again. The girls were transferred to another boat and were back at sea. After spending two more days on the water with minimum food and water, they arrived at yet another island. She soon would learn it was the Grand Cayman Island, one of three islands that form the Cayman Islands. She was the only one removed, and then the boat set sail again. Even though she was thankful to finally be off the boat, she was scared to be separated from the others.

She was quietly whisked away in the back of a black cargo van in the middle of the night. The ride would take thirty minutes, and the driver told her to make herself presentable.

Maria saw the black bag at her feet and opened it. Inside were wet wipes for cleaning herself and a blue dress. She held up the dress. A price tag was still attached: *$800*. That amount of money could feed her entire family for two months. She ran a hand over the fine silk.

She moved over to a corner that was somewhat out of view of the driver and changed out of her dirty clothing. Then she did her best to use the wipes to clean her face, arms, and legs. When she finished, the driver tossed a small bag toward her. She opened it and nearly fainted. It was jewelry. There were two rings, a diamond bracelet, and a pair of diamond earrings. She quickly put them on.

Jayden spoke, making Maria's thoughts fade and bringing her back to the present. She asked him to repeat himself, then nodded. The girls continued to chatter in the back seat, this time in English, as directed. They were so clueless. Just like she had been when she had left her homeland. Fairy-tale stories had been sold to her by a young woman who claimed to have left a year earlier for a better life. So, she had hugged her family goodbye. She was going to America for work. She just needed a few years, and then she would send for her family. All a lie. Everything the women had told her was false. For all she knew, her family were now dead from civil war, famine, or disease. It was only by chance that she had caught the eye of her handler and she had been spared the life that awaited these girls.

The black nondescript SUV slowly turned into a gated neighborhood. The houses were large and well maintained. Whenever they arrived at one of these homes, the girls were sure to be in awe. Maria turned and spoke her rehearsed line: "Girls, we are here."

She heard squeals of delight, causing her to pause. She patiently waited for them to settle down and then continued. "Remember, you are a lady. You must show poise and talk little, but praise and compliment the gentlemen. There is no guarantee they will choose you, and if they don't, you will be shipped back home without the clothing and jewelry."

The youngest of the three said, "We will not let you down. You have been so generous. We only want the life you have: to be a princess."

Maria held back her emotions and smiled. "And you shall have it, if you remember and do all that I taught you."

All the girls nodded and promised to do so as the SUV came to a stop in front of a two-story white mansion with large columns surrounding a beautiful porch with a balcony above. The girls were starstruck as Jayden pulled into the garage and the door closed behind them. Jayden exited the car and opened Maria's door first, then the back door, helping each girl stand in their three-inch heels. As expected, no one questioned why they had entered through the garage instead of driving up the circular driveway and entering the home through the impressive glass double doors on the front porch.

A young man wearing a black tuxedo opened the kitchen door. He smiled and bowed for them to enter. Maria watched as he took in the beauty of the three girls. He took the hand of each and kissed it, then slowly spun the girl around for inspection. The girls only smiled at his admiration. He looked back at Maria and nodded.

That was her cue. "Ladies, we have champagne. How about a toast?"

With utmost trust, the girls watched as Maria lifted an open bottle of champagne sitting on ice that was on the island in the large kitchen. She poured each a glass and then her own. Her well-manicured hand raised her glass. "To a life of happiness."

The glasses clinked, and Maria rested hers at her lips as she watched the girls drink from their glasses.

Laying on his charm, the young man whisked the girls away into the living room. Maria set the drug-laced glass of champagne down on the counter and motioned for Jayden to check the pantry. He walked over, retrieved a briefcase, and scanned the contents. He nodded his approval.

She took one last look at the doorway where the girls had exited. She waited another ten seconds for any hint of trouble. When she heard laughter, she turned and left the same way she had entered. Her job was now complete.

***

*One Day Later; Five Miles Away*

Dr. Cassandra Rose's neck muscles were tight as she pressed the correct floor on the elevator. She looked at her watch. It was now 1 p.m. She had left Keith a message around 8 a.m., saying she wouldn't be long.

The elevator door opened to the parking garage, and Cassandra pulled out her phone and pressed her number one contact. Keith answered on the third ring, and she replied, "Hey, hon, I'll be there in five. Just getting in my car."

"Perfect timing."

She smiled. Not every doctor had a spouse as supportive as hers. She had just assisted in a heart transplant that had lasted five hours, an hour longer than expected. Their patient, a sixteen-year-old, had just gotten a new heart thanks to another teen who had unfortunately been riding in a car with her drunk boyfriend.

Cassandra had been home on Davis Island packing a bag when she had gotten the call from Dr. Potter. Today was supposed to be the start of a four-day break, something she hadn't received in the last five months. Since Keith hadn't been due home until noon, the surgeon junkie had eagerly said yes, jumped in her Lexus convertible, and driven the half mile to Tampa Memorial General Hospital. But he was a workaholic as well, running his own multimillion-dollar investment company, Rose Investment Firm. That had been among the first qualities that had attracted her to Keith from the beginning: hard-working, successful, and driven.

"Got the dingy ready to go?"

He laughed at their inside joke. The "dingy" was a small yacht valued at the same price as their eighty-four-hundred-square-foot residence but was only half the price of their beach house, Rolling Tides, twenty-five miles away at Clearwater Beach. "All packed, just waiting on you. Hurry. I'll be on the dock."

Cassandra ended her call, fired up the engine, and shifted to reverse. As she checked her rearview mirror, she braked as she saw a man wearing a black T-shirt and dark jeans leaning against a concrete pillar, staring at her and smoking a cigarette.

An uneasy feeling washed over her as she glanced around the parking garage. Then, when she looked back at the mirror, he was gone.

She backed out and proceeded out of the parking garage, going down two levels without seeing the man again. She convinced herself that he was probably just taking a smoke break or needed to get out of the hospital for a while due to a family illness or tragedy. Once on the street, she drove straight for about a minute and then made a quick right into her driveway. She pulled into the garage, cut the engine, and lowered the garage door behind her, never thinking of the man again.

She quickly walked into the house and straight to the master bedroom. Her open luggage with a few necessities already packed from earlier sat on the made bed. She ran to the closet, grabbed a few more things, stuffed the clothing inside, and zipped the bag. She glanced around the room and decided she was finally ready. Grabbing the bag, she left the bedroom.

Once outside, she glanced around their pool in the backyard. Quiet. No children running about. Only the water running down their eight-foot waterfall. No toys or balls floating in the water. She thought back to the last time Keith's three girls had visited. Had it been one or two months ago? There had been toys, goggles, and towels everywhere, with Keith behind the barbecue grill. A smile formed on her lips; it had been a beautiful day.

"Hey, you!"

Cassandra turned and found her husband of two years standing along the walkway of their pier.

"Oh!" She laughed. "Caught me daydreaming, that's all."

She watched as he neared and took her bag. He hugged her tightly and planted a kiss on her lips. "Is this what you're dreaming about?"

She deeply kissed him back, then stepped away and grabbed his hand, pulling him along toward the boat. "You have no idea. Let's do this."

Keith smoothly maneuvered the *Cassidy Rose* through the many passages surrounded by canal homes until finally entering open sea in the Gulf of Mexico. Cassandra lifted her binoculars and scanned the coast of Clearwater Beach until she saw Rolling Tides, a tall and narrow, three-story house painted blue with white balconies across the entire back of the structure. She smiled. She knew their cleaning lady would already have tied the lounge chairs' cushions in place and set a rolled towel on each in anticipation for their arrival later tonight. The refrigerator and bar would also be well stocked with her requested items. Keith had called earlier and made the arrangements for their yacht at Clearwater Harbor. She lowered the binoculars.

The boat slowed to an idle, and she heard the winch. Cassandra stood from her padded lounge chair and walked down below to get Keith a cold beer. She opened the refrigerator door and scanned over the selection of drinks. Settling on a bottled water for her and a Corona for Keith, she pulled them out and set them on the granite counter, then quickly rinsed and cut a lime. Picking up the bottles, Cassandra climbed the stairs back up to the top.

"You read my mind." Her husband took the offered beer and looked out at sea. "Wow! *Wow!* We couldn't ask for a better day. Weatherman got it right. Calm seas and beautiful sunshine all weekend long." He looked at her. "What more could we possibly ask for?"

He took her hand and guided her over to the lounge bed. Taking their drinks, he placed them both on the table, then pulled her down on top of him. They rolled around and kissed under the bright sun without a care in the world.

"This feels so good," he said as he rubbed his hand down her flat, warm stomach. "And I don't think you need this anymore." He untied her purple swim top and tossed it to the deck.

"Careful. You don't want to know how much that top cost," she said with wink.

He glanced down and saw the shiny fabric close to the boat's edge. "Let it fall over. Tops are useless anyway."

She giggled while rolling her eyes as his mouth dove to her chest. They made sweet, passionate love as the boat slowly rocked over the clear-blue water. After three years together, days like today still felt like the honeymoon stage, with neither getting enough of the other.

Cassandra heard a seagull above, bringing her out of her love daze. "You might want to lather the girls up, or you're not going to be able to touch them again this entire weekend."

He laughed. "Where's the sunscreen? I'll get it."

She stood. "Thanks, but you'll never be able to find it." She reached for her cover-up, but he stopped her.

"Not needed." He looked around. "There's not a boat anywhere near us."

She looked around to confirm. The nearest boat was too far away for its occupants to see them. There was not a single soul in sight. "There are telescopes in the beach houses," she pointed out.

He chuckled. "Then if someone is watching, we already gave them one hell of a show."

She smiled, then left him with his eyes on her tight derriere, the result of cycling a minimum of five days a week. Down below, she found their bags stored in the large berth that held a modest-size bed. Picking up the small pink makeup bag, she dropped it on the bed and caught her reflection in the floor-length mirror attached to the closet. Her hands went to her face. She spent a lot of time indoors at her job and was always careful with sunscreen and a hat when spending time in the sun.

She took a step closer to the mirror. Her hands ran over her full chest, her nipples raised and raw from their lovemaking. She turned sideways and looked at her toned stomach. Studying to become a doctor had caused her to marry later in life, and she hadn't borne any children yet. Now she was thirty-five. Would the timing ever feel right? Did Keith really want another family?

Everything about their relationship had been a leap of faith. Keith was divorced with three beautiful girls. When they first met, he hadn't been interested in trying marriage again and starting another family. But they had connected, and everything had changed. Several months into their relationship, when questioned again about having a child with her, he had replied he would do whatever would make her happy. A week later, he had popped the question. Nothing he had done or shown her with his own three girls should have given her any reason for doubt, but still, there was something she just couldn't quite place. Did he really want to do the baby thing all over again? Or was he just trying to make her happy?

Her mind wandered over the last few weeks. Keith had become distant. He was traveling more with work and when he was home, meetings had been scheduled at night. When she questioned him, his answers were always vague stating *it's just work*. She pressed her hand over her belly. This weekend, they needed to have a heart-to-heart conversation about their future. No matter what excuse he gave, there was something bothering him. She was determined to find out exactly what that something was before Monday rolled back around.

She heard Keith's voice from above, and she dropped her hand. Unzipping the bag, she grabbed the sunscreen and headed back up. She was about to ask what he had said until she saw him on the phone. Work.

She stood for a moment, studying his backside as he leaned on the railing, one foot standing on the string of her top. Keith was still fit at forty-three, and she had no qualms about his ability to be a good father. She sighed. Maybe all this doubt was coming from her. No way was she going to stop practicing medicine or cut back on her hours after having a child.

She slowly walked toward him and tapped his thigh. He turned, then looked down and removed his foot from her two-hundred-dollar patch of material. She picked it up, took a seat on the lounge bed, tied her top on, and began to apply sunscreen. Still in conversation, he gazed at her, and her eyes rested on the scar across his chest, reminding her of the first time they had met. She had made that incision, saving his life.

He turned away from her. Cassandra picked up her bottled water and took a long swig. The water had gotten hot. She reached for Keith's beer; it was warm too. She rose, and just as she picked up both bottles to replace them, she heard a boat fast approaching.

She quickly threw on her cover-up. Keith ended his call as Cassandra tried to identify the boat. It was tan with a red stripe. It was too hard to make out the name on the side. She racked her brain trying to guess which friends the boat belonged to. Looking down at her sheer cover-up, she grumbled, "I need to change, damn it!"

She picked up her bottoms off the lounge bed and headed below. As she walked back to the berth, she pulled off her cover-up, grabbed her one-piece tank, and pulled it on. As she changed, the other boat slowed its engine as it approached.

She heard her husband talking to a man; he knew him. A sense of dread washed over her. She had secretly hoped they were strangers. She needed this alone time with Keith to figure out her future. Now she would be expected to socialize. She checked her appearance in the mirror and left the berth.

Just as she started to climb the stairs, she heard Keith raise his voice in anger. She carefully poked her head up and saw a man holding a gun. She quickly retreated to the berth and locked the door.

\*\*\*

An alert sounded on a computer at the FBI Tampa Field Office. Special Agent Aiden Greene sat up at his desk and read the message: *WIRE TRANSFER ROSE INVESTMENT*. He quickly clicked on the message and saw the amount: $5 million.

Aiden yelled for his partner, who was down the hall, grabbing coffee. "Jonas, where is Keith Rose right now? We got a hit on five million!"

Special Agent Jonas Parker ran toward him. "The last update was when he left the house with his wife on their boat, *Cassidy Rose*. They were going to Clearwater Harbor."

"Let's get a chopper up and get eyes on them. The wire transfer went to an overseas account. They could be on the move."

\*\*\*

A man standing on the deck of a chartered fishing boat anchored a half mile offshore lowered his binoculars as the last of the flames from the *Cassidy Rose* were extinguished as the turquoise water consumed the small yacht and it sank below. Two boats were speeding toward the black smoke that lingered above.

Foreign-accented directions were given to the captain, and then two men standing on the deck retracted their fishing lines. The winching sound of the anchor was heard as all the gear was stored away.

The man went below, closing the door to the American men left on deck. For the next hour, he remained out of sight as the fishermen above tried to render assistance and answered the coast guard's questions about the boat tragedy. Finally, the sound of the engine came roaring back to life as the boat shifted into gear and was guided to the marina.

He finally relaxed, releasing his phone that he was holding and realizing for the first time the throb in his knuckles from the tight embrace. He flexed his fingers on his large, rough hands and rolled his shoulders, trying to release the tension that had built in them.

Picking the phone back up, he placed a call. When the other party answered, he said simply, "It's finished."

# CHAPTER 1

The small jet smoothly touched down on Davis Island. Addison Shaw tightly grabbed the armrest as the single-engine plane came to a roaring stop. There was no flight attendant to see her discomfort. She didn't mind flying, just the takeoff and the landing. Also, it didn't help that she was all alone with no one to talk to. Of course, she could have pressed a small button at any time to talk to the pilot, but she had felt it best just to let him concentrate on getting her from Atlanta to Davis Island in one piece.

Her eyes scanned the cabin and found the liquor cabinet. She wanted another drink. But there was something haunting about drinking from an open bottle of her dead brother-in-law's bourbon. Keith and Cassandra's lawyer had repeatedly told her it was to be all hers now. She just needed more time to process everything that had happened was all.

Addison picked up the small tumbler and drank the last swallow. The smooth liquid valued at God only knew how much burned as it trickled down her throat. She understood what she was set to inherit, but no amount of time would ever get her used to the idea that her only sister was now gone and never coming back to this world. A tear slowly slid down her cheek, and she wiped it away as the FASTEN SEAT BELT sign turned off.

The pilot's voice filled the space. "It's safe to move around the cabin, Ms. Shaw."

13

She unbuckled her seat belt and walked to the cabinet but didn't open it. She placed the glass in the small sink and waited on the pilot. A few minutes passed, and the cockpit door opened. "How was the flight?"

She forced a smile. "Good, thank you."

"Excellent." He stared at her with interest.

Panic filled her. *Oh God, am I supposed to tip or something?* She fumbled for her purse. She was so out of her league her head was spinning and she couldn't think straight.

"I'm very sorry for your loss, Ms. Shaw. The Roses always treated me with kindness and the utmost respect, and I enjoyed flying for them. I'm going to miss them."

She dropped her purse onto the seat and looked at the man, who appeared to be in his late forties. His smoky-green eyes looked sincere. "You are very kind. Thank you for sharing."

She watched as he moved past her and pulled a handle forward and up. The door slowly opened, and the July Florida heat quickly consumed their airspace. A young man was rolling a staircase toward them.

The pilot gestured with his hands. "Please, go on ahead. I'll bring your bags down."

She opened her purse and pulled out her wallet.

He shook his head. "That's not necessary, Ms. Shaw."

She felt her face turn red. "I . . . I . . ." She gave a nervous laugh. "This is all so new, and I don't—"

He took a step closer and gently laid a hand on her arm. "I'm sure it is. It's okay." He removed his hand, pulled out a card from his jacket, and handed it to her. "My salary for the year has already been paid. So just call whenever you're ready to pick up your son."

He remembered her son. Shame consumed her at the thought of what else he might have remembered from her visit last summer. He was the pilot who had flown her to Atlanta while Riley had stayed with her sister. It all had been Cassandra's idea. She had called the pilot, made reservations for two at the finest restaurant in Atlanta, and arranged for a car to pick Addison up at the airport. When Addison had arrived home to surprise her husband, she was the one who had gotten the shock of her life when she had found Kristy, his skinny little blonde coaching assistant, wearing only his T-shirt. They were lounging on the couch, eating Chinese takeout with a bottle of wine open before them. Returning to the jet an hour later had been a blur. Addison couldn't even remember what she had said to this man.

Pushing the memory away, she read his name—*Caleb O'Brien*— and saw his phone number. "Mr. O'Brien, I don't know how long I'll be staying. There's still so much to sort through."

"I can imagine. Just know that I'm only a call away. My set off days are listed on the back, but if you give some notice, I can switch some things around to be available. I hope the lawyer explained why I wasn't available last week when you needed me."

The memorial service flashed before her eyes. She slowly nodded and picked up her purse. As she descended the stairs, a sleek black SUV with a driver was waiting on her as planned. It felt silly; she was just going three miles to her sister's canal home. But it was what the lawyer had arranged; he had communicated by email.

She watched as the pilot pulled out two large suitcases from the cargo hold and handed them to the driver. Then he opened her door. "Have a nice evening, Ms. Shaw."

"Thank you."

He closed the door, and she looked around at the leather interior.

A bottle of wine was chilling just in her reach. Then she saw a large envelope with *The Law Office of Greer & Cruz* printed in the left top corner. Her name was written below. Inside were the keys to Cassandra and Keith's belongings. Soon to be hers.

She reached for the bottle of wine that had already been uncorked. She read the fancy label and poured a glassful, thinking that money would be wasted if she never took a sip. She watched as the driver got behind the wheel and pulled forward. His wedding band upon his left hand flashed when the sun hit it. *Nah,* she thought. The wine would've been taken home to his wife.

"Ma'am, if there's anything you need, my name is Peter Marks."

"Thank you, but if my memory is correct, it's a short ride."

"Yes, about five minutes."

"Then I'm quite fine, thank you."

The tinted glass slowly rose between her and the driver and Peter disappeared.

Addison looked out the windows at all the private jets. She shook her head. *What the hell do I need a private jet for? I'm a schoolteacher, for Christ's sake.*

The SUV pulled out of the airport and turned right. Davis Island wasn't that big. It held about a hundred canal homes, along with a hospital. The same hospital Cassandra had worked at since her residency. One exquisite estate home passed by after the next. Then the car slowed, and Addison saw Cassandra's enormous stucco and red-tiled-roof home appear. Peter pulled around the circular driveway and stopped.

An old memory of Cassandra walking out the front door to greet her arose. It felt like a month ago, not a year. Cassandra had been wearing scrubs, just home from the hospital. A driver had picked up

16

her and Riley. She had hugged Addison tightly and kissed Riley, who had been two at the time, all over his face. A faint smile appeared on her lips at the image of Riley trying to wiggle free. They had only stayed that one night before leaving early the next morning for the beach house in Clearwater.

The sound of the trunk closing jarred her mind back to reality. Cassandra would never be home to greet her again.

She picked up the envelope and stepped out. She immediately noticed there was a white FedEx envelope propped up against the door. She reached down and picked it up. It was addressed to her, with the return address of a bank in Clearwater. Since obviously it did not require a signature upon delivery, she assumed it must not be that important. It could wait. She tossed it in her computer bag and shrugged. *Add this to my to-do list as well.*

Peter carried her bags to the front door and waited patiently as she searched for the keys in the envelope, all individually marked with a tag. Finally, she found the one marked *28 Davis Island, canal home.* When she inserted the key, Peter stopped her. "Ma'am, do you know the security code?"

"Oh, the security code. Thank you!"

"Yes, you will only have a moment to punch in the numbers once you open the door, or the alarm will go off and the police will come. If my memory is correct, the alarm panel is right by the front door."

She juggled the handful of keys and then dropped them in his offered hands. Inside the envelope was printed directions. She scanned the pages until she found the one for 28 Davis Island, along with the security code, and announced, "Thanks. I got it."

She opened the door and quickly deactivated the alarm. When the light turned from red to green, she breathed a sigh of relief. She would have to get used to all the alarms. Her small apartment didn't have an alarm, and all those buttons made her nervous. She stepped toward the doorway and found Peter back outside, having placed her luggage inside the foyer. "Thank you."

He reached into his pocket and retrieved a card. "I'm contracted till the end of the year. My number is listed on the card. The Roses usually texted me when I was needed. I just ask for a day's notice where I can plan accordingly. If I'm unavailable, my brother will pick you up. We're a family business."

"Alright, well, I'll keep that in mind. I believe there are three cars parked in the garage for me to use."

He smiled. "I understand. But sometimes driving in the city can be tricky. Just let me know how I can be of assistance. Is there anything else you need this evening?"

Addison shook her head. "Not that I can think of. Thank you and drive safely."

"Yes, ma'am."

She closed the door and flipped the lock. She looked at her luggage: worn and old, out of place. Just like her: out of place.

Slowly, she turned around. What once had been an inviting home now seemed so cold and empty without Cassandra fussing over her and Riley. Addison closed her eyes and leaned up against the solid oak door. She took deep breaths, settling her nerves. Finally, she opened her eyes and pushed off the door, leaving the suitcases behind to explore.

The home was twice as large as the beach house. She couldn't remember how many bedrooms and bathrooms filled the Mediterranean-inspired house. She did remember the enormous kitchen with the dark-wood cabinets and the accented stone-covered wall surrounding the cooktop. The massive backyard held a resort-style swimming pool and outdoor kitchen. She turned a corner and saw the pool through the floor-length windows, glistening with the last rays of the shining sun.

She walked across the travertine floors and stood at the glass door leading to the backyard. Suddenly, a memory of Cassandra playing with Riley appeared before her. She pushed him in a little raft boat that had a water gun attached. Riley laughed and giggled as he sprayed everyone and everything around him, even Keith, who was flipping burgers at the grill. It was a perfect evening filled with laughter. The next day, Keith stayed behind with work as Cassandra drove her and Riley out to the beach house. Cassandra had managed to take off four full days during her and Riley's ten-day visit.

The memory faded. Addison looked away and headed toward the kitchen.

The counters were void of any bread or fruit baskets. She opened the stainless-steel fridge and found it clean and empty except for bottled water. She opened the freezer next, and it was empty of food as well. She vaguely remembered the lawyer's comment about how both homes had been cleaned with all trash removed. She walked over to the pantry. Nonperishable cans and goods were stacked neatly in rows. Eyeing a bag of chips, she grabbed them and closed the pantry door. She opened the bag and began to eat as she climbed the stairs to the second floor. She would go to the master bedroom, located on the ground floor, last.

Upstairs, all the doors were open, each revealing clean and tidy rooms. Three of the doors had the names of Keith's girls: Natalie, Brandi, and Layla. They had rarely visited, according to Cassandra. Addison tried to remember their faces at the memorial service, but it was all such a blur. She had only seen them once before that, at the wedding. She wondered how the girls were coping and was thankful they still had their mother, Reba, whom she had only met briefly at the service.

Addison pushed the grim thoughts away as she walked on down the hall and found the second master bedroom suite. It had been the room she and Riley had slept in for one night. Her eyes drifted to the French doors that led to the balcony overlooking the pool. She walked over, opened the door, and stepped out.

The sun was setting, and the wind had picked up. As the palms shifted in the wind, the boat dock came in sight. There was no *Cassidy Rose* tied up. It was gone too, just like Keith and Cassandra. Emptiness filled her heart, and grief descended upon her once again. The ache in her chest came roaring back. She closed her eyes and concentrated on breathing in through her nose and out her mouth. The pain in her chest slowly resided, and she opened her eyes.

She pictured Cassandra's smiling face. Not only had Cassandra been a gifted surgeon but a precious soul who had moved people with her presence. Addison hadn't seen it while growing up since Cassandra had been five years her senior, but they had reconnected four years ago when she had finished her residency. Both had looked at each other differently: Cassandra, a respected heart surgeon, and Addison, a third-grade teacher, pregnant with her first child. Neither were the spoiled, selfish brats they had remembered from their teenage years. *If only I'd reached out sooner after that fight.* Shaking her head, she couldn't even remember all the details. *Stupid. So stupid.*

Just as Addison turned to go back into the house, she saw movement by the pier. She took a step toward the railing just as a shadow passed over the walkway. She looked to the right and to the left: there were only houses hidden behind tall shrubbery. She tried to remember if there was a walking path that connected all the docks and homes, but her memory failed her.

Suddenly, the waterfall turned on, and she jumped. Gripping the railing tightly, she scanned the pool area and backyard. Again, the palms rattled as Addison remembered a storm was predicted tonight.

*Get a grip, Addison!* she thought. *The waterfall is on a timer, and it's just a storm rolling through.*

She slowly released her tight hold of the railing and returned inside. She secured the door and locked it with anticipation of the evening storm.

As she descended the spiral staircase that was the focus of the grand foyer, she heard a faint knock. She paused briefly, then continued stepping down, her footsteps silent along the carpeted staircase. She walked to the front door and looked out the small hole. No one was there.

She heard the knock again, but it was coming from behind her. She checked the front door to make sure it was locked and then headed toward the noise. The living room soon came into view, but she didn't see anyone at the glass door that led to the backyard.

She stopped and looked around the room, trying to decipher the noise. She waited a full minute but didn't hear the knock again. She crossed her arms over her chest and tried to relax. She needed a drink. Spying the wine cellar located off to the corner, she grabbed a bottle of red and headed to the kitchen for a glass, turning on lights as she went since the house had grown darker. There was just a hint of the sunset as the gray storm clouds rolled in.

She opened a glass cabinet and marveled at the array of glasses to choose from. Then she poured a glass, turned, and leaned up against the counter as she drank. She saw her purse sitting on the kitchen counter, along with her phone. She needed to call Owen, her ex, and let him know she had arrived safely. And if Riley was still up, she wanted to tell him good night. Sadness filled her once again. She had no family left now except Riley and Owen, who was about to marry that blonde bimbo next month.

Owen answered on the fourth ring, and she responded in a tired voice, "Hi, I made it. Is Riley still up?"

"No, Addy, the little bugger was wiped clean out. We went to the pool today."

She didn't have to ask who "we" were. "Okay. Will you call me in the morning when he wakes? I just want to hear his little voice, you know?"

"Yeah, sure."

"Okay, thanks. Goodbye."

"Wait, Addy!"

Addison heard his voice and brought the phone back up to her ear. "Yeah, I'm still here."

"Um, how are you? You okay doing this by yourself?"

His question and concern left her speechless. Since when had he cared in the last year if she was okay? She was about to give an ugly reply before she stopped cold. Owen was Riley's father, and that one fact was never going to change, no matter how much he had hurt her with his affair. She pushed the negative energy away. There was no point in making this more difficult than it already was. "I'm managing. It's just been a long day."

"Yeah, I bet. Hey, Menard asked me what your plans were for the fall."

Dick Menard was her principal. "What? When did you see him?" she asked.

"He was at the high school today. We ran into each other in the hall. He was just concerned about you, that's all."

Addison took a long sip of the red wine as she doubted his words. Owen sleeping with his coaching assistant and their divorce had been the hottest gossip to sweep the district all year. For the upcoming school year, there would be a new Mrs. Shaw, and Addison had debated about retaking her maiden name. The anger slowly rose in her throat, and she tasted bile. "What did you tell him?"

His voice was defensive. "Nothing. I don't know your plans."

"Have I given you the impression that my plans were changing?" she exclaimed.

He sighed loudly. "Addy, you are set to inherit millions. Nobody has a clue what you're doing, but we all just assumed going back to teaching at sixty thousand dollars a year is not on the agenda."

"So, I'm the talk of the district once again. Great. Thank you very much, Owen. Just what I needed to hear tonight!"

There was a long silence. Then he lowered his voice. "Look, if you need me to fly down to help you, just ask. Riley and I can leave tomorrow."

He sounded sincere, as if he did care. Then he again showed his true colors when he added, "Of course, you need to send that fancy jet of yours. Flights to Tampa are outrageous in the summertime on a day's notice."

Addison tuned him out. It was too much. She looked around and studied the large kitchen before her, void of smells, food, or laughter. Void of Cassandra. Her heart sank. She so desperately needed Cassandra in her life. Whom was she going to talk to now when Owen drove her insane? She turned right toward the hallway that led to Cassandra and Keith's bedroom. It was time to go in. She needed to do this tonight.

She heard part of what Owen was saying and rudely cut him off. "No, thank you, Owen. I'll call again tomorrow morning to talk to Riley. But in the meantime, don't go around spouting off my so-called changed plans for the fall."

Addison ended the call without hearing his reply. She picked up the wineglass and drained the liquid. She picked up the bottle of wine and hesitated. One drink on the plane, a few sips on the drive over, then the full glass. She shrugged; she had no responsibilities tonight without Riley. She quickly justified that if she wanted to get drunk, she had every good reason to. She poured another glass and headed to the bedroom.

\*\*\*

A man dressed in black waited in the shadows as he watched Cassandra Rose's sister walk throughout most of the home, flipping lights on and off as she went. On the main level, she hadn't made it to the study; she had kept mostly to the living room and kitchen. Now she was headed toward the master bedroom where Keith and Cassandra had slept.

He smiled as she continued to drink from her wineglass as she talked on the phone. She had checked in with someone. He thought of her son back in Atlanta. Cute little kid. If things went south, at least the kid would be getting a new mommy next month. If Addison Shaw needed to be in a car accident and the money was right, he was prepared to make that happen.

Glancing at his watch, he needed her to go to bed. Lurking around at night in this privately patrolled neighborhood was making him a little uneasy. The sooner he got in the house and got back out, the better.

# CHAPTER 2

Maria made her way down to the guesthouse at the oceanfront estate. Inside were five new girls. None of them had been led to believe they were going to America for a better life. No, they had all been sold because their families couldn't feed them. Her job was to convince them that just because those were the circumstances that had led them to America, it didn't mean that what was going to happen was going to be a bad thing. The best way to do that was to show them. She dressed every day in designer clothing and fine jewelry. She looked and acted the part of a well-kept princess: always happy and willing to please. She unlocked the door and entered with a big smile on her face.

The youngest girl, Constance, stood up from the couch. "Maria is here!" she called to the other girls. Soon the other four came out from their bedrooms.

"How are your accommodations? Nice?" Maria asked.

The custom guesthouse contained seven bedrooms and three bathrooms. There was a small kitchen and one common room with a washer and dryer. The house was a perfect square with an open courtyard and swimming pool in the center. There was only one way in and out, and it could only be accessed with a key from the outside. There were no windows.

The oldest and the one most likely to stir up trouble, Tatiana, replied, "I don't know what to say. I've never had my own room or clothing all to myself."

Her attitude had changed since first arriving two days ago. Tatiana had been very upset that the door was locked and she couldn't walk out on her own free will. Maria had explained that it was for their protection, and they would only stay there for a few days before leaving for America. They could go out to the courtyard and enjoy the weather and their own private pool at any time of day or night.

Maria smiled. "Please, let's all have a seat." She waited briefly while the girls sat and then continued. "Today's agenda will be to go over what is expected of you at a fine restaurant."

Bianca's eyes widened and she smiled. She was the most beautiful girl in the room. "We will get to eat at a restaurant?"

"Of course, all the time in America. Now it's my job to teach you what silverware to use and how to order. Tomorrow, we will focus on your hair and makeup." Maria paused to look over each one carefully. "You only have a few short days to learn what is required. So please pay close attention. I want to find you suitable husbands who will make you just as happy as I am."

Tatiana asked, "Are your diamonds real?"

Maria looked down at her well-manicured hands. "Yes. I have lots of fine jewelry to choose from, and you shall too once we get to America, and I find you your perfect mate."

Constance giggled. "I've never had a ring before. I was given a necklace once from my grandmother, but it was later sold." Her eyes turned sad.

"Well, don't you worry. With your beauty, Constance, you will have lots of rings. I promise you."

She looked at Anna and Hanna, who could pass as twins. They were sisters aged eleven months apart. Neither had spoken much since arriving. She asked them, "How are your rooms?"

Anna spoke in a quiet voice. "Nice, thank you."

Maria looked at Hanna and waited for her response.

"I used the pool. Our mother taught us to swim."

Maria smiled. "That is good, Hanna. Make sure you use sunscreen. You need to protect your beautiful porcelain skin, like mine." She looked at all the girls. "That goes for everyone. Now I shall go." She stood. "I will return at six p.m. sharp. Please wear one of your nice dresses and heels. You must practice walking in them. We will go over a few rules, and then dinner will be served at six thirty. I hope everyone is hungry for steak and lobster."

The girls shrilled with excitement and began hugging one another. Maria knew they had probably never in their life been served steak and lobster. She smiled at them and was able to relax somewhat. She needed as many happy moments with the girls as possible because the dangerous voyage to America was nothing to look forward to. Once on the boat, they would be terrified. She needed moments like this to remind them it would only be temporary. Once they arrived in America, things would be different. Maria stood and excused herself. No one questioned her when she left, locking the door behind her.

She turned to start up the hill toward the main house when she bumped right into her husband, Sebastian. He was so much taller than she with his height of six feet three, and his body was as strong as an ox even at his age. An age of which she still had no clue. He had never told her when they had married; she had only been seventeen. She had never even seen the marriage certificate but knew there was one since he had introduced her as his wife several times when she was lucky enough to attend community events.

She smiled. "I didn't know you were home."

He placed both hands on her shoulders and rubbed her arms affectionately. "Yes, only for a bit. The staff said I could find you down here. How are things going?"

"Surprisingly, very well. I was most concerned with Tatiana, but she seems to be settling in nicely."

"That's good. We will drop her off first in Miami, just to be on the safe side." He then leaned in and kissed her gently on the lips. "I missed you this morning."

He took her hand, and they climbed the few steps back to the main house. Once up the hill, they entered the grand estate, and he led her toward the bedroom, where he shut the door, undressed her, and guided her backward toward the bed.

Maria knew this routine well. He would indulge her every desire and then coddle her in bed for another hour. It was his way of keeping her satisfied and accepting of this life that he had created for her. The after-sex attention was what she craved the most: his strong arms holding her and him telling her she was his everything while continuing to promise a plentiful life with anything she wanted. As she lay naked across the bed, watching him undress, she reminded herself that he had held true to his promise. He had only taken five girls this time, unlike the package of eighteen that had been unbearable.

She watched as he climbed on the bed and straddled her. Then he picked up her leg and began to kiss his way upward. She closed her eyes briefly, then she turned her head and saw the wrapped present on the nightstand as her body began to quiver with his skillful touch. She turned her attention back to him and let go as her body began to melt.

Two hours later, she was dressed in a silk robe while sitting on her balcony, enjoying the view of the water below and admiring her new diamond bracelet. Sebastian had left for the office. She picked up her tablet and hit a button. A screen with live footage from every room of the guesthouse came in view. She tapped on footage of a room where Constance, Tatiana, and Bianca were gathered. All looked good as they lounged on the furniture, watching TV. She clicked on another window and found Hanna and Anna. They were sunbathing in the pool.

She closed the window and set the tablet down. For now, she had nothing to worry about. All was good. She just hoped it would continue.

***

A young boy with blond, curly hair like his mother was snuggled up beside his father as he read the boy's favorite bedtime story. Tonight, he was determined to stay awake till the end. He almost made it, but his tired blue eyes betrayed him once again.

Isaac Mullins eased out of bed and pulled the covers up around his son's chest. His eyes rested on his son's face as he took in the sight of four-year-old Oliver, who was the spitting image of his wife of seven years. A few moments passed before he finally determined Oliver was out for the night. Isaac flipped the light switch and eased out of the room with the T. Rex night-light still showing enough light in case Oliver woke back up.

"That was fast."

Startled by his wife's voice, he jumped. A smile slowly crept upon his face as he took Demi in his arms. "He was wiped out from the beach. What about Annabelle?"

"Sound asleep," she whispered as she pressed her lips to his.

The kiss jump-started an awakening deep within, an effect Demi still had on him with just the simplest touch. He stepped back, grabbed her hand, and led her down the hallway toward their living room. "We got a storm rolling in later; let's make the most of it. Want to sit outside?" He grabbed the bottle of wine off the wet bar, along with two glasses.

"You read my mind. Let me just grab the baby monitor from the kitchen."

Isaac opened the French doors and stepped out onto the balcony overlooking Old Tampa Bay. Placing the glasses down on the outdoor bar, he uncorked the wine. Just as he poured a glass, his phone vibrated in his pocket. The glass door opened, and he turned to Demi. His hand stilled around his phone at the sight of her wearing nothing but heels and holding a baby monitor. He smiled as she placed the monitor by the wine bottle and stepped into him, wrapping her arms around his neck.

Demi looked at the skyline. "You said, 'Let's make the most of it.' Just thought I would save some time."

Isaac forgot about the call until he felt the vibration again. "Naked is good." He pulled his phone out, and she saw that he was getting a call from an unlisted number.

She smirked. "Don't be too long."

Taking the wineglass, she walked by, kicked off her shoes, and descended the stairs toward the pool. He followed her backside as the last rays of the setting sun gave just enough light for him to appreciate the show.

He glanced at the number on his phone, and his gut clenched. Poor timing as always. He answered as Demi eased into the water and turned to face him, sipping from her glass of wine.

"We got a problem."

A frown quickly appeared on his face, and Isaac turned away from his seductive wife. "What?" he asked with little patience.

"The sister came back. She's in the house."

"Damn it! This is what I was talking about. We should've taken care of this last week." A brief silence went by, and then he asked, "She got the kid with her?"

"No. She's alone and drinking pretty heavily."

Isaac's thoughts played out all the unknown factors and scenarios as Demi lifted herself up upon the tanning ledge and stretched out. "What's the plan?"

"We got the key and the code; he's going to go in tonight when she's asleep."

Demi raised her foot and raked it over her outstretched leg as she continued to sip from her wine. His patience started to shatter. "Look, I don't know about this. Hell, the Feds could be watching her—or worse, have contacted her already."

"Decision's made. I was just keeping you in the loop. I'll call when it's done."

"No." He picked up his wineglass and walked toward the pool. "Call only if there's a problem." He pocketed his phone and stepped down the stairs to the pool.

"Everything okay?"

With those simple, soft-spoken words, desire swept over him like never before. He was the luckiest man alive. Demi never nagged him or questioned him about his work. It was what it was. She was perfectly content with being a housewife and taking her husband whenever she could get him. As the founder and owner of Sunshine Properties, he was always on call, and she had supported him every step of the way as he had built his real estate company into a multimillion-dollar business.

He unbuttoned his shirt. "It is. Just a client confirming tomorrow's appointment."

She watched as he pulled his phone back out and placed it on the edge of the pool, then removed his shorts. "Good." She placed her wineglass down and eased over on the ledge for him to join her. "An unlisted number?" She raised her eyebrows, teasing him. "For a moment there, I thought I was going to have to share you."

He smiled. "Not tonight, babe. Not tonight."

Wrapping her up in his arms, he rolled her off the ledge and into the pool.

\*\*\*

Addison flipped the light switch, and Cassandra and Keith's room came into full view. A king-size poster bed dominated the room with its plush white comforter. She walked toward the oak bed and ran her hand across the bedding. Then she turned to the large dresser with a mirror across from the bed. A framed picture of Cassandra and Riley caught her eye. A tear escaped as she walked across the room and picked up the picture.

The memory of taking the photo came flooding back. The three of them had been on the beach last summer. Cassandra was sitting in the sand, playing with Riley. He joyfully clapped as Cassandra unveiled another perfect sandcastle when she lifted the bucket. Addison had snapped the photo. When she had returned home, she had downloaded all the pictures and had sent the framed photo to Cassandra on her birthday. Cassandra had called and said it was the best gift ever, just don't tell Keith; he had bought her a new Lexus that she claimed she didn't need.

Addison set the frame back down and lifted the lid to Cassandra's jewelry box. It was empty.

*What? Where's her jewelry?*

Fear consumed her as she thought of their mother's ring. She rushed into the bathroom to find the closet.

32

Addison desperately tried to remember what the lawyer had said about Cassandra's personal belongings. Her breath caught as she stood before the closed double door that led to the oversize custom closet. What had he said? No answer came as she timidly opened the door, not knowing whether she would find it empty or not. Relief washed over her when she saw neatly stacked boxes with labels: *Keith's suits, Keith's leisure wear, Cassandra's dresses, Cassandra's shoes,* etcetera.

She pushed boxes aside until she found the one marked *Jewelry.* She opened it and found her mother's wedding ring. Relief immediately washed over her. She placed it on her left hand. A perfect fit where her wedding band had been. She glanced through the rest of the jewelry, which had all been placed in small mesh bags. She briefly wondered why the lawyer had chosen to box the valuables instead of placing them in a safe.

She was overwhelmed by the need to smell her sister's fragrance. She tossed boxes until she found one labeled *Cassandra's shirts.* She tore it open and removed a pink knit blouse. She brought it to her face and inhaled. She couldn't smell her. Tears streamed down her face as she pulled out blouse after blouse, trying to find Cassandra's scent from her favorite perfume. Finally, she found a green cashmere sweater that hadn't been dry-cleaned. Surrounded by clothing, she sunk to the floor and cried.

Unknown time had passed before Addison awoke to the sound of thunder. Her eyes felt tender and puffy as she slowly opened them. She rose to a sitting position and wiped her face with her hand. Lightning flashed through the bathroom windows and skylights, making shadows dance along the closet walls; another loud wave of thunder followed. She pushed herself up and left the closet, closing the door behind her. Once she returned to the bedroom, the lights flickered.

"Oh, surely not!" Addison looked at the clock on the nightstand, but it was now blinking *12:00.* She looked at her watch and gasped. "Eleven thirty? Can't be, can it?"

The lights went out again, staying out a little too long for comfort before finally coming back on. She rushed to the nightstand and opened the top drawer. It was empty; no flashlight. She opened all the drawers. All empty.

As Addison made her way to the kitchen in search of matches to light some candles, she didn't know how she felt about a stranger going through Cassandra's things and packing up all her belongings. It felt like an invasion of privacy. While opening and closing drawers, she wondered what someone would find in her own bedroom drawers. She shuddered at the thought.

She finally found matches in a drawer in the kitchen island. She quickly walked over to the living room and lit the three candles sitting in an iron scroll on the coffee table. Just as she finished lighting the last one, lightning struck nearby. Thunder rattled the house, and the lights went out again.

"Damn!"

Ten seconds later, they came back on. Oh, that was right: the house had a generator. She laughed. Of course, Keith and Cassandra would have a generator, living on the coast with power outages and such.

Addison blew the candles out and looked at the iron scroll. Then she busted out laughing. She had just lit decorative candles that had never been lit before.

*Oh Cassandra, what am I doing in this house? It's so big; too big for me and Riley.*

Sitting all alone in the middle of the storm, part of her wanted to grab the keys to Cassandra's Lexus and bolt from the house as quickly as possible. But where would she go? To the beach house? A hotel? She had tried running from her marriage problems before and knew how that had turned out. *No, better to face the music now,* she thought. Cassandra and Keith were dead. Eventually the houses would be her responsibility.

She stared out the windows to the dark backyard. Every now and then, light would flash across the yard from the storm. For the first time, she allowed herself to think about her future. What was she going to do in the fall? It would take time for the estate to settle but she did have access to the house and some of the cash. Was it even possible to pour her heart and soul back into teaching in just short of three weeks?

Teaching was safe. There would be a routine again, week in and week out filled with lesson plans and short weekends. Owen's and Kristy's faces came into view. The district was small. She would bump into them time and time again with work, and then there was Riley. She still had to walk him to the door of Owen's new house that he now shared with Kristy. A three-year-old just couldn't be dropped off at the curb on his weekend visits. She had to see them whether she liked it or not.

But, for the first time, she realized she had options. As much as she loved teaching, she hated dropping Riley off at preschool and leaving him all day until 4 p.m. Then, after fighting traffic and getting home around 5 p.m., she was exhausted from teaching and entertaining nine-year-olds all day. Maybe she would hire a full-time nanny and Riley would never have to set foot in another daycare ever again. That would free up at least one hour of the day due to the back-and-forth traffic. And she could buy one of those big houses in the neighborhood across the street from her elementary school. *Yes, that just might work,* she thought.

Getting off the couch, Addison went into the kitchen, refilled her wineglass, and returned to the bedroom. There was something about this room that felt warmer than the rest of the house. She again looked at the framed photo sitting on the dresser and smiled as she realized why.

Suddenly, her clothes and skin felt gritty, and the idea of a bath lured her into the bathroom. Soon the large garden tub was filling with bubbles and hot water. Stripped down, Addison slowly submerged herself in the thick foam of bubbles. She laid her head back and closed her eyes, trying to relax and ease her mind of all the tension and grief from the day. She remembered this morning when Riley had cried as she had dropped him off at Owen's house. Then she had driven back home, emptied her trash, and packed up two suitcases of clothing. She glanced at her wrist; it was now midnight, fourteen hours after saying goodbye to Riley.

Picking up the wineglass, she took another long sip. The wine was good, and with the hot bath, she was feeling tired. Very tired. She closed her eyes again, thinking she would just sit there another minute or two before forcing herself to get out of the tub so she wouldn't drown.

Her mind drifted back to Riley. How nice it would be to stay home with him till he started kindergarten, then resume teaching. She pictured herself playing with him, then taking trips to the park. The images faded as the wine and exhaustion gradually took over and she fell asleep, her head lying on the little padded cushion elevating her face just high enough from a potentially watery death.

A loud noise sounded, and she jolted, her left arm landing in the bathwater and splashing her face. Shock registered as she realized she had fallen asleep and the bathwater was stone cold. The noise! What the hell was that noise?

Finally, everything registered in her murky brain: the house alarm was going off.

She screamed, "Shit, shit, shit! Why is it going off?"

Addison quickly rose and wrapped herself up in a towel. She carefully walked across the slick tile created by her wet feet. She found the alarm panel in the bedroom; the number four was illuminated. She tried guessing the code from earlier, but it didn't work. She remembered Peter's words: "The alarm will go off and the police will come."

She walked into the kitchen and picked up the printed directions from the lawyer and found the code again. Needing to get dressed before the police were sure to arrive, she ran toward the foyer to the alarm panel and her suitcases. She quickly flipped the white lever and entered the code. The deafening noise ceased.

She opened her large suitcase and pulled out the first item on top. She yanked the gray T-shirt dress over her slightly wet hair and body just as headlights flashed through the side windows. She closed her luggage and opened the blinds. Two uniformed policemen were walking up the stone staircase. She unlocked and opened the front door to greet them.

"I'm Officer Don Jones and this is Officer Frank Williams. We have a report of a house alarm. May we come in?"

"I'm so sorry. It's not my home, and I'm not sure what . . ."

Realizing what she had said, she quickly corrected herself, but it was too late. Both policemen were looking at her with suspicion.

"Just come on in. I can explain."

She watched as they looked at the luggage on the floor and studied her. Feeling self- conscious about her appearance, she covered her chest by crossing her arms.

"I was taking a bath, and the alarm went off. It took me a while to get dressed and find the code. This was my sister and brother-in-law's home—Keith and Cassandra Rose. They were killed two weeks ago in a boating accident. I just arrived today."

Officer Jones, the older man, removed his hat that had shielded his face from the rain. "I'm sorry for your loss, ma'am."

Officer Williams walked over to the alarm panel. "You got a number lit up. Mind if I check the house?" He turned and faced her.

"Sure, I came straight through to the front door. I have no idea what the numbers go to."

Officer Williams saw the bath towel lying beside the partially opened luggage. He said nothing as he walked on down the hallway past the kitchen and into the living room. "Don, in here."

Addison watched as Officer Jones placed a hand on his gun and followed his partner's voice. She followed as well. When she reached the living room, her heart stopped. The back door was wide open.

"Ma'am, did you open this door?" asked Officer Williams.

Addison couldn't form words, so she shook her head.

Officer Jones stated, "Take us where you were when the alarm sounded."

Addison pointed back toward the kitchen that led to another hall-way. "The . . . the master bathroom."

Officer Jones left her with the other officer and walked in the direction she had pointed. Addison watched Officer Williams intently as his hand rested on his gun. A few moments passed, and Officer Jones returned to guide her back to the bathroom.

"Stay here and lock up," he commanded.

She nodded as he spoke into his radio, requesting backup. As soon as he closed the door, she locked it.

Time stood still as she strained to hear their footsteps and movement throughout the house. The unnerving quietness got the best of her as she racked her brain trying to remember if she had ever checked the back door. Had it been locked? Had housekeeping accidentally left it unlocked? Had the storm blown the door open? She tried to calm down; after all, the storm had been strong enough to knock out the power. Wind off the water could be forceful enough to open a door if it wasn't shut and secured properly.

She turned and caught a glimpse of her appearance in the mirror. Her face was streaked with mascara from crying earlier. Her dark-red hair looked as if a rat had taken shelter in it, as it was messily piled high upon her head. Just as she opened a drawer in search of a brush, a loud knock sounded. She jumped with fright, then relaxed when she heard Officer Williams's voice as he identified himself on the other side of the bathroom door. Addison turned the lock and opened the door.

"House is all clear, ma'am. The storm must have blown the door open."

Relief washed over Addison. "I was telling myself just that. I never checked the door when I arrived. I can only assume it was locked when the cleaning staff left."

"Might want to verify when they left. Was the alarm set when you arrived?"

"Yes, it was. But I don't remember resetting it." She watched as he studied her with a critical eye. "It's been a long, exhausting day," she said quietly.

Finally, the awkward silence was broken when Officer Jones appeared. "Ma'am, is there anything else we can do for you tonight?"

Addison saw Officer Jones look around the bedroom. Then he looked her way. Now both men were studying her. She forced a smile.

"No. I think I'm just going to try and get some sleep now. It's late, and like I said, it's been a long day. I appreciate you coming. I'll walk you out."

Addison followed the men back into the kitchen and stopped when she saw a tall man wearing street clothing. At first, she was alarmed but then realized the officers knew him. He heard them approach and turned.

"Addison Shaw?" He stuck out his hand.

Addison nodded and stepped forward. "Yes."

His handshake was strong, and he had a kind smile that showed a hint of a dimple in his right cheek. "I'm FBI Special Agent Aiden Greene. Glad to see everything's okay tonight."

"FBI? I didn't realize a special agent would be called for backup."

That smile again lit up his face as his soft-blue eyes scanned over her. "No, not normally, ma'am."

Addison felt her cheeks warm. She tried patting down her hair and wiped hard beneath her eyes at the mascara streaks. It was hopeless. She crossed her arms over her chest, feeling half-dressed without a bra. She was just about to explain her situation when she heard a woman's voice fill the room from Officer William's radio: A request for backup on 1900 Collins Street was announced. Officer Williams looked at everyone. "We need to go. Good night, ma'am."

Addison followed them to the front door with Agent Greene a few steps behind. After closing the front door behind the policemen, she turned and faced him. "I wasn't expecting all of this tonight and surely wasn't expecting company." She again tried to fix her hair and smooth out her wrinkled dress.

He smiled, trying to put her at ease. "I'm sure you weren't." He handed her a card. "I was the agent who worked your sister's case. I'm sorry for your loss."

She reached for the card just as a flood of emotions hit her again. The FBI had been called in to investigate the boat explosion due to Keith being a high-profile self-made millionaire. The Tampa newspapers had made it their front-page story for a week until investigators had concluded it had been an accident. She blinked back the tears along with the images. "Thank you."

"You need anything, you give me a call anytime." She nodded and he added, "Even at one o'clock in the morning."

She forced a smile. "Okay, I will."

She watched as he neared the door and then opened it. He turned one more time as if to say something but stopped. "Well, good night, Ms. Shaw. Lock back up and reset your alarm."

"I will, thanks."

Addison turned the lock and lifted the wood blinds on the window to watch him walk down the driveway and get into a black truck. When he pulled away, she went to the alarm panel and reset the alarm, this time remembering the code. Then she walked back over, zipped up her luggage, and wheeled both pieces to the staircase. She stopped, then turned with the luggage and went back into the bedroom. She knew it would seem odd to others, but she wanted to sleep where Cassandra had slept. Somehow, she thought that would give her more comfort and peace.

The sheets were fresh and clean as Addison slid in between them, still wearing her gray T-shirt dress. She had no desire or energy left to change. Then she closed her eyes to sleep, but she kept replaying the events of the last thirty minutes. She had fallen asleep in the tub. How dangerous that could have been! Then the storm blowing open the door and the alarm going off. And the last thought that crossed her mind before sleep finally took her was the lingering comment from Agent Greene: "You need anything, you give me a call anytime. Even at one o'clock in the morning." Why would she need the good-looking FBI agent? And why had he shown tonight—in the middle of the night, no less?

# CHAPTER 3

Aiden left the ritzy Davis Island community and drove south along Bayshore Boulevard toward his two-bedroom condo. During the thirty-minute drive since leaving the Rose estate, he had thought of nothing else except the new heiress, Addison Shaw. She had played the role of a distraught sister perfectly. She had told the officers that she had been in the bathtub when the alarm had sounded, but according to the officers, the water in the tub had been cold. Her makeup had been smeared, but had it really been due to tears of heartbreak, or had she been half-asleep and drunk? He had noticed the empty bottle of wine sitting on the counter.

Earlier today, Aiden had gotten a call when the Rose jet had landed at Peter O. Knight Airport. It hadn't taken long for Cassandra Rose's sister to arrive and make herself at home. He had been wrong about her arriving alone; he had thought she would have her three-year-old son with her. All his research had led him to believe Riley was her number-one priority in life. Why had she left him?

Aiden remembered walking into Keith Rose's study. There had been four boxes, with only two labeled *Documents*. All had been opened. What had Addison been looking for? Did it concern the missing $5 million from Rose Investment Firm? He had only had enough time to scan the files labeled on top, looking for one name: Wayne Keaton. No such luck. He shouldn't have been surprised. After months of heavy surveillance, Keith Rose had made no mistakes.

The man he was investigating was Wayne, the owner of three Tampa strip clubs: Angels, Dolls, and Tampa's Wild Things. He also owned The Chandelier Bar. Wayne had come across their radar nearly three years ago when a young woman had recognized him in a photo stack at the Tampa Police Department. The woman, Eva, had entered the country on a boat at night. From her recollection, she had been one of fourteen girls, all from Colombia. Eva had claimed that once they had arrived in Tampa, they had been separated. Like the other girls with her, Eva had been sold into a life of sex trafficking. Like many similar stories, she had been held in a low-budget hotel against her will. Luckily for her, she had escaped the day before, and someone had brought her to safety at a local hospital.

When Eva had singled out Wayne, it really hadn't been a big surprise, considering his choice in entrepreneurship. But when pressed, she claimed she only remembered seeing him at the docks when she had arrived, and the girls were separated. She never saw him again. When they pressed harder, she then changed her story to that he looked like the man in the photo. From a prosecutor's standpoint, that would never hold water, but it was enough to add Wayne to the FBI's watch list and begin monitoring the dealings of Wayne Keaton Enterprises.

Soon The Shores apartment complex came into sight. He turned and parked his black truck in a secure garage, then took the stairs up three flights to his condo overlooking Hillsborough Bay. His unit was the first on the hallway. He lived alone, and after two years, he still only knew two of his neighbors out of the sixty-four apartments that were neatly arranged in three buildings lining the sandy shoreline. They thought he was a construction foreman, not an FBI special agent working the human trafficking division.

After checking the hallway, he unlocked the door and slowly entered his apartment with his hand resting on his gun. His German shepherd stood at attention.

"At ease, Sam."

After a six-year-long relationship that had ended with her wanting someone with a normal career, he only had his dog of two years to run to him and greet him with kisses. Aiden pulled out a treat from a glass jar and tossed it on Samantha's bed. The dog ran to the far corner of the room and lay down to chew on her reward.

With his loyal companion settled for the night, Aiden walked down the short hall that led to a second bedroom that he had converted into his study. He flipped the light switch and faces and names of Keith's lucrative clients and a photo of Wayne appeared along the walls. In the middle of the groupings hung pictures of Keith and Cassandra. The words *Missing, Presumed Dead* were stamped across their smiling faces. With Samantha on duty, everything was as it should be.

He walked over to a small desk and picked up a sheet of paper. He made notes from tonight about Addison and the opened boxes. More questions about her entered his head, but the answers would have to wait. Tomorrow would come way too early.

***

The sound of birds chirping woke Addison. She slowly opened her eyes to darkness. For a moment, she was confused by her surroundings. Then she remembered she was in Tampa.

She turned toward the wall of windows and remembered she had lowered the night shades late last night. She turned back to her left and saw the alarm clock still flashing *12:00*. Raising up, she reached for the lamp and turned on a light. Keith and Cassandra's bedroom came into full view, bringing reality crashing back.

She looked at her watch: 10:15 a.m. She questioned the time until she saw the tiny black line beating slowly around the numbers. She couldn't remember the last time she had slept this late.

She flipped some switches, and the ceiling lights and fan came on first, then the sound of the window shades slowly rising. She watched as a beautiful, sunny morning came into full view without a hint of the passing storm. Wow, to wake up to this every morning. How had Keith and Cassandra ever gotten out of bed? Thinking of Cassandra's busy work schedule brought back sadness. She probably had rarely had the opportunity for coffee in bed. Addison got out of bed and pushed the thoughts away as she headed to the kitchen to make herself some coffee and to find her phone to call Riley.

The built-in expresso machine took a few minutes to figure out as she tried to remember Cassandra's instructions from over a year ago. Finally, she got it working. Eyeing her cell phone, she thought of Riley. She picked it up to call Owen but noticed immediately it was dead. She had failed to charge her phone last night. She dug into her purse, found her charger, and plugged it into the wall. Soon the phone came to life with two missed calls: one from Owen and another from a number she didn't recognize.

She pressed Owen's name, but there was no answer. She frowned, then left a message that she had just woken up and please call back. She looked at the other number again, but there had been no message. She ignored the call, assuming it was a telemarketer or another nosy reporter sniffing around her business. Then she left for the bedroom to get dressed.

Twenty minutes later, Addison stood in front of the mirrored vanity, combing her wet, tangled hair. Her dark roots were starting to show again. Blowing her red hair dry, she wondered if it had been a good decision to change her hair color after her divorce. Cassandra had told her when she had first seen it on a video call that it looked nice, just different. Had that been code for "I liked it better dark brown, but since you're going through a hard time, honesty isn't always the best path"?

She wondered who had cut and colored Cassandra's hair; it had always looked perfect. No dark roots and no evidence of early gray. Cassandra had gone from brown to blonde at eighteen and never went back. Blonde had suited her. She imagined most of her friends and colleagues—or Keith, for that matter—wouldn't have recognized her with dark hair if she had walked right past them. She turned off the dryer and made a mental note to fix her hair while she had the time without Riley.

Back in the kitchen, Addison refilled her coffee cup and picked up the printed instructions she had received yesterday from the lawyer. As she read them and sipped from her coffee, she realized the words made no sense when she turned the page. She flipped back and saw a three on the bottom of the page and then a five on the next page. A page was missing.

She folded the paper back and looked at the staple. A tear was visible. Why was page four missing?

She looked back at the heading on page three: *Rose Investment Firm, 1405 Druid Lane, Suite 1900, Tampa, Fla. 33612*. Then back at page five with a new heading: *Rolling Tides, 18 Pelican Way, Clearwater Beach, Fla. 33755*. It was the directions for the beach house.

Addison flipped back to the front of the handout and found the phone number listed for Greer & Cruz. She called and talked to the secretary, who told her someone would call her back very shortly.

With a piqued interest in Rose Investment Firm, Addison decided to locate Keith's study in the meantime. There were two doors at the end of the hallway. She opened one and found a state-of-the-art gym. She walked around the mirrored room and envisioned Cassandra riding her fancy computerized bike. They often had chatted while she had exercised. She eyed a scale and walked over. When stepping on it, the computer screen came to life and read her weight. "130!" She hadn't noticed the weight loss over the last two weeks. Finally, she had something to smile about. She left and closed the door.

The other door opened to the study, and Addison stepped back. Something felt wrong. There were only four boxes, and all were opened. She read each of the labels. The two marked *Personal* were filled with memorabilia such as framed pictures and awards. The two marked *Documents* were filled with files. Who had opened the boxes?

She thought of the alarm last night, the open door, and now the torn page from the directions. A wild scenario was forming in Addison's head as she timidly read through the files. Nothing stood out as

strange or sinister. Home and car insurance policies, college documents, tax documents along with the years, banking and credit card
statements. Nothing from Rose Investment Firm. She stood up and
looked around the room. Of all the boxes in the house, these were the
only ones that had been opened.

Suddenly, the phone rang in her hand. She recognized the Tampa
area code. "Hello?"

"Is this Addison Shaw?"

Thinking it was the lawyer, she didn't hesitate. "Yes, it is. Thanks
for calling me back so quickly."

There was a brief silence, and then the male voice replied, "I'm not
returning your call."

Leaving the study, Addison thought it was another pesky reporter.
She rudely demanded, "Excuse me, but who is this?"

"A friend of Cassidy."

An uneasy feeling washed over Addison. Cassandra hated to be
called Cassidy, even though Keith had named their boat *Cassidy Rose*
after her. The boat had been a surprise, and Cassandra had confided in
her that she hated the name. But since Keith never referred to her as
Cassidy, she just let the issue slip. After all, *Cassidy Rose* was already
printed on the boat.

Addison kept that information to herself. "What do you want?"

"I don't want anything; I'm just calling to warn you."

She immediately felt uneasy. "Warn me from what?"

"Go home. You are not welcome here. Go back to your son in Atlanta and don't return."

Addison turned a full 360 in the living room, sensing that she wasn't alone. She walked over to the alarm panel, and it was still active from last night. She looked at the lock on the front door. It was locked. Then she rushed to the back door and found the lock turned. She was safe.

She heard laughter, and she nearly dropped the phone as chill bumps covered her arms and her spine tingled. Was he watching her?

She demanded, "What do you know about me and my son?"

"Only that you are in danger if you stay. Go back to Atlanta, and you and your son will live."

The line went dead.

"Hello? Who is this?"

The sound of the doorbell caused her to nearly faint. She spun around and stared down the hallway, debating what to do. The bell sounded again, and she found herself slowly moving toward the door.

She stepped into the foyer, still clutching her phone, and stopped at the door. She took a deep breath and leaned forward to look out the peephole. No one was there.

She caught the door handle, trying not to slide to the floor in fright. Taking another deep breath, she stepped to the right and slowly opened a blind. Her heart skipped a beat as a brown delivery truck pulled away from the curb. She looked down and saw the package on the doorsteps.

After turning off the alarm, she opened the door. She stepped out on the porch and looked around at the empty driveway. A woman was walking a brown-and-white schnauzer along the sidewalk, paying her no attention. Addison picked up the twelve-by-twelve box weighing a few pounds and closed and locked the door behind her. She had expected to see Cassandra's or Keith's name on the box, but instead, it had hers. No sender was listed. Weird. Had to be from the lawyer's office.

Just then her phone rang. This time, she was sure it was the lawyer's number. She left the package on a small chair by the door and walked into the kitchen. "Hello?" she said with a cracked voice, still quite shaken from earlier.

"Ms. Shaw, it's David Greer returning your call."

Relief washed over her. "Oh, I'm so glad to hear from you. Thanks for calling me back so soon."

"Certainly. Is everything okay?"

She debated how much to tell him. "Not really, but I'm still trying to adjust to everything."

"Understandable. How can I assist you today?"

"Did you send me a package—a small brown box?"

"No. Just the envelope with the keys and instructions."

She looked at the printed handout on the kitchen counter. "Yes, the instructions you left me. I'm missing a page."

"Missing a page? I don't understand."

Addison picked up the pages and flipped through them again. "Page four is torn out. And according to the heading on page three, it concerns Rose Investment Firm."

"That can't be. I read and checked over the document myself, sealed it in that envelope with the keys, and hand-delivered it to Peter Marks, your driver."

"Then how is it missing?"

An image of the open back door from last night flashed before her eyes. Someone had been in Cassandra's house.

She felt ill. "I'm sorry, but I need to call you back."

"Yes, but I'm deeply concerned someone opened that envelope before it was delivered to you."

Addison remembered breaking the seal in front of Peter. "No, I was the first to open the envelope."

"Then I don't understand," David stated.

Addison thought of the opened boxes in the study and how everything of Cassandra's had been packed away in boxes before she had arrived. "Um, on second thought, I'd like to drop by your office. I have some questions. Can you make time to see me today?"

"I will make the time. I'll be here until six o'clock."

"Thank you. I appreciate that."

Addison ended the call. Then she picked up the card on the counter from Agent Greene and pressed the number listed for the FBI agent. It went straight to voicemail. She waited a moment, then said, "This is Addison Shaw. We met last night. Please give me a call. It's important."

She tucked her phone in her purse and tried to push all doubt aside. She wasn't imagining any of this. Someone had been here last night. She hadn't been alone. A cold pin trickle crawled down her back. She no longer felt safe in the house.

She quickly thumbed through the keys until she saw the one marked *Lexus*. Then she took the instructions and the remaining keys and placed them back in the envelope. She ran to the master bathroom and threw her toiletries into her luggage, then zipped up her suitcases. She set the alarm, then drove away in Cassandra's black Lexus. The forgotten unopened box still sat on the chair in the foyer.

# CHAPTER 4

A slick dark-blue Mercedes pulled into Sunshine Properties and parked in the *Reserved* spot for the owner and founder. Isaac stepped out, wearing an expensive tan summer suit Demi had just bought him last week. He nodded at one of his realtors who was talking with potential clients as they climbed into her Land Rover. As they sped away, he opened the front door and sighed with relief as the cold AC washed over him. "How's it going, Georgia?"

His highly competent receptionist replied, "Perfect timing!" She stood with a big grin and handed him a file. "We just got an offer on Stacy's listing at 168 Cliff Drive. Just two hundred and fifty under; can you believe it?"

Isaac tried his best not to look at her gaping blouse as he took the file. Demi hated Georgia Fountain based only on the fact that she was knock-dead gorgeous, which was one of the reasons he had hired her to greet potential clients. The fact that she was smart, and a hell of a time manager was just a bonus.

He scanned the terms and smiled. "This is good. Has Stacy called the owners yet?"

"Not yet. She's at a closing."

"Okay, keep me posted."

She took the file from him and slid back into her leather chair. Isaac was only a few steps away from his office door when he heard her call out, "Oh, did Mr. Martini get in touch with you?"

He spun back around. "When did he call?"

"About an hour ago. Should I have interrupted your appointment?"

A forced smile appeared on Isaac's face. "No."

Relief washed over her perfectly painted features. "That's what I thought. I know how demanding the Millers can be."

"Yes, they can. Hold all my calls please."

Georgia responded, but he kept walking and closed his office door behind him. Taking a seat, he pulled out his cell phone from his jacket and scrolled through his recent calls. He saw a different area code around the suggested time frame. He had been too busy with the Millers to take any calls. Not recognizing the number, it had to be another one of Wayne Keaton's burner phones. He pressed the number and didn't have to wait long for an answer.

A raspy voice answered. "Busy morning?"

"Why are you calling the office number?"

"You didn't answer your cell, and we need to meet today."

He immediately knew this wasn't good. He asked, "Where?"

"The docks. Park behind the old boat shed on the north corner."

Isaac noted the time. "I can leave in five minutes."

"See you around noon." The line went dead.

Isaac ended the call and leaned back in his chair. The photo of

54

Demi and their two kids smiled back at him from the corner of his desk. An uneasy feeling consumed him as he contemplated the location. He tried shaking it off.

He remembered the day that Wayne, also known as Jack Martini, had walked into his office looking for a property. A deal that was too good to be true was signed. At the time, he had made light of the logic, relying on the old adage "If I don't ask, then I don't know." So, he had just focused on the much-needed money. When he had left his realty firm to strike out on his own, it hadn't been as easy as he had hoped. Then Demi had gotten pregnant and wanted a bigger house.

Now, several years later, Isaac didn't need Wayne's money. Every deal made now left Wayne the loser and Isaac the winner. Isaac had made sure that Wayne needed him more than he needed Wayne. Isaac had been greedy at first, but stupid he was not.

But everything had changed with the hit on Keith Rose. When Wayne had discovered the FBI were watching Keith, Wayne's boss, the Russian, had ordered that Keith be eliminated. If Keith could be eliminated, then so could he. A thought that had not been lost on Isaac; therefore, he just had to be smarter. It was time to get out, but the questions remained: Could he? And when?

\*\*\*

Aiden hadn't noticed the missed call. He was knee-deep in questioning an exotic dancer who had just come forward on claiming harassment from her workplace, Tampa's Wild Things, owned and operated by Wayne Keaton for the last twelve years. Aiden had hoped she would be a good fit as a mole, but after an hour of listening to Babs Goodshoe, he had his doubts. She wasn't the one to help bring down Wayne and his sleazy downtown strip joint. Babs was not a victim of human trafficking. She was a United States citizen born in Jackson, Mississippi, who had taken the dancing job to support her two school-age girls after her sugar daddy had run off.

Aiden walked out of the interview room of the Tampa Police Department. He caught the eye of Police Chief Rudy Gomez and walked his way. Rudy had been overseeing the Tampa police office for eight years now, and Aiden had grown to respect his strong work ethic. He was also tough on crime and criminals. Their working relationship had been vital to each other's investigations over the years, and they continued to support each other well.

"Thanks, Chief, for the tip, but we're not interested."

Rudy looked past him to the woman still sitting in interrogation room three, talking with one of his officers. "Well, it's not every day they walk in of their own free will. Thought maybe I had something for you."

"No offense, but she's as dumb as the fake rocks on her fingers. And besides, she's not one of Wayne's elite dancers. She works on weeknights."

Rudy chuckled. "Oh, you're looking for a rat with the whole package. Well, good luck on that one."

Aiden frowned. "I'll find her. Circumstances and bad choices lead the women to him. The right one will come along. I've just got to be patient."

The police chief tapped him on the shoulder. "Yes, you do. You're doing great work, Special Agent Greene."

"Thanks, Chief. I appreciate that."

"But, hey, keep us in the loop. I don't want to accidentally pick up your rat on prostitution charges."

Aiden laughed. "No kidding. Later and thanks again."

Aiden took an elevator to the garage to retrieve his truck. When he stepped off, he saw he had four missed calls. On the third voicemail, he heard Addison's voice. He began running to his truck. Firing up the engine, he contemplated how he needed to handle her.

Keith and Cassandra had been ruled legally dead. But only a few people knew that no bodies had been found. Reba, Keith's ex-wife, had insisted on a memorial service.

Under FBI Supervisory Special Agent Quincy Aikens's direction, Aiden had been leading a quiet investigation into Keith, a prominent Tampa businessman. With the help of his partner, Jonas, and another agent, Trevor Reid, they had been investigating Keith for the last six months. With their hard work, they had gotten close to finally nailing him with money laundering when his boat had exploded. Add the event to the wire transfer of $5 million, and now there were more questions with very little answers. Someone had wanted the Roses dead or to give the impression that they were. Either way, it didn't sit well with the FBI's monthslong investigation.

Aiden and Jonas had discovered Keith when they had been tailing Wayne one night when he had left Angels at 11 p.m. and gotten lucky when Wayne hadn't driven straight home. Instead, he had driven to a secluded park on Davis Island. A man in a jogging suit had approached him by foot and gotten inside his car for a five-minute chat. When Wayne pulled away from the park, they followed the other man to 28 Davis Island. From there, an intense investigation into Keith and Rose Investment Firm had begun.

Aiden replayed Addison's voicemail and frowned. He pressed Save and called Jonas. "Got a minute to spare?"

"Only for you. I still owe you lunch," Jonas replied.

Aiden laughed. "You owe me more than lunch. Are you at the office?"

"Yeah, you heading this way?"

"Yes, just left the Tampa police station on a dead-end lead. I'll be there in about ten minutes."

Jonas, at thirty-two, was just a year older than Aiden and was also a Tampa native. Aiden had known him since the academy. They had been made partners four years ago when they had been added to the human trafficking division that covered the Tampa Bay area. Jonas's wife, Alanis, was Puerto Rican, and she had welcomed Aiden with open arms into their home that they shared with their two children. It wasn't unusual for her to feed him and Jonas her mouth-watering tripleta sandwiches at 1 a.m. following a late-night stakeout. Add the Sunday night football games and long talks over ice-cold beer, and their working relationship had evolved into a true friendship. There was no one he trusted more or enjoyed working with in the FBI than Jonas.

Aiden drove quickly through traffic and parked in the gated garage of the FBI Tampa Field Office. Taking the stairs to his office on the second floor, he made it there in eight minutes. Seeing Jonas sitting at his desk, he motioned him over to his office.

Jonas entered and took a seat in front of Aiden's desk. "This about the Rose case?"

"Yep." Aiden pulled a file from his locked cabinet and placed it on the desk. He opened it, and a picture of Addison getting out of her car in Atlanta appeared. "The doctor's sister is in town."

Jonas picked up the photo. "Addison Shaw. Well, that didn't take long."

"No. The Rose jet landed at six last night. I would've called you earlier, but I knew you were on the Baker case."

"Yeah, we finally nailed the scumbag at two in the morning, leaving the back door of the laundromat. I was just finishing up the paperwork."

"Well, you weren't the only one burning the midnight oil."

Jonas laid the photo back down. "What happened?"

58

"The house alarm at the Rose canal home at 28 Davis Island went off a little after twelve. Officer Williams, one of the patrolmen on Davis Island that we contacted earlier, called me. He and his partner found the back door wide open. After searching the home, they assumed it was the wind from the storm. The island had lost power. Seems the Rose estate wasn't the only alarm going off."

"Did you get a look at the house?"

"I was able to get a quick peek at the study. There were four boxes, all opened."

"Do you think it was Addison who opened them, searching for something?"

"I don't know but listen to this." Aiden replayed her voice message on speaker.

"Sounds upset. You call her back yet?"

"Not yet."

"You think she's in on it? Or worse yet, Keith and Cassandra are alive, and they're using Addison to help them? After all, we have no bodies from the accident."

Aiden replied, "If Keith is alive and he's using Addison to help him, then why is she reaching out?"

"Damn. This case can't get any more complicated," Jonas announced.

Aiden looked at the thick file on Addison. The estate would take a long time to settle, but Addison would become the largest beneficiary of the Rose estate. It made no sense. Keith's brother, Marty Rose, would receive ownership of the business, and Keith's three daughters from his first marriage would each receive a million which was pennies compared with the bulk of the estate, which was worth $89 million. A lot of the money would be tied up with Rose Investment Firm, but Addison still was looking at over $50 million when everything was settled. "It's a lot of money that was given to her. Raises a lot of questions, that's for sure."

Jonas flipped through the photos and picked up one of Cassandra. He shook his head. "How does a smart, classy-looking woman like her end up with the likes of Keith Rose? I don't get it."

"Me neither. All her hard work to make it as a surgeon, then she climbs in bed with a criminal who could drag her to prison for life," Aiden replied.

"Maybe she didn't know. They do say love is blind. After all, she did save his life, so maybe she did fall in love with her patient. Just look at the first Mrs. Rose. She was clueless."

Aiden chuckled. "Yeah, well, the first Mrs. Rose turned a blind eye to a lot of things. She didn't care to know what her husband did every day, just as long as he brought in the money. She never traveled with him, and he would be gone for weeks at a time." He looked closely into Cassandra's blue eyes. "But this one, she was smart. Why work so hard to save lives just to hook up with a man involved in money laundering and human trafficking? That's what doesn't make sense. They don't go together."

"That's my thoughts on it. I mean, she did log over sixty hours most weeks. No way to keep tabs on her husband's daily affairs. And if she didn't know, then why would her sister?"

Aiden flipped through paperwork until he found Addison's bio. He reread it, then said, "Last record of visit was last summer. Next planned visit wasn't supposed to be until the end of July. Cassandra had worked straight through the Christmas holiday, and Addison had stayed home over her spring break. As far as we can see, their only contact had been phone or email."

"No communication through social media?"

"The doctor had accounts, but they're basically nonexistent. She had no time." Aiden lifted up a financial statement for Addison and passed it over to Jonas. "She was barely getting by. There's no record of large deposits other than the one for her student loan; a gift from Keith at Christmas."

"I'd like to know whose idea that was."

"Yeah, me too. It was the exact amount of the loan. So easy to trace."

"Maybe she found out something on Keith and it was a payoff."

Aiden's brow creased as he contemplated Jonas's idea. "You think she knew of the money laundering and was blackmailing Keith?"

"Paying off a student loan as a Christmas gift is quite generous. No one ever did that for me."

"That loan was a drop in the bucket for Keith. And besides, I don't think Addison had the time or resources to investigate him. And why would she, when Cassandra gave the impression to everyone we talked to that she was happily married?"

Jonas threw his hands up. "I'm just saying it would be a motive. Nothing explains why Addison received the bulk of the estate."

"Then she sells them out and her sister ends up dead?" Aiden frowned. He looked at Addison's picture again. The memory of the night before came back. "Last night, she told the officers she had been in the bathtub when the alarm went off, but the water in the tub was cold."

"Cold?"

"Yeah. One of the Officers felt the water. They saw an empty wine glass too. She might have been drunk. You should have seen her; she looked a mess. Makeup smeared all over her face. Red, puffy eyes."

Aiden tossed the picture and picked up another photo of her pushing Riley on a swing at the park near her apartment in Atlanta. "Her life truly seems a mess: a newly divorced mom working in a small school district that pays shit. I just don't know; I can't seem to read her."

"Well, I say it's time you get to know her. Call her back," Jonas suggested.

# CHAPTER 5

Once she was safely out of the house and down the street, Addison pulled over. She tried to collect herself and push all her fear and images of strange men chasing her out of her mind.

She removed the paperwork from David Greer's office envelope. Then she typed in the address in the car's GPS and pressed *Go*. The office appeared on the map five miles away in Downtown Tampa.

Just as Addison placed the car in drive, she second-guessed herself. Maybe she should go to Rolling Tides first. It was a gated community, so surely, she would be safe there as she processed everything. Addison didn't want to just show up at the lawyer's office without a complete picture of what was going on. Placing the car in park, she typed in *18 Pelican Way* and immediately noticed it was saved under Cassandra's favorites. She re-pressed Go and pulled away from the curb.

Rolling Tides was only twenty-five miles away, but with summer traffic, it was scheduled to take over an hour. Addison cautiously drove the speed limit while constantly checking her rearview mirror. She kept tabs on cars and trucks that slowed, passed, and sped by her. Her mind was racing when her cell phone rang in her purse. She carefully pulled it out while keeping her eyes on the road, chastising herself for not hooking up to Bluetooth. "Hello?"

"Ms. Shaw, this is Agent Greene, returning your call."

At the sound of his voice, relief washed over her. "Thank you so much for calling me back."

"You sound upset. What happened?"

"I think someone might have been in the house last night."

"Why do you think that?"

"There was a handout on the kitchen counter from Keith and Cassandra's lawyer. A page was torn out. I already called the lawyer to confirm; Mr. Greer checked the document himself and sealed the envelope. Yesterday, he gave it to Peter Marks, my driver, and then I opened the envelope."

"You think someone was in the house and ripped a page out of some documents?"

"I do."

A brief silence went by, then Aiden asked, "Where are you now?"

"I had to leave the house because I was so rattled staying there. In the study, there were some opened boxes that looked like someone had gone through them." More unnerving silence passed. "Are you still there?" she asked.

"Yeah. So you're saying you haven't opened any boxes in the home?"

"No . . . well, I mean, yes. But nothing from the study. Look, I only just went into the study this morning when I noticed that the page missing from Mr. Greer's notes was concerning Rose Investment Firm. Someone else opened them!"

He asked again, "Where are you?"

"Um, heading to Cassandra's beach house in Clearwater."

"I'll meet you. I can head over there now. Do not go in without me. There's a coffee shop across from the gated entrance. You know the one?"

"Yes, in the shopping center, right by the ice cream shop."

A horn blew, and Addison swerved as a large truck passed her on the right. She hadn't been paying attention and had accidentally crossed over into the other lane. With caution, she moved to the slow lane. "I'll meet you there, probably in another forty-five minutes, depending on the traffic on Memorial Causeway."

"That's fine. Just get there and sit tight. I should be there soon after."

She hung up, deciding to wait to tell him about the phone call from the stranger. She had enough on her mind and wanted to arrive in one piece at the coffee shop.

*** 

A loud siren blasted to warn of an incoming cargo ship. Wayne Keaton turned and watched as the vessel was guided into a vacant slot. Men readied themselves to receive the shipment as a crane moved toward the boat to begin removing large crates with Japanese writing plastered on each one.

Gravel crushing beneath tires caused Wayne to turn back around. It was Jayden Hart, arriving right on schedule. He walked to the black BMW and quickly slid into the front passenger seat. He wasted no time with small talk.

"So, what did you find at the house? Anything?"

Jayden, the Russian's top hired hand, reached into the back seat and grabbed a locked briefcase. "It wasn't easy to get. The bitch wouldn't go to sleep, then a damn storm rolled in, but I found a file with your name on it."

"Christ!" Wayne mumbled as he watched Jayden insert a key in the lock and then heard the sound of the locks twisting.

Jayden handed him the file.

"This everything?" Wayne asked.

"I can't be sure. But the boxes were labeled. Sure made my job much easier."

"Labeled!" Wayne cried.

"Oh yeah! The damn lawyer's hired help labeled every damn box. Anybody could have walked in and opened the box labeled *Documents* and seen your name jump out."

Wayne saw his name written in black ink on the manilla file folder.

"We got lucky. Just numbers and references, but the boss is worried because if Keith's threat holds true—"

Wayne interrupted, "Then we can still be in danger." He thought back to his last meeting with Keith. He had been jittery and awfully nervous. He had also said if anything happened to him, there was insurance and the whole organization was going down. "Where is Addison Shaw now?"

"She's on the move, but I've got a tracker on all three cars. I'm just waiting on the boss to give the word. Juan's watching her now."

Wayne took a deep breath and closed his eyes as he thought about all that could go wrong. He worried because Juan Diego wasn't as good as Jayden, but Jayden couldn't be everywhere. He looked back at Jayden. "I hope he doesn't screw up." He then looked down and began reading page after page of numbers. "What is this?"

"It's a code for something. But it's ours now. Even if Keith did leave this behind for someone to find, now they'll find nothing."

Time ticked away as Wayne carefully scanned each page. Finally, he set them all down and closed the briefcase. Looking at his watch, he stated, "It's almost noon."

Jayden looked up toward the entrance and found the one-way driveway empty. "I should go. No need for me to be present unless I'm needed." He glanced back at Wayne. "Am I needed?"

"Not yet."

Wayne opened the door, leaving the briefcase behind, and stepped out. The scorching sun held nothing back, as the sky was void of clouds. He watched as the BMW kicked up rocks while it sped away. Walking toward his Lincoln, he took a quick look around and then climbed in behind the wheel. He started the engine and adjusted the AC. When he looked back up, he saw Isaac's blue Mercedes approaching. Wayne motioned for Isaac to come to him.

Isaac parked his car but left it running and removed his jacket. Then he stepped out of the car with a frown as he looked below at the ships docked and the men working. He opened the door to the Lincoln and climbed in. "I don't know why you picked this location."

Wayne looked at all the commotion. "Because it's busy. They could care less who's sitting up here. Besides, we know the owner."

Isaac cut to the chase. "Did we get into Keith's house?"

Wayne nodded. "We did."

"And?" Isaac spoke with little patience.

Wayne lied, "Nothing. We're good."

Isaac shook his head and looked around nervously. "I think we need to lie low and cease all contact between us."

Wayne frowned. "We can't right now."

"Why the hell not? You know the FBI is still out there monitoring everything and everyone."

"We need a property."

"What?" Isaac was flabbergasted.

"Can't be helped. There was a shipment mix-up within Rose Investment Firm.  Something we couldn't control at the time."

Isaac smirked. "I hope you don't think this will be the only one with Keith gone."

Wayne looked at him with a serious expression. "Look, the boss is coming to town with the shipment. We can't screw this up. Can you get the property by nightfall or not?"

A brief silence passed before Isaac reluctantly agreed with a nod. "After this, though, tell your boss to chill for a few months."

Wayne chuckled. "This is why you've never met him. You don't make demands."

"Trust me, I don't want to meet him or even know his name."

Now Wayne smirked. "Allows you to continue with ignorance or your guilt-free conscious."

Isaac sat back and rubbed his face. Then he slowly turned to Wayne. "We're getting greedy, Wayne. Keith knew it too. It's been a good run, but at some point, it can't continue."

Wayne laughed. "Oh Isaac. Once you sign with the devil, there is no going back."

# CHAPTER 6

It took thirty minutes for Addison to maneuver through Memorial Parkway; after all, it was July, the height of the summer season. She pulled into a slot closest to the coffee shop. When she cut the engine, she realized her hands were shaking. She rubbed them along her thighs, trying to calm her nerves.

She heard a tap on her window and jumped. It was Aiden.

She closed her eyes briefly, then grabbed her purse and stepped out.

He immediately apologized for scaring her. "I thought you saw me."

"No. Too much going on in my head."

"Let's go inside and talk in the AC."

Aiden closed her door and gestured for her to go first. They walked down the sidewalk, and he opened the door to the coffee shop for her. "Why don't you take a seat here? Can I get you anything? Coffee or iced tea?"

She glanced at the menu with way too many options for her brain to comprehend. "Some sweet tea would be nice."

"You got it; I'll be right back."

Addison watched as he placed the order and couldn't help but notice how the twentysomething behind the counter smiled at him. She laughed at something he said and gave him the change. When he pocketed his wallet in his jeans, Addison found her eyes lingering a little too long on his backside. He turned, catching her. She quickly looked down at her purse and pulled out her phone, trying to hide her embarrassment.

"I hope you like peach tea."

Addison looked up and their eyes locked briefly. "Yes, peach is great, thank you."

He smiled, and that small dimple appeared again. She reached for her tea and noticed he didn't wear a wedding ring. She pushed the thoughts out of her head. That was a road she did not need to go down.

"Why don't we start from the beginning? Tell me everything you've done since arriving."

She nodded. With rapid speed, Addison recounted every event since landing at Peter O. Knight Airport. He interrupted her a few times to ask about communicating with David Greer since the memorial service. When she told him about the warning phone call, he immediately became agitated.

"Wait, this happened back at the house before I talked to you earlier?"

"Yes." She followed his eyes and noticed how he scanned the café and the cars in the parking lot. "You're scaring me."

He looked back at her. "Tell me again exactly what the man said."

She narrowed her eyes. "Honestly, the more I think about it, it must be just another sleazeball reporter who thinks it would be funny to scare me. Mr. Greer warned me about this. Everything about me and my son has been plastered all over the news for over a week now." She used her hands to make air quotes as she said, "The new heiress with millions." She rolled her eyes.

He didn't comment, so she continued. "Why did you show up at my sister's house last night? You're an FBI agent. What interest would you have with a house alarm going off?"

He avoided her question. "May I have your phone to look at the number that called you?"

She sighed with frustration. "I wish you would just level with me."

She picked up her phone and slid the screen open. She pressed an icon and scrolled down to the number with the Tampa area code. She gave it to him and watched as he made a call with his own phone. She listened to him rattle off the number and waited.

"Got it, thanks." He ended his call. "It's an untraceable number."

"You mean like a burner phone?"

"Yeah, just like the movies."

She grinned at his joke and studied him. Trust was something that she just didn't hand over easily anymore thanks to Owen.

"Anything else?" he asked.

She thought about telling him about the package as well, but her mind was racing with wild theories. What if the package had been sent to her at Cassandra's request? Sent by a colleague in event of her death? No. She wouldn't tell him about the package just yet. She didn't quite trust this special agent who had just appeared at the house. Why now? Why not introduce himself earlier when she had been in town for the memorial service? No. Until she spoke with the lawyer, she would give nothing more to this man. Keith and Cassandra had been good people. Whatever was going on, she needed to know before she would allow just anyone to blight their reputation.

Suddenly, she stood. "I'm going to my sister's beach house now. Then I plan to see Mr. Greer today. I don't like how all Cassandra's belongings were packed up. I should have been the one to do that. Not some stranger or housekeeper."

He stood. "I'll go with you."

She shook her head. "No. My gut tells me you're not being totally honest with me. Something's going on, and I'll figure it out myself with Mr. Greer's help."

She turned away. He grabbed her arm to stop her, then looked around. "Please allow me to accompany you to the beach house." He lowered his voice. "We can talk more there."

His grip was firm. She looked him in the eyes. "Are you giving me a choice?"

"There is always a choice." He released her arm. "But please, Ms. Shaw, allow me to accompany you to the beach house. It's important."

"Fine." She walked out the door with him on her heels.

His black truck stayed right behind her as they stopped at a gated entrance. Addison typed in the code listed on the paperwork. The gate opened.

Addison no longer needed the GPS; there were only three more turns before reaching Pelican Way. Soon the multicolored, three-story beach homes that dotted the coastline came into view. Then she saw Rolling Tides, and with it came a flood of memories.

This place had been the setting of so much joy in her life as well as Cassandra's. The house was Keith's; he had bought it after divorcing Reba. Addison remembered Cassandra's phone call the day after she had met Keith: "I'm in love. Is that possible? Is there really such a thing as love at first sight?" Addison had listened to all the stories over the next several months as Keith had worked to fully recover from his heart attack. By a year later, they had married at this house, with Addison and Riley in attendance, along with Natalie, Brandi, and Layla.

Addison parked the Lexus and stared at Rolling Tides. She and Riley had vacationed there every summer since he had been born. She had never known just how much money Keith had until the accident. Of course, she had known of his generosity firsthand, with his paying off her student loans and all the flights to and from Atlanta. But also, Cassandra had shared how no prenup had been signed like the one with his first wife. The day Cassandra had said yes, Keith had paid off her student loans accumulated over the last decade as she had studied to become a surgeon. Two days later, he had moved Cassandra out of her downtown apartment and into his canal home. Everything of his had become hers.

*And soon mine.*

Her eyes left the house and looked in the rearview mirror just in time to watch Aiden pull into the circular driveway behind her.

Addison cut the engine and looked at the envelope from the lawyer resting on the passenger seat. She pulled out the document and keys labeled *18 Pelican Way*. Scanning a few paragraphs, she found the security code. She instantly smiled; it was Riley's birthdate. After tucking the document back into the envelope, she wiped moisture from her eyes. Seeing the FBI agent standing outside his truck waiting on her, she finally gathered up everything and stepped out. The Lexus chirped as she hit the lock button.

"If you don't mind, I'd like to do a walk-through first." His hand rested on his gun clipped to his jeans as he spoke.

Addison turned away and scanned the front of the house. All the wood blinds were shut, and the double garage doors were securely closed on the ground floor. She walked to the cascading staircase that would take her to the entrance on the second floor. "If you think that's necessary. The neighborhood is gated."

"Just a precaution, Ms. Shaw."

She climbed the stairs without responding, then inserted the key and unlocked the door. She carefully opened the solid door and pushed it forward. She immediately heard the alarm beeping. "I'll need to enter the code."

He followed closely behind as she disarmed the alarm. Then she stepped back and took in the quiet house. All looked clean and untouched. Aiden informed her to wait as he stepped around her and began searching the home.

Addison slowly walked over to a small sitting room with bookshelves filled with books and pictures. Photos of the past few summers of the four of them—Keith, Cassandra, Riley, and her—caused her breath to catch. She immediately turned away.

On the wall was a photo of Keith with his three girls. They were all dressed in white, and Layla was sitting on top of Keith's shoulders. Natalie and Brandi held hands. They were so young. She couldn't help but wonder what Reba must be going through raising them alone: divorced and now a full-time single parent.

Time seemed to stand still as the only sound she heard was the click of Aiden's boots along the tile floors. He reappeared in the foyer. "Stay put. Just need to check the top floor."

Addison waited till he disappeared up the staircase before walking to the wall of windows that overlooked the large balcony and the Gulf of Mexico. She saw hundreds of families dotting the coastline, enjoying the hot summer day. There was no seaweed; the water was calm and clear. Children were building castles and riding the soft, gentle waves out in the water. A perfect beach day. Her eyes lingered on the horizon. Two boats were present: one a small yacht and another a fishing boat. Her gut clenched at the thought of the *Cassidy Rose* exploding on a normal day just like this.

Something touched her shoulder and she jumped.

"Sorry. The house is all clear." As if sensing what she was feeling, Aiden added, "I'm very sorry about your sister and brother-in-law. Were you close?"

"Yeah. We were."

He nodded. "Let's take a seat. There are some things I'd like to share with you."

She studied him, searching for sincerity. Finally, she agreed and walked around a table to the couch. He sat across from her on a loveseat.

"I don't think the explosion was an accident."

The words rocked her, and a wave of nausea consumed her. "What . . . what did you say?"

He got up and sat beside her, placing a hand on hers. "I know this may come as a shock to you."

"A shock?" she cried out. "Who would want to hurt my sister? She did only good. She . . . she saved lives. There are many people who are so grateful and—"

He interrupted. "Keith was the target."

She jerked her hand away, stood, and began pacing. "I don't understand. Why are you saying this? Keith was an honorable businessman. He was generous. He was . . ." She stopped and faced him. "Why are you saying these things to me?"

She read his bleak expression, and the threatening phone call immediately came roaring back in her head: "Go back to Atlanta, and you and your son will live."

Addison swayed to the side and caught herself on a table. The call hadn't been from a crazy reporter after all. Deep down she knew that wasn't plausible. But at the time, she couldn't wrap her head around why anyone would want to harm her.

She began to process everything aloud. "Someone was in the house last night. They tore a page from Mr. Greer's notes . . . It was about Rose Investment Firm." She pushed off the table. "I've got to go. I'm getting that page from him, and I'm going straight over to Rose Investment Firm and find out what the hell is going on!"

He tried to gently grab her by the arm as she ran by him. "Ms. Shaw, please don't. It's not safe for you."

She jerked her arm away. "My sister is dead. Never coming back. I must do this."

"Think of Riley, Ms. Shaw."

She stopped dead and looked back into his blue eyes. "What do you know about my son?"

"The same as the men who killed your sister."

# CHAPTER 7

The warm Caribbean breeze ruffled his long salt-and-pepper hair as he stood on the large white stone balcony facing a picture-perfect image of the alluring turquoise sea below. Most would say the Cayman Islands were a fine substitute for his homeland, Russia. But when Sebastian Hawks looked out into the ocean, it only saddened him as he thought of his motherland, still suffering the economic hardship that had followed the Cold War.

So many people he knew had left in the early nineties, searching for a better life for their families. Sebastian had been twenty-five when his mother had fallen ill with tuberculosis. He had left the following month after her death. His father had died fighting alongside the Russians in the Cabinda War in Angola back in '75. His mother was all he had had left in this world. When she had died, he had taken her necklace of Saint Peter and boarded a cargo ship to Turkey. From there, he had made it to the Caribbean and settled in the Caymans.

He spent his first years as a fisherman, learning the strength and powers of the ocean. Then he began seeing things that made men rich beyond his dreams. Young, beautiful women traded from all over the world, mostly from his homeland and Eastern Europe. With his Russian accent and burly sea body, he was well liked. A simple captain's job turned into something more when others realized his connections to Russia. He became an asset. Now he ran his own business and called his own shots. The man who had hired him was dead; his body would never be found. You can only have one captain on a ship.

Sebastian lifted his binoculars and scanned the coastline. There in the distance was his shipment, right on schedule. He had chosen this oceanfront home for the view of the shipping passage. He could see all cargo boats coming in from the Atlantic Ocean. He lowered his binoculars at the sound of his name. He turned and saw his Hungarian wife lounging on a cushioned chair by the sparkling pool. She was holding lotion up in her delicate hand for him to apply to her back. He set the binoculars down and approached her.

Maria turned over and untied her swim top. "Why don't you join me?" she asked in perfect English.

"Not now, my love. I have much work before tonight."

Maria pouted her lips and flipped back over, exposing her breasts. "Are you sure you don't have just a few minutes to spare? It's going to be a long night."

He took a seat beside her. Tonight, would be unpleasant for Maria. Maybe the attention would help ease her mind. He needed her to be her best, with no mistakes.

He looked at her perfect breasts waiting to be touched. Slowly, an awakening stirred within Sebastian. Why wouldn't it? Maria was twenty-four: young, vibrant, and healthy. He thought back to the day he first saw her. With her long, blonde hair; porcelain skin; and her virginity intact, he had been set to make top dollars off her. But instead, he had chosen to keep her. He needed someone in his home to help with the girls he brought to his estate. But after a few months of her in his home, he had become insanely smitten with her. So, at the age of forty-eight, Sebastian had finally taken a wife.

The arrangement worked well. By day, she taught the imported women English and skills, and by night, she fulfilled his every desire. He had made Maria a princess, and she was forever loyal and grateful. No other man had ever touched her, and no other woman had ever touched him since.

Her hand raked across his exposed chest above his buttoned shirt, and then she leaned in, kissing him slowly, her lips wet with desire. Sebastian scanned his property; two men were on guard with full view of his wife's display. He snapped his fingers and called out in Russian, and the men left.

He stood and quickly removed his trousers. Maria moved to the edge of the chair and began her magic. Sebastian raked his hands through her blonde tresses and then lifted her to her feet. Guiding her over to the outdoor bar, he untied her swimsuit bottoms and watched with anticipation as they hit the concrete. He turned her around and pushed her down on the bar. She cried out with delight as he pushed her harder into the granite, pleasuring her just as much as himself. He turned her back around and lifted her to his waist. He walked her over to the pool and descended the smooth slope into the warm water.

An hour later, Sebastian left the house a happy man. When he got to the docks, his shipment had already been unloaded and was heading toward his warehouse, all on schedule. No one asked what had delayed him.

Climbing into his open-door jeep, he drove two miles inland to his warehouse. Crate after crate of fine furniture and hardwood were directed by his foreman, Gabriel Hoffman, to their correct location. Sebastian smiled, put the jeep in gear, and sped around to the entrance of his warehouse where the showroom for customers was located. He parked in a slot by the front door and walked in. Vivian Birch, his floor-room manager, greeted him warmly.

"Beautiful day, Vivian."

"Indeed it is, Mr. Hawks." She handed him a folder, and he took it with him down a small hallway that led to his office.

Premier Design was one of the most profitable custom-design furniture stores in the Caymans. Sebastian imported the finest hardwoods and furniture from Europe and Asia to sell or refurbish. Vivian and her team had furnished and decorated over fifty estate homes on the island and countless others dotting the many Caribbean islands around them. Sebastian had won several coveted business awards and was known as one of the Caymans' richest proprietors. He also attended local events and donated to various charities. A true gentleman in the eyes of the islanders.

Settling in his leather chair behind a solid oak desk imported from his Russian homeland, he opened the file Vivian had given him. Inside was a printout of the week's sales. A smile crept upon his face. Business was good.

He heard a knock on his door. He looked up and found Gabriel.

"Inventory's looking good. Packaged well."

"Good to hear." Sebastian closed the file on his desk and inserted a key into his bottom drawer. "I've got five packages that need to go with the Cuba shipment this evening." He removed a brown envelope from the drawer and handed it to Gabriel. "Pickup is at seven. Boat leaves at seven thirty sharp."

Gabriel opened the envelope and glanced over the documents that would accompany the furniture shipment to Cuba. He stated, "This is the Miami package."

Sebastian noticed his demeanor. "Maria will be there to assist. I expect no problems. It's a small number this time around."

Gabriel nodded. "That will help, that's for sure."

"Are you up for this, Gabriel?" Sebastian asked in a concerned voice.

"Yes, of course. It's only five. A lot easier than last time."

Sebastian nodded. "Good. I'll be on the four o'clock flight. Call me when it's done."

Gabriel took the file and left.

Sebastian returned his attention to his open laptop and checked his flight status to Miami. On time. Later this evening, he was scheduled for drinks and dinner with the owner of a furniture store in Downtown Miami at 8 p.m. The owner, Valerie Blake, was an heiress of Blake Fine Furniture, a franchise with six stores throughout Florida. She had made the contact and was very interested in doing business with him. Another cool million was expected for Premier Design. Sebastian checked and composed a few emails, then shut his computer down and packed it up. It was time to go to Miami.

Once in his jeep, Sebastian made the call to Jayden to inquire about his little problem in Tampa. Jayden answered on the first ring.

Sebastian asked, "What's the situation?"

"The box was delivered, but she didn't open it. I made the call, but she's still here."

Sebastian frowned. "Damn! Where's she now?"

Jayden glanced at Rolling Tides and saw the parked Lexus, along with a truck. "She's at the beach house. She's got company."

"You run the plates yet?"

"Yeah, tag registered to a Doug Wood. Looks like a cop. What do you want me to do, boss?"

Sebastian let out a deep sigh. "Keep watching her. For now, I need her alive until we find out what she knows."

"Yes, sir."

The jeep pulled into the Owen Roberts International Airport parking lot. Sebastian ended his call but made no move to get out. He sat contemplating Addison Shaw.

Keith Rose had become a problem. A problem that had been taken care of. Now he had to discreetly move his investments to another firm. Had Keith left a paper trail? Had he really followed through on his threat if something happened to him he would reveal them all? If Keith had confided in his sister-in-law, she could waltz right into Rose Investment Firm and screw him with a click of a few buttons. Had that been his plan if he turned up dead? He had clearly given her enough money to disappear. Why hadn't he left the money with Marty, his brother and business partner? More scenarios played out in Sebastian's thoughts.

He thought back to his last meeting with Keith. He had seemed nervous and agitated, just as Wayne had described. It was understandable at the time since the FBI had discovered him through Wayne. He had assured Keith he would take care of it. But as weeks had gone by, Sebastian's gut instinct had told him something didn't feel right, and he couldn't chance Keith cutting a deal with the FBI.

Sebastian finally opened the jeep door and stepped out. It was time for him to find out firsthand what Addison Shaw was up to in Tampa.

***

Addison checked her rearview mirror and saw Aiden following her three car lengths back. They had agreed she needed to go to the law offices of Greer & Cruz to find out exactly what was supposed to be in that printout concerning Rose Investment Firm. She had been instructed to park in the adjacent garage, and he would park nearby to watch and see if anyone was following her.

Addison was nervous and her driving reflected it. She had missed two turns downtown. Thank goodness the Lexus's GPS continued to redirect her to the law office.

The garage was open to the sunlight outside. Addison drove up three floors until she found a parking spot near an elevator. She was still spooked even with the FBI agent watching out for her. She checked her surroundings and finally got out of the car and walked swiftly to the elevator. She faced the parked cars as she waited on the doors to open. At the sound of the chime, she turned and rushed ahead straight into another woman, causing her to drop an envelope.

"Oh, I'm so sorry!" Addison reached down and picked it up for her.

The other woman gave her a polite nod and continued on her way.

Addison pressed the first-floor button. While she was going down, she read the sign that explained a catwalk on level four that would take her across the street. She pressed the number four just as the elevator stopped on the ground level and opened.

Just as the door was about to close again, a man rushed in wearing blue jeans and a white T-shirt. Addison's gut tightened at the thought that this was the man who may have called her. She stepped to the far corner as the man stared at her, watching her every move.

Finally, the elevator came to a stop on the fourth floor and the doors opened. Addison dashed out with the man right on her heels. Panicked, she looked around for the walkway.

"Ma'am, are you lost?"

Addison swallowed her fear. "The catwalk."

"Just over there."

She looked to where he was pointing and then faced him again. He had neared within two feet. "I'm heading there myself."

Addison watched as he moved ahead of her before she followed. A few times, the man turned around and looked at her with curiosity. Up ahead, two women in business attire walked toward them. She began to relax.

On the other side of the glass-enclosed walkway was a security guard standing behind a desk. She quickly approached him and inquired about Greer & Cruz's office.

"Go around the corner to the set of elevators. They're on the eighth floor."

Addison turned back around and no longer saw the man from the elevator.

"Ma'am, your purse."

She took a deep breath and faced the security guard. She hadn't realized she had set her purse on his counter. "Thank you."

With no further incidents to send her into full panic mode, Addison walked into the office of Greer & Cruz. The woman behind a desk greeted her with a pleasant smile. "How may I help you?"

"I'm Addison Shaw. I'm here to see Mr. Greer. I called earlier, and he said I could just drop by."

"He's been expecting you. Please follow me."

Addison couldn't help but notice how the furnishings, fixtures, and pictures among the walls screamed wealth. But that shouldn't have surprised her. Keith would have insisted on the best lawyer money could buy. The woman knocked briefly on a double oak door, then opened it. "Mr. Greer, Ms. Addison Shaw is here to see you."

David Greer, a man in his late sixties, dropped a paper he was holding and immediately stood. "Thank you, Caroline."

Addison turned and watched the impeccably dressed woman close the door behind her. Then she walked forward and met him halfway. They shook hands.

"I've been waiting on you. Please, let's have a seat on the couches."

To the right of his desk was a wall of windows that overlooked Downtown Tampa. Leather couches sat with a coffee table in the middle. A wet bar was in the corner. Addison noticed right away a file with Keith's name lay on the table waiting for her.

"May I get you something to drink?"

She was about to decline until she saw bottled waters stacked nicely in the glass-door refrigerator. Suddenly, her throat felt parched. "Water would be nice. It's very hot outside."

"Yes, it is. My wife runs away every summer to our lake house in Upper Michigan."

Addison gave him a warm smile as she took the offered drink and had a few sips.

He waited patiently, taking the seat across from her. When it appeared she was done with the water, he asked, "I was very concerned when you called earlier. May I see the printout I sent to you?"

Addison nodded and pulled the stapled papers from her purse. She handed them to him. "As you can see, I'm missing a page."

He studied the handout and shook his head. "I checked the paperwork and sealed it myself. Did you break the seal to the envelope?"

"I did, and I'm positive someone broke into the canal home last night and took the page."

Shock registered across David's face. "What?"

"The house alarm went off."

"Did you call the police?"

"I didn't have to. They showed immediately." Addison stood and walked toward the wall of windows. "The power had briefly been knocked out by the storm, but the generator had kicked on and then I guess when the power was restored it triggered the alarm." She turned and faced him. "The back door was open. At the time, we all assumed it was just the wind from the storm, but now . . ." Her voice trailed off.

"You think someone broke in and stole a page?" He shook his head. "But why? I mean, why not take the entire packet, keys and all, if someone was trying to rob you?"

"That's why I'm here. What exactly was printed on the missing page about Rose Investment Firm?"

David opened the file on the coffee table as she walked back over and took a seat. "I took the liberty to reprint it. Here is the document in its entirety. But there is nothing about Rose Investment Firm that would benefit someone. There are no keys or password codes. Just a list of names of the people who sit on the board of directors and a brief summary. That's it. And anyone has that information at the tip of their fingers if they look up Rose Investment Firm on the internet."

Addison took the handout and read it. It stated exactly what he had explained. It was just a summary of Rose Investment Firm. The same introduction she had read on the company website a week ago.

"I just wanted you to have an idea what Rose Investment Firm does. You will control a share of the company, but you will have no leadership role or the ability to change Rose Investment Firm. That will all be in Marty Rose's hands now—Keith's brother."

Deep in thought, her eyebrows creased. In a soft voice, she asked, "Why did Keith and Cassandra leave me so much of their estate?"

David walked around the table and sat beside her. His kind eyes and soft voice displayed years of wisdom. "Like we discussed before when we first met, I only carried out their wishes. But let me assure you, Keith was adamant about leaving the bulk of his estate to you if something happened to him and Cassandra. They hoped it would somehow bring you much happiness in the event of their deaths."

A tear silently escaped from Addison's green eyes. Keith and Cassandra had planned. They had talked about death. *Riley,* she thought. She hadn't made any plans. But of course, Owen and she had rarely traveled without him when they were married, but that was no excuse. She closed her eyes and pushed all her clouded emotions away. Then she opened her eyes and wiped them gently before facing David. "At the house, everything of Cassandra's and Keith's had been boxed up. Why?"

"Again, all Keith and Cassandra's wishes. They didn't want a loved one to have to do all of that. They had thought it would be too emotional for you or his daughters in the event of their deaths."

"And the study with all their files?"

"Yes, well, Marty will come by soon to collect any of the ones marked *Rose Investment Firm.*"

"Are you sure he hasn't already?"

"He doesn't have access to the house, only you."

Thoughts were running through her head. Could Marty have come by when the cleaning staff was there? They probably knew him and wouldn't think anything of letting him in. Or maybe Keith had given him a spare key years ago. After all, he was trusted to run Rose Investment Firm.

Suddenly, Addison stood. "There were only four boxes in the study. None were marked *Rose Investment Firm*, and they were all open."

He seemed rattled. "You didn't open the boxes?"

"No. Add that fact to the missing page, and you see why I think someone may have been in the house. I don't think the wind opened the door or the generator triggered the alarm."

David quickly rose to his feet too. "I see why you are upset. I'll get in touch with the packing company and find out exactly when they finished the job. I can also call Marty."

"That would be great." Addison reached out and shook his hand. "Thank you for your time. I really appreciate you seeing me today."

David followed on her heels. "I will be in touch as soon as I hear anything. And Ms. Shaw, please don't hesitate to call. My office is here to help with anything you might need."

Addison turned around. "Is your retainer for the year paid for as well?" Shock registered on her face, and a hand flew to her mouth as soon as she spoke the words. "Oh, forgive me, I'm not myself. I'm . . ."

He reached out and touched her hand. "No apologies necessary. I can't imagine being in your shoes right now."

She slowly closed her eyes and shook her head, silently chastising herself for always speaking whatever came to her mind. Then she looked him in his deep-blue eyes. "You are very kind. Thank you."

He opened the door for her, and as she stepped away, he replied, "My retainer is paid by Rose Investment Firm. You will always have access to my services. Anything you need, just ask."

She nodded and walked down the hallway toward the entrance.

When she was out of sight, David walked over to his desk and took a seat. He picked up the phone.

"Marty Rose, please . . . Yes, tell him it's David Greer. It's urgent."

# CHAPTER 8

Tucked away in a quiet golf course neighborhood was a forty-one-hundred-square-foot vacation home for the Marx family who lived in Denver, Colorado. Sunshine Properties had taken on the maintenance of the property three years ago when the husband, Dr. Jim Marx, had stepped into Isaac's office looking for someone to care for his home. For a nice fee, Sunshine Properties checked on and cleaned the home every two weeks.

Sitting in his Mercedes in the driveway of the Marxes' home, Isaac stared at the set of keys in his cupholder. Earlier today, he had examined ten homes before settling on this one. The Marxes weren't set to return until Thanksgiving. He hesitantly grabbed the keys and stepped out of his car. He had contemplated parking in the garage but then had realized it was common to see a vehicle parked in front of the home due to Sunshine Properties providing services. If anybody did see him, they would see him doing his job: checking on the property.

On the front porch, Isaac turned around and looked at the other homes in view. Five were visible, but only three could see the coming and goings of the house due to the large tree-lined lots. Two were unoccupied: One was for sale, and the other managed by his property as a vacation home recommended by Jim himself. The third house was home to a young married couple, both busy professionals uninterested in the comings and goings of their neighbors. It was the retired residents who had him most concerned. But looking at all his options, this home was his best choice for Wayne to use on such short notice.

He inserted the key and the door opened. After attending to the alarm, he checked each room in the house. All was as it should be: beds made; refrigerator cleaned, with only bottled waters and sodas lining the door. From there, he walked into the study and disconnected the internet to the security cameras. With the summer storms, this would be something he could easily explain if anyone ever noticed.

He returned to the kitchen, opened the pantry, and found some canned dried goods left over from the Marxes' visit from two weeks ago. He quickly took a plastic bag from under the sink and packed it all up. Next, he counted the water and sodas. Those he could easily replace when needed. He carried the plastic bag out the front door and pressed his key remote. His trunk popped open. He placed the bag inside and grabbed three other bags from the local grocery store just down the road. Balancing the bags, he glanced around and saw no one. He closed the trunk and reentered the house.

\*\*\*

Addison pulled Cassandra's car into the garage at the canal home. She looked in her rearview mirror and watched as Aiden stepped out of his truck and walked her way. She had filled him in once she was safely back in the car, using Bluetooth while driving. They had agreed to return to the canal house and look through the boxes in the study.

He entered the garage and pressed a button on the wall, closing the garage door. Once it was secure, he motioned for her to get out of the car. They entered the home, and just like the night before and at the beach house, Aiden searched it for any sign of an intruder or disturbance. Addison stood by the front door as commanded while he climbed the stairs to the second floor. She immediately noticed the box that had been delivered earlier today. She picked it up and flipped it around in her hands, looking for any sign of who could have sent it. Nothing.

She looked up the stairs for Aiden. He was nowhere in sight. She tapped her fingers on the box, waiting impatiently for him to return. She knew she probably shouldn't open it, but the idea that Keith could have been involved in something shady that had resulted in his and Cassandra's deaths was mind-blowing. Doubt filled her mind.

"Screw it! The FBI can be wrong."

Addison took a seat on the small chair and opened the box. Inside was an object wrapped in white tissue paper. Had Cassandra entrusted someone to send her something in the event of her death? That would explain the lack of return address.

She peeled the paper, expecting to find something precious. Then she screamed.

Aiden ran down the spiral staircase, his gun raised in midair, searching for the source of danger. Seeing no one, he lowered his gun. "What is it?"

She tilted the box toward him, revealing a child's stuffed animal along with a note written in red: *Go home!*

"It's Riley's dragon. It's . . ." Her voice trailed off.

As he neared, he removed a pair of gloves from his pocket and pulled them on. Then he took the box from her, careful not to touch the items inside. "Are you sure it's his?"

She slowly nodded. "That stain—it's from chocolate ice cream. I didn't have a chance to wash it before I left." Addison reached into her purse. "I've got to call Owen."

The call went unanswered. "Pick up the damn phone, Owen!" she screamed in agony of the unknown.

"What's Owen's address? We'll send someone over to the house."

"Three forty-eight Hackberry Lane, Atlanta."

She tried again; still no answer. She watched as the special agent made the call. When he lowered his phone, she asked nervously, "How long will it take for someone to get to them?"

"The nearest highway patrol is about five minutes away. We'll know something soon."

Her phone rang and she jumped. "It's Owen." She pressed the Answer button. "Owen, do you have Riley?" she shouted.

"What? Of course I do."

"Do you see him right now?"

"Addy, what's going on?"

"Do you see him?" Her voice cracked.

"Yes, take it easy. He's sitting at the kitchen table eating his dinner."

"Oh thank God!" She sank to the floor and buried her head in her hands.

Aiden walked over and held his hand out for her phone. She gave it to him.

"This is FBI Special Agent Aiden Greene. We have a highway patrol car heading to your house. We have reason to believe Riley could be in danger."

Addison felt weak. The room began to spin, followed by ringing in her ears. She lay on the tile, feeling the coldness on her cheek. She closed her eyes, fighting the lightheaded sensation. She didn't want to faint, not now, but it was hopeless. She fainted.

Aiden kneeled beside her and placed a hand on her forehead as he continued explaining the situation to a very unhappy and worried Owen. The dragon could not be found at his home. No one had seen it, and Owen claimed Addison hadn't packed it. Finally, Aiden ended the call when the highway patrol arrived.

"Hey, Addison."

She slowly opened her eyes, and static sounded in her ears. She was confused at first, then she realized that she had fainted.

"Here, sit up." He gently guided her to a sitting position, both hands resting on her shoulders to prevent her from fainting again and hitting her head. "Have you eaten today?"

She shook her head.

"Let me go find you some juice. Do you need to lie back down?"

She nodded.

He eased her back down and went to the kitchen. Addison closed her eyes. She wanted to curl up into a ball as guilt washed over her for leaving Riley. She felt his hand upon her forehead again and opened her eyes. This kind man was trying to help her.

Once she was back in a sitting position, he held on to the glass while she drank, her hands covering his. The juice was starting to help. Soon, she felt stronger and was no longer lightheaded. She pushed the glass away. "I can stand now. Thank you."

Aiden helped her up. "When did this arrive?"

"Earlier today. There's no return address. I had forgotten all about it till now when I saw it. How can this be happening?" She slowly walked away from him, leaving him in the foyer, the box again sitting on the chair. Then she heard him quickly catching up, following her into the living room.

She stopped and looked out the windows to the backyard. It was littered with palm trees from the storm last night. All looked a mess, just like her life. She turned around.

"My sister is dead. My son and I have been threatened, and the brother-in-law that I've adored for the last few years . . ." Her voice cracked. ". . . is the cause? What did he do?"

Aiden frowned. "That I can't tell you. Like I stated earlier, the investigation is ongoing."

He reached out and placed a hand on her shoulder. She balked.

"Yeah, yeah, it was ruled an accident to protect the investigation. But don't you think I have the right to know now? Someone just threatened my son!"

"Ms. Shaw, I am very sorry. Believe me, I understand how—"

His phone vibrated, and he held up his finger as he reached for his phone with his other hand. He read a text message, then announced, "Someone will be by shortly for the box."

She crossed her arms, waiting on him to say something more.

He frowned again. "The investigation revolves around other individuals. To say more would jeopardize our case. When something changes, I will update you if I can."

"So I'm just supposed to pack my bags and leave?"

"It would be the best for you and your son, yes."

She shook her head and turned, rolling her eyes in frustration as she stormed off toward the hallway that led to the study. "I'll figure it out on my own. I don't need you or the FBI's help."

Aiden followed her into the study, where she kneeled and looked at each label on the boxes. She chose to start with the one labeled *Documents*.

Aiden patiently waited for her mood to dissolve. He watched but never offered to help her. Finally, after all four boxes were carefully picked over, she stood.

"I don't see anything in here from Rose Investment Firm. Either there was nothing here to begin with, or Marty Rose already came by." She snapped her fingers and added, "Or someone took it last night!"

The doorbell sounded. "They're here for the box. I'll be right back." Aiden left her in the study.

Addison checked all the built-in drawers and file cabinets to make sure the study was indeed empty and the moving company that David had hired hadn't missed anything. When she was satisfied, she left the study in search of Aiden. She found him signing some paperwork, and then the other agent left. Deciding there was nothing left to do, she grabbed her purse.

Aiden stepped toward her. "Where are you going?"

"To find Marty Rose. If Keith was involved in something crooked, he had to know."

"If you do that, you risk tipping our hand, and the people responsible for your sister's death will never be brought to justice."

She looked him in his eyes. "Then what am I supposed to do?"

"Go home to your son and let us continue our investigation."

She shook her head. "Not until I meet Marty Rose. I have every right to know if he has been in this home. I need to know who opened these boxes, and I would think it would be easier for your investigation if I just casually asked him myself."

Aiden sighed. "Are you always this stubborn?"

She smirked. "Yes. In fact, I am. So are you going to follow me over, or am I going on my own?"

He took another step toward her. "Okay, I surrender. But can you at least wait until tomorrow when we have a better plan?"

# CHAPTER 9

*South Beach, Florida*

Check-in was as smooth as always at The Tides South Beach, located on Ocean Drive. Sebastian had booked the nicest room, the Presidential Suite, overlooking the powder-white sandy beach. South Beach lured thousands of visitors per week to bask in the sun and enjoy the clear water and the fine-dining options at night. Like most hotels on the strip, The Tides was across from Lummus Park, which bordered the beach. What Sebastian liked most about The Tides was the layout of the swimming pool. By 7 p.m., he was dressed for his evening meeting and lounging poolside under his private air-conditioned cabana with a gin and tonic in his right hand.

The poolside scenery was as expected. Many women wearing minimum clothing could be seen in all directions. Most weren't alone, having made this trip with their significant other. But there were still many single women to choose from if he so desired. A dark-haired Brazilian beauty caught his eye; she gave a small smile as she returned her attention to her group of women friends. Sebastian took a sip of his drink and scanned the entrance of the pool. He recognized no one. An illicit one-night stand was easy in South Beach, but Maria had already fulfilled his needs earlier. He was content as always since marrying her. He continued to watch the guests as he self-consciously twisted his wedding band along his ring finger.

No small talk was made except for with the waitress who had delivered Sebastian another drink. He drained the last liquid from the ice cubes and stood. A driver would be waiting on him in the lobby to take him downtown. Grabbing his briefcase, he left the cabana and walked among the small crowd around the pool and loungers.

In the lobby, guests were huddled in small groups and more were checking in, but the concierge immediately greeted Sebastian and showed him to his car. Outside, the dinner crowd was already in full force, packing the sidewalks as each restaurant tried to lure potential customers in with their sweet talking and beautiful hostesses. Sebastian tuned it all out when he noticed his driver standing by a black Lincoln.

"The Palms at 159 Coconut Grove; correct, sir?"

"Yes. Thank you."

The drive took the expected time, and Sebastian arrived five minutes before eight. He immediately was shown to his table and introduced to Valerie Blake. Her picture on the website hadn't done her beauty justice. She stood, wearing a seductively sheer white dress with nude lining. Her curves and sexuality were on full display. Her bio immediately flashed in Sebastian's mind: heiress to Blake Properties, thirty-five, mother to one child, recently divorced. She was clearly on the prowl.

"Ms. Blake, good to finally meet you."

"Likewise." She took a seat and raised her wineglass. "I hope you don't mind. I started without you."

"Gin and tonic," Sebastian told the waiter who approached and quickly disappeared. "Long day at the office?"

She smirked. "Long week."

"Just one more workday to go." He smiled.

She looked at his briefcase sitting beside them. "Let's enjoy the dinner and getting to know each other first. Business can wait till dessert."

Sebastian politely nodded. "As you wish, Ms. Blake."

She smiled. "Call me Valerie. All my friends do."

"Alright then, Valerie." Sebastian set the menu aside. He could play this game. He smiled at her again. "Let's start with you. Tell me something about yourself that I couldn't find on the internet."

"Ah, you've been reading about me," she teased.

"Of course. We are about to be business partners." His drink arrived, and he lifted it in the air for a toast. "To us and getting to know each other."

She clinked her glass. "Yes, indeed."

*** 

The night air smelled stale. There was little to no breeze as the Royal Liner sailed its final leg from the Bahamas. The vessel had made the twenty-two-hour trip across the Caribbean Sea, around Cuba, and into the Gulf of Mexico. Once it passed the Florida Keys, the ship had sailed into the Atlantic Ocean toward the Bahamas.

Maria, along with her five passengers, hadn't had to endure the entire trip. Once leaving the Caymans, the cargo vessel filled with furniture had stopped in Cuba. From there, they had boarded a small plane and flown to the Bahamas. Within minutes of landing, they were quickly carried to another cargo boat, this one owned and operated by one of Sebastian's business associates who lived on their island. The money and trade-off they had received from each other had been profitable for both parties.

A light wind began to blow across the Atlantic as they inched toward PortMiami. Maria looked at the time. Thirty more minutes would pass as she quietly endured the sticky conditions of July humidity. She wiped the sweat beads from her forehead with a white linen cloth and looked over her five passengers as she tried to console herself. August was worse, and there would be no more trips this month.

The girls between the ages of fifteen and eighteen sat before her, their right hands each bound to a rope that was securely tied to a metal hook on the wooden plank floor. Maria hated the restraints but knew there was no way around it. One late-night journey had almost cost them everything when a young woman had jumped from the boat. Luckily, they had found her before she had been able to solicit help from a nearby cruise liner. Sebastian had found out, and the way the women were transferred had never been the same.

There was just enough rope that allowed each girl to use a small, makeshift toilet behind a blanket that gave very little privacy. Maria was thankful for the calm seas tonight, for seasickness was contagious. The only difficulty was the sweltering heat. Maria checked the fan once more. It was still on the maximum speed. She walked back over and took a seat.

"What have you become?" Constance, the once shy fifteen-year-old, questioned boldly in her native Hungarian. Maria's scowl did nothing to deter her. "Why do you do this to our people?"

Maria looked away and glanced at the other four girls. For days, she had fed them, clothed them, and showered them with fine trinkets as she had brainwashed them with new hope into thinking their lives were just beginning. Now they were all staring at her, waiting for her response. She knew this had been triggered by their current conditions. The small room and the rope that bound them were the complete opposite from how they had been treated since arriving on her doorstep in the Caymans.

"For a better life; you just don't see it now. This . . ." Maria lifted the rope. "Can't be helped. It's for the best. Your protection."

A haughty gasp sounded from Tatiana, the oldest. "Protection? If we had to protect ourselves, we wouldn't be able to with these ropes." She lifted her arm and pulled. Then she asked, "What have we done to lose your trust?"

Maria gave her a hard stare. "Nothing. You did nothing. These are the rules, and I follow the rules." She then looked at each of them and tried to comfort them. "This is almost over; maybe just twenty more minutes. I promise that you will all have a better life once we get settled in America. A life that will be tenfold better than your war-torn and parched land. And if I must remind you, your elders knew the decision they were making when they took the money."

Spit flew across the small space and landed on Maria's exposed leg. She angrily wiped it with her linen cloth. She stood, peeled off a strand of thick tape, and covered Tatiana's mouth, then looked at the others daring them to misbehave.

This group was small, but they were much different from the last one. These girls had been purchased. There were no lies of finding jobs in America and then sending for their family once they were settled. They knew their families had sold them. It was Maria's job to fool them into thinking they would have a life like hers, so she had spoiled the girls over the last several days. And they had seen firsthand how Maria lived, coming and going freely from her mansion. Slowly, the girls had come around and started to look at the positive instead of dwelling on the past. Their parents couldn't afford them and survive. She just hoped they would now think of the positive and not their current conditions.

Ten more minutes passed before the lights appeared brighter in the night sky. They were near their destination. Maria reached for the tape again and began tearing off another piece. She remembered Sebastian's words: "They must not be able to call out for help."

When the fifth strand was cut, Constance spoke again. "Do you remember Rebecca, my sister?"

Maria was slightly caught off guard before raising the tape to Constance's mouth. She hadn't known of any families who had sold more than one child. Sebastian had explained it wasn't good business. Too risky.

Constance quickly muttered before Maria could apply the tape, "You were her friend in grade school."

Maria's hands fell to her sides as the room immediately felt smaller. She took a quick breath as her mind raced, conjuring places and names from her childhood home. Rebecca? An image of a laughing, green-eyed blonde formed in her memory. Sweet Rebecca, to whom she had confided her deepest secrets up until the day she had left home?

To confirm she did indeed know Maria, Constance gave her surname—O'Malley—along with the name of their small village: Boanne.

Maria tried to lift her hands to apply the tape, but she couldn't. This fair-complexioned girl couldn't possibly be Rebecca's younger sister, right? She studied her eyes. Green like Rebecca's. She did the math in her head. Eight years had passed. Could this be the Constance who used to annoyingly follow them around?

"You remember me, don't you? I've only just now remembered you. I kept telling myself there was something about you that looked familiar."

Maria looked at the girls. They were all listening carefully to Constance.

*Do they believe her?*

Maria quickly shook off the past. A past that had to forever stay buried if she was to keep her sanity and her posh life.

She raised the tape again. Just before she applied it, she heard Constance's dreadful words.

"Rebecca's dead."

A chill formed along Maria's spine beneath her damp cotton dress. Constance's eyes had turned sad, and Maria knew she had spoken the truth.

She applied the tape and quickly turned away from the girl, running up the stairs to the deck above. It was dangerous to be seen among the men and cargo, but Maria could no longer breathe. She had to get some air. Somehow, some way, her past had come roaring back.

She ignored the hard stare given by a deckhand as she ran past him to the railing. She leaned over with anticipation of getting sick, but only numbness filled her lips and tongue. She gripped the railing and closed her eyes.

To acknowledge Rebecca and Constance from her village was to acknowledge who she was: the daughter of a proud farmer who had broken down with shame as he had hugged Maria one last time. "You will find a good job. One that will feed you and take care of you. You will have a better life." He had spoken more to convince himself than her. For years, she had justified leaving would also help save money to help feed her brothers and sisters. Hunger had already taken their mother.

Gabriel Hoffman, Sebastian's hired foreman who lived on the island with them, touched Maria's arm. "Are you okay?" he asked with sincerity.

Maria turned and nodded. "I'm sorry, I just couldn't breathe."

He frowned. "I really need you to get below. You could endanger the entire mission." Gabriel led her away from the railing.

She dutifully followed, then paused and looked out at the lights of PortMiami. Her husband would be waiting on her. A man who had taken care of her. She looked down at her wedding ring: a diamond so large she had questioned its authenticity. Sebastian had laughed at her naivety, saying, "It's only the beginning for you. I will shower you with riches." And he had.

With slow, deep breaths, Maria pushed her old life away, burying it deep beneath her soul. Finally, she turned from Gabriel and returned below. She would continue to speak her father's words as he had done to her: *"You will have a better life."*

# CHAPTER 10

A team of FBI agents departed from the canal home, leaving Addison with Aiden. Staring into the dark backyard, she sipped from a glass of wine, lost in thought. Her son had been threatened, and someone had entered the house while she had been passed out in the bathtub last night. She had never felt so alone. Over the last year, Cassandra had been her rock and her sounding board when her world had been turned upside down. Now she had no one. She took another sip and closed her eyes.

Hearing him near, she opened her eyes, turned, and faced Aiden.

"Are you doing okay?"

She nodded. Earlier, she had agreed to allow the agents to take a closer look at the house and dust for prints. She had gone outside, planning to straighten up from the storm and try to busy herself, but had soon found herself stretched out on a lounge chair, drinking wine.

"Did you know the security cameras are broken?"

Addison's face registered shock. "No, I didn't." Then she laughed. "I have no clue how to work them or where they are."

He grabbed her hand to try to bring some comfort. "I don't want you staying here tonight. It's not safe knowing someone has access to the house."

She looked at his hand. He cared. Slowly she nodded. "I'll stay downtown, somewhere near Rose Investment Firm."

"So, you haven't changed your mind. You're still going tomorrow?"

Thoughts of Riley filled her mind once more. She couldn't risk endangering his life. Losing Cassandra was bad enough. Losing her son would kill her.

"Yes, but after I meet with Marty Rose tomorrow, I'm flying home. I'll figure out what to do with all this property later. I still have time before the estate is officially finalized. Whatever Keith was or wasn't involved in doesn't make a difference now. Cassandra isn't coming back. I have to think of Riley."

"For what it's worth, I think you're making the right choice. I just think you should skip Rose Investment Firm."

She looked back down at his hand, and he slowly removed it. "No. I want to see him and talk to him in person. I want to know what he knows about Keith's affairs."

Aiden frowned.

She clarified, "Casual conversation. Just an introduction. Look, if he had something to do with Cassandra's death, I'll know it."

"You telepathic?" He chuckled.

She walked away from him, but he followed her into the kitchen. When she placed the empty wineglass in the sink, she looked him in the face.

"I'm good at reading people. Besides, he should know someone was here and was snooping around. What if he's next? In some kind of danger as well and doesn't even know it? I have to—"

He interrupted, "No. You don't. The FBI is most likely in his home now as we speak, asking questions." He gave her a stern look. "It's best you leave all of this to us. Go home. Give this some time. I promise I will reach out when it's safe to do so."

She turned away and grabbed her phone that had been charging. "So he'll know someone broke in. Looks like I won't be spoiling any of your investigation then, will I?"

"Please, Ms. Shaw."

"I'll sleep on it. But for now, I plan on going first thing in the morning." She opened her purse and grabbed the two cards given to her yesterday. "I have a driver and a pilot. Isn't this ridiculous?"

He saw the pain in her eyes, as well as the signs of drinking too much wine. "I can take you to a hotel."

She looked at the time and then back at him. "Okay. Thank you, I would appreciate that."

After removing her luggage from the trunk in the garage, Aiden checked the house one last time. Addison set the alarm, and they walked out the front door.

The drive downtown was quiet as Addison searched for the closest hotel to Rose Investment Firm. She was in luck: a room was available two blocks away at the Grand Hotel. She dropped her phone back into her purse and gave him the address. He nodded, not bothering with his GPS.

A few moments of silence passed as Addison chose her words carefully. "How long have you been investigating my brother-in-law?"

She watched as his jaw tightened, eyes still on the road. Just when she thought he wasn't going to answer her, he said, "Several months."

A tear began to form. "Did you reach out to my sister?"

Another long silence passed as she watched his every move.

"I never had the opportunity to meet your sister. That's all I can say. Sorry." He looked at her briefly. "Was she as stubborn as you?"

Addison grinned. "Yeah, we got that from our dad." The thought of being all alone again caused her to look back at the highway. He must have sensed her sadness because he asked nothing else and the rest of the trip was made in silence.

At the hotel, he flashed his badge at the valet attendant; his truck was to remain out front until he returned. Check-in was fast, with no lines at eleven forty-five at night. Addison didn't bother to respond when Aiden insisted on riding the elevator with her to the tenth floor and checking over her room.

After he cleared the room, she followed him to the door. He stopped and turned toward her.

"I never suspected your sister of any illegal activity. From what I can tell, she was very busy with her work at the hospital. What little free time she had, she spent at the beach house."

Addison closed her eyes and bowed her head. Her hand went to her forehead, shielding herself from his view.

"Someone will escort you tomorrow. Please do not leave this room until you hear from me. Try to get some rest."

She looked back up. "Is that really . . ." She quickly shook her head, remembering the threats against her. "Okay. But I want to leave here at nine thirty sharp."

"Someone will be here." He opened the door and checked the hall. Just before closing the door, he gave another command. "Order room service. Don't leave for breakfast."

She nodded. "If I don't see you tomorrow, keep your promise. I want to be informed."

His eyes turned soft. "I will. Good night, Ms. Shaw."

She closed the door and rested her body up against it, exhausted once again.

***

*South Beach, 1 a.m.*

The door opened as she placed a magnetic card over the black box. Maria slipped into room 605, closed the door, twisted the dead bolt, and pulled the gold lever, securing an additional lock at the top.

She turned and found Sebastian sitting on the balcony overlooking the pool below. The door was closed to keep the cold air in, but the curtains were open. He appeared lost in thought as he sipped his preferred drink. She was glad he was still awake at this hour.

Her eyes looked over the well-appointed suite as she made her way to the sliding doors. She stepped out onto the balcony, and their eyes locked.

"You waited up?"

He placed his drink on the glass table beside him and rose. "And that always seems to surprise you."

She gave a half smile, then stepped into his waiting arms.

"How was the trip?"

Her eyes closed as she felt his embrace bring her much needed comfort. Her answer was never a simple "Good" or "Bad." She had to tell him everything. Leave nothing out. Sebastian's attention to every detail was what had enabled him to elude the authorities for years.

He pulled away and placed a hand under her chin. "You look tired. Let's go in to talk and then get you a shower."

She nodded.

They stepped inside, and he closed the door to the outside world. He led her to the couch and then grabbed a bottled water from the minibar. She took it and drank. He patiently waited, knowing that if something had majorly gone wrong tonight, Maria would never have shown up at The Tides. Instead, it would have been Gabriel.

"Anyone lurking when you found the key?"

She shook her head. The key had been hidden in the lobby. Really, it was in plain sight if anyone had been looking for it. "No, and I rode the elevator alone."

He touched her cheek and traced her lips with his hand, then pulled it away. "Something's wrong. I can tell." He grabbed her hands and affectionately held them. "You can tell me anything, Maria, good or bad. I hope by now you know that without a shadow of a doubt."

Maria closed her eyes and took a breath. Then she opened them and stared directly into his. "The girl Constance is from my village. She recognized me."

A frown immediately formed on Sebastian's face. "What? You tell me this now?"

Maria frantically shook her head. "No, no! She only called me out tonight. I had no idea. She was just a little girl when I left. I would have never recognized her."

Sebastian pulled away and rubbed his face with his burly hands.

She reached out and touched him. "I'm being honest, Sebastian. I would never lie to you." A tear started to roll down her cheek.

He wiped away the tear. "I know, my dearest Maria, I know." He pulled her in for a tight embrace. Then he slowly released her and asked, "How did you handle Constance?"

Maria told him about the tense conversation on the boat, holding nothing back. Once she had composed herself, she had returned below and explained to Constance that she was mistaken. She was hurt that the girls would turn on her the way they had; she had treated them so well and prepared them for this mission. Didn't they understand she had just as much to lose as they did? She once again explained why the rope to tie them was necessary, and as soon as they got off the boat and into the car, she would remove their tape. From there, things calmed down and the girls complied.

Sebastian patiently listened and did not interrupt. When she finally finished with as much detail as she could remember, he asked, "So how was the exchange?"

"All as planned, but Mr. Banks refused Tatiana. He wanted Constance instead."

A quiet rage consumed Sebastian. He stood and paced. Bill Banks had agreed to take three girls of Sebastian's choosing. The other two were to be transported to Tampa and given to Wayne to use in one of his clubs. Tatiana had been considered the higher flight risk, so he had planned to leave her in Miami. Wayne was already on edge since Keith's death. Constance had been the quiet one, rarely speaking or causing trouble—well, until tonight when she had questioned Maria about her past.

Sebastian stopped pacing and returned to his seat. "Why did Banks refuse Tatiana?"

"Said she looked too old for his club. Claimed you misled him."

Disbelief filled his face. "Too old? She's eighteen!"

Maria nodded. "I know, but he said she looked older."

"How did she act?"

"Surprisingly, good. She never spoke, just like she was told." Doubt filled Maria's face. "What was I to do? Should I have forced him to take her? Did I mess up?"

"No. I will deal with him later. I'm sure you did the best you could." He raked a hand through her blonde hair. "So, the girl who recognized you, she's in Miami now with Banks, correct?"

Maria nodded.

He asked, "With the sisters, Hanna and Anna?"

Again, she nodded. "They were quiet as usual. A little confused but gave me no trouble."

"Alright, my dear. Go get cleaned up. You must be exhausted." He held out a hand and helped her to her feet. "Tomorrow, you have another big day in Tampa with Tatiana and Bianca."

"Thank you." She released his hand and walked through the double doors into the master bathroom.

Sebastian waited till the water was turned on, then picked up his phone.

"I need you in South Beach. We have a problem."

"I can leave now," Jayden responded.

"Good. Call Gabriel when you get here. He will explain."

Sebastian then called Gabriel, explaining what needed to be done. When he finished, he looked at the closed bathroom door with his young wife behind it. He pictured her naked body under the spray and was immediately consumed with lust. There was no hesitation. He undressed and headed to the shower.

Maria was washing her hair under the spray with her eyes closed when he entered the shower and touched her. She jerked at first, startled. Then she lowered her hands by her sides and watched as his eyes scanned her entire body from head to toe.

He grabbed her and spun her around, facing the wall. He spread her legs as she braced herself for his quick entry. Soon the shock factor wore off, and she began to enjoy herself just as much as he. Then he dragged her to the bed and pulled her on top of him. It was his favorite sexual position, as he loved watching Maria bounce up and down, riding him. Finally, she cried out and sank into his chest. He rolled her over and held her tightly, wishing he could bottle up this moment in time and have it forever.

# CHAPTER 11

A shrilling noise woke Addison from a deep sleep. She raised herself up and looked around a dark room, trying to remember where she was. A light blinking to her left just above a door and some light filtering in from the windows from the right reminded Addison she was at the Grand Hotel. The fire alarm.

Addison quickly slipped her shoes on and grabbed her purse. She opened the door to the hallway wearing a T-shirt, shorts, and sandals, tightly clutching her purse. The noise was becoming deafening. She looked both ways and saw no one. "Where is everyone?" she screamed out in disbelief.

She ran toward the sign marked EXIT for the staircase. She opened the door and ran down a flight of stairs. Just as she hit the landing to the next floor, a door swung open, and a man dressed in black grabbed her. She dropped her purse as he lifted her in the air. She kicked, losing her sandals as the power of his arm bore down on her neck, trying to crush her throat. Grabbing his strong arm, she pinched and pulled, but to no avail.

Her oxygen wasn't flowing anymore, and her head began to pound along with her lungs. She started to fade. Just as she closed her eyes, a vision of Riley appeared. She opened her eyes and pulled one last time on his lock, kicking as well.

She woke up, her arms flailing in midair and her feet kicking off the bedsheets. Addison slowly sat up and pushed her sweaty, clammy body against the headboard. The hum of an air conditioner was the only sound that could be heard. The time was 6:05 a.m.

She flipped on the light beside her. Her top sheet and blanket were lying on the floor. Addison grabbed her throat and couldn't shake the sensation of being choked. She quickly gathered up the sheets and blanket and remade the bed. Settling back under the covers, she flipped the light switch off and lay down, closing her eyes.

Sleep would not come. Addison huffed and threw the covers off her body. She knew she needed the rest, but her mind was racing. No way was she going to be able to return to sleep. She felt a sharp pain in her stomach, and she remembered how she hadn't had a decent meal since arriving in Tampa. After a quick glance at the room service menu, she ordered breakfast.

While she waited on her food to be delivered, she sat at the small desk in the corner and got on her computer. Once logged into the internet, she paid bills and then checked her emails. Someone in her department was having a back-to-school party and hoped she could make it. The next email was from Dick Menard, her principal, asking her to call at her convenience. She didn't have to guess what that was about, not after the conversation she had had with Owen. Addison sat back in her chair, contemplating how to respond to her boss.

A knock on the door broke her train of thought. She heard a voice outside. "Room service."

She looked out the peephole and saw a young man dressed in hotel attire holding a platter. She opened the door. He greeted her politely, asked if she needed anything else, and left.

Addison bolted the door again and felt her mouth water at the smell of fresh coffee and bacon. When she sat down to eat, she allowed herself to wonder what it would be like to live like this. She and Riley could travel the world until he started grade school. They could see Europe. Oh, how Riley would love seeing the castles, just like the ones in the storybooks she read him.

She took another bite and continued dreaming. David's words filled her mind once more. Cassandra and Keith had wanted her and Riley to have everything. With all that had happened since arriving in Tampa, that one thought brought a reassuring peace. She thought of Cassandra's kind smile and gentle touch with Riley. She had loved Riley like he had been her own.

She placed her fork down and closed her eyes. Decisions had to be made. Big, life-changing decisions. She slowly shook her head, then looked at the date on her watch. School was restarting in three weeks; she would report in two. But she had to get there a few days earlier than that to get her room ready.

She opened her eyes and stared at the large breakfast sitting before her. She had been starving when she had ordered. Now, just after a few bites, she was already full, losing her appetite at the thought of everything before her that was still left to do. After forcing herself to finish the eggs and bacon, Addison shoved the remaining food to the side and showered. The hot water felt good, and she found it easier to concentrate on what she needed to do next. She always did her best planning in the early hours of the day.

By 7:30 a.m., she was dressed. She unzipped a compartment in her computer bag to grab her notebook and paused when she noticed the white FedEx envelope from the bank. She had totally forgotten about the envelope that had been sitting on the porch of the canal home when she had first arrived. She reread the label: National Bank of Clearwater was the sender. She walked to the couch and opened the envelope.

Inside was a white legal-size envelope and a one-page letter with the typed message: *Please deliver this envelope to Cassandra Rose in the event of my death. If Cassandra's death proceeds mine, please deliver to her next of kin, Addison Shaw.* It was signed *Keith Rose.*

Addison sat temporarily stunned. This was strange. Up to this point, David had handled everything. Why had Keith arranged for the bank to send a letter upon his death? Why had the letter just been dropped off at the canal home with no required signature?

She realized her hands were shaking and forced herself to relax. She set the letter down and opened the legal-size envelope. She saw a handwritten note and read it. She read it again and then again.

She closed her eyes as the words floated in her head: *In the event of my death . . . I'm sorry to ask this of you . . . Cassandra loved you so much . . . Lockbox 18 . . . Come alone . . . Don't tell.*

She opened her eyes and fought back her emotions. None of this made sense. Again, she thought of the lawyer. So far, he had taken care of every detail of Keith's estate, so wasn't he in charge of the lockbox? This was odd. And why go alone and not tell anyone? He obviously trusted his lawyer, so why didn't he trust David with the lockbox? And if this letter was so important why didn't the bank demand a signature upon delivery?

Her thoughts slowly turned to Aiden's statement that Keith had been the target of the boat explosion. Keith had owned an investment firm that made millions. *How exactly did he make all that money? Whose money did he invest?* Clarity and shock began to register. *Had Keith been laundering money?* A tear rolled down her cheek.

*Oh dear God, Keith. What did you do?*

By 9:30 a.m., she had called Owen; Caleb O'Brien, the pilot; and Peter Marks, the driver. She packed her suitcase and shut down her computer. She had requested a late checkout, and if she didn't return, they would retrieve and store her bags downstairs.

She heard a knock at the door. It would be Special Agent Parker, the man whom Aiden had called about earlier to say he would greet her. She walked to the door and looked out the peephole. A man in his early thirties with blond hair and green eyes stood before her. His clothing description was also a match. She opened the door.

"Hi."

He produced his FBI badge. "Good morning. I'm Special Agent Jonas Parker, Special Agent Greene's partner."

She gave a small smile. "I'm Addison Shaw. Thank you for coming. Hopefully, this won't take too long. I really don't like to be a bother."

"No bother, Ms. Shaw. So, where to?"

She remembered Aiden's words: "Go home to your son and let us continue our investigation." She pushed the thought away.

"I'm sure you already know, and I haven't changed my mind. We're going to Rose Investment Firm. It's just a few blocks away on Druid Lane."

He smiled. "Yeah, he didn't think you would change your mind. You ready?"

Addison nodded and they left the room. They rode the elevator down in silence. Jonas's red SUV was parked out front waiting where he had left it. He opened the door for her, and she couldn't help but notice how he surveilled their surroundings as she climbed inside. The drive was short, just two blocks like she had stated. He turned left toward the sign for the parking garage and entered.

They continued upward until the fourth floor. Jonas was looking for the right parking spot near the elevator. She couldn't help but remember she had done the same thing just yesterday before meeting with David a few more streets down. He checked his side mirrors, cut the engine, and turned to her. "Are you ready?"

"Yes."

"Stick close to me. We'll take the elevator to the lobby. There, you'll have to sign us in."

"You plan on going upstairs with me?"

"Yes. Aiden told me not to let you out of my sight."

"I understand, but I want to talk to Marty Rose alone."

Jonas hesitated before replying. "I can't tell you what to do or drag you to a plane kicking and screaming." He smiled, breaking some of the tension, then continued. "But please, Ms. Shaw, just have a friendly conversation with him and introduce yourself. Try not to conduct your own investigation or interrogation. It really will hamper our investigation."

She sat back and reflected on his words. "I wouldn't want to do that. I want you to catch whoever killed my sister."

He smiled again. "Okay. Then we're good. I'll escort you to the office and then wait outside."

She nodded, and they stepped out of the SUV. The walk to the elevator, the ride down, and the sign-in process went smoothly. It only took about five minutes before a young receptionist walked them to the office elevator. She stepped inside, swiped her card over a magnetic box, and pressed the button for thirty, the top floor. "Someone will greet you upstairs." With that, she left with a smile.

They went straight to the top, and true to her words, another young woman greeted them. "Ms. Shaw and your friend, Jonas Parker?"

"Yes." Addison stepped forward.

"Follow me. Mr. Rose will see you now."

The hallway was short and stopped at a dark-stained door with the words *Marty Rose, CEO, Rose Investment Firm*. She thought, *that didn't take long. It's only been two weeks.*

The receptionist tapped on the door and then opened it. Addison looked at Jonas before entering. "I'm sure she can show you to a reception area."

He smirked. "I'll be right here. Just yell if you need something."

Addison rolled her eyes. "I'm sure that won't be necessary."

Just as she turned, he touched her arm. "Remember what we discussed?"

She didn't respond, as she heard a male voice within the office say her name. She entered the room, passing the receptionist, who closed the door behind her.

\*\*\*

*South Beach*

Maria awoke in a fright at the sound of an alarm clock. She reached over and silenced the alarm, then slowly rose to make out her surroundings. She wasn't in a field working under the hot sun like in her dream.

As if to reassure herself this hotel room wasn't the dream, she looked down at her hands. They weren't bleeding or scratched. They were the hands of a lady, a well-kept lady with fine jewels upon her fingers. She looked at the rare blue diamond, and then her thoughts turned to Sebastian and their intense late-night lovemaking.

A hand went to her stomach. Oh, how she longed for a child. She had secretly stopped taking her birth control pill a few months ago. Now she just had to wait. Surely once she was pregnant, Sebastian would stop this horrid business and just focus on his furniture store. Then her dreams would be of walks on the beach with Sebastian, holding the hand of their child, instead of nightmares of her past or dangerous night voyages filled with faceless young women.

She got out of an empty bed. Sebastian was long gone on his way to Tampa. He had set the alarm for her. She had to be dressed and gone by checkout at noon. Looking at the clock, she had two hours. There was to be no record of Maria at the hotel. She had illegally entered the country and would leave again late tonight the same way she had entered. As for the US Customs report, Sebastian had arrived alone for business.

A dress hung on the bathroom door. Sebastian had removed it from his luggage, along with a fresh pair of undergarments. She stood and walked around, noticing he had taken her clothing with him from the night before. A small makeup bag had been left by the sink, along with her handbag. A handwritten note was beside it that read: *Thanks for a good time.* She cringed as she walked into the open-door shower. The note wasn't for her benefit; it was for the cleaning staff. If there was any suspicion two people had shared this room, the note would give the idea that Sebastian had had a one-night fling.

The warm spray washed over her body, but she still felt numb. The night she had shared with Sebastian had been a temporary fix to her emotional state. Constance's words still rattled her. She turned the lever toward hot but couldn't break the chill. She couldn't get the girl's voice out of her head. Rebecca was dead.

Soon, a dam of emotions burst, and tears ran down Maria's face. Shame consumed her. She hadn't even had the decency to acknowledge Rebecca as friend, let alone inquire about her death.

It took twenty minutes before Maria composed herself and turned off the hot water. She stood in front of the fogged-up mirror. Wiping the glass with a towel, her red, splotchy body and sad, haunting eyes appeared before her. She took a deep breath and picked up a brush to begin detangling her long, blonde tresses. She continued with her beauty regiment after convincing herself that this would be it. Surely, she was finally pregnant. She would take a test as soon as she got home.

By the time she was done dressing, she had pushed all thoughts of her nightmare, Constance, and Rebecca from her mind. Packing her makeup in her designer bag, she walked over to a chair and slipped on a pair of six-hundred-dollar shoes. She stood, looked in the floor-length mirror, and saw the woman she had become. She touched her hair that was tightly smoothed into a knot, then removed a pair of shades from her purse and left the room. She would finish this job and make Sebastian so proud that he would be elated by starting a family and a new adventure with her.

# CHAPTER 12

Marty Rose was not what Addison had been expecting. He was much younger than Keith, at least by ten years. He introduced himself as he stuck out his hand. She stepped forward and shook it; a very hard, firm shake. "Addison Shaw."

Addison said, "I'm sorry, but I don't remember meeting you at the chapel. The whole memorial service is still quite a blur for me."

"Yeah, I know what you mean." An awkward silence passed before he spoke again. "Keith was very fond of you and your son."

"Thanks for saying that." She reached for his hand. "Can I be honest?"

"Of course." He squeezed her hand back.

She released his grip and looked at the floor as she spoke. "I'm a little overwhelmed by it all. Why on God's green earth would Keith give me so much money?" She slowly looked up and met his eyes and continued. "Reba and the kids must hate me." She added sheepishly, "And, well, you too, probably."

He laughed and surprised her by giving her a hug. "Oh Addison, I love you already." He squeezed her tightly, then let her go. "But there's no doubt Reba hates you, though!"

Addison cringed.

He laughed again and then motioned to a sitting area. "Please, let's have a seat."

She sat opposite from him as he took the chair. He continued. "Their children are still too young to understand the provisions of the will." He crossed his arms. "Now, for me, I don't hate you. Keith left me the controlling interest of this company. I can grow the business and make my own fortune and legacy. I don't have a wife or children. I can live and breathe this business and make it my own. But something tells me you don't have a clue what your plans are going to be."

Addison was speechless. He stood and walked around the coffee table and sat beside her. It was her turn to laugh. He put her at ease, making conversation easy. She relaxed. He was charming, handsome, and self-confident. Definitely Keith's brother.

"I have some decisions to make, that's for sure."

He nodded. "I can help, you know. After all, it's what we do here. We help people invest and grow their money."

"Which is one of the reasons I wanted to come by. I know nothing about this business."

"I wouldn't expect you to. You're a teacher, right? Am I remembering that correctly?"

"Third grade."

"And you're a single parent." His eyes locked on hers. "Your life is busy."

"Yes."

He nodded. "Well, Keith was very generous when he gave you twenty percent of the company as well. I don't won't you to worry

126

about Rose Investment Firm. I'm sure the lawyer explained Keith had no desire for you to play a role in this company. You have the luxury of no stress. You just get your share of the profits every quarter. Pretty sweet deal if you ask me."

"He gave you forty-five percent. Obviously, he trusted you and knew you could handle the stress of running this company."

A look of pride filled Marty's face. "He did. But I still have to answer to a board of directors. If I can't make this company successful, I'll be replaced."

"Do I get a vote?"

Humor filled his face. "I know this probably sounds odd, but no. You get no vote. Keith set it up where the board of directors places your vote.

"How can that be changed?"

Marty gave her a serious look. "You want to play a role in this company? An industry you know nothing about?"

She had struck a nerve. She had to tread carefully. "No, of course not. That came across all wrong; sorry. I was just curious how the company was set up."

The tension on his face relaxed. "The seven board members make up the other thirty-five percent. They each own five percent of the company. Any restructuring would require a vote. But still, your vote is determined by the board." He smiled. "It was truly Keith's wishes for you not to be involved." He grabbed her hand and squeezed it again. "Just take the money every quarter and enjoy a stress-free life. You and your son have the means to go and do anything you want."

She pulled her hand away, then reached out and picked up a glass of water on the coffee table. She drank slowly, trying to process everything. *"Just take the money."* But what about the letter and the lock-box? she thought.

He looked at his watch, indicating he was a very busy man. "Is there anything else I can help you with today?"

Addison placed the glass down while pushing Keith's letter out of her mind. She had to stick to the plan. She would not tell a soul until she had the contents of the lockbox. "Did you by chance come by the canal home and go into the study?"

He smirked. "I heard about that last night when I had a surprise visit from the FBI. No, I did not."

"Aren't you concerned?"

"Well, yes, but not from a business point of view." He saw her confusion and immediately explained. "Keith was one of the best at this business. My brother was the smartest man I've ever known. Look, you have to understand his work ethic. It made him who he was, and the success of this company is a result. Keith would have never taken home files from this office that would jeopardize our accounts. We have strict rules here. Nothing leaves, and everything is kept locked down at all times. Keith's rules. Trust me, there was nothing in his study concerning Rose Investment Firm."

*But he kept a lockbox at the bank?* she thought and then asked, "How can you be so sure?"

He smiled. "You didn't know my brother like me. I worked with him every day. You only knew the Keith that was married to your sister."

An image of Keith holding Cassandra down in the sand on the beach as Riley buried her filled her vision. Everyone was laughing. His face froze before hers, and she looked at his brother. They had some of the same features: tall, broad shoulders, and charming brown eyes. Keith and Cassandra had rarely talked about Marty. She didn't know anything about this man who stood before her now and, apparently, she hadn't known Keith either.

"You okay?"

She shook off the memories. "Yes, sorry. But if the boxes weren't related to the business, why were they opened, and who opened them?"

He shook his head. "I'm clueless, and I told the FBI that. Look, Keith and Cassandra have made the front-page news the past few weeks. It could be anyone trying to cash in. Every household has the standard files. You know—the credit cards, warranties, insurance statements, maybe some medical folders Cassandra kept. It wouldn't be that hard for a good thief to figure out where they lived." He saw the tension in her face. "Hey, I'm sorry to scare you, but honestly, I wouldn't worry too much. My brother was smart. Someone would have to try really hard to succeed in stealing his identify."

"You think this is identify thief?"

He shrugged. "Addison, I don't know. But what I do know is Keith had a plan for everything. It would be very difficult for a criminal to steal his identity. Keith would have taken every precaution against fraud. But yes, on the other hand, you should worry. The locks and alarm code need to be changed immediately. I told the FBI the same thing last night. And besides, it's going to be your house soon." He sat back and shrugged. "Could have been Reba. She's not happy about the will. She probably still has a key."

"Reba. I didn't think about her."

"And don't give her another thought. I told the FBI that Reba was a very bitter woman. They'll be talking to her."

"But would she really break into the house?" Addison asked.

He laughed. "You ever have a conversation with Reba that lasted longer than a minute?"

"No. At least, I don't think so. Like I said, the memorial service is a blur."

He turned serious. "Take my advice: stay away from Reba. And she drinks. Like a lot."

Addison sat back and studied him. *Who is this man? He acts as if he adored and worshipped Keith. Should I trust him? Or does this act mean he's involved too? Did he know Keith was being investigated? Is he just as guilty for Cassandra's murder?*

She looked into his eyes. They appeared genuine. *Was she reading him wrong? Was all this a sham? Had he gotten tired of living in Keith's shadow and sold him out? Was he responsible for the explosion?*

"Why are you looking at me like that?" he asked.

Addison turned red from embarrassment. "What?"

"I make you nervous. Why?"

Addison sat back up. "What? No. Sorry, it's been a long two days."

A brief silence formed between them. Finally, Marty broke it. "I'm sure it has been. Are you still going to stay in the house?"

She shook her head. "I stayed in a hotel last night."

"Good. I think that's wise for now. Maybe you should start to think about selling the canal home. It's a big target with it being empty." He smiled and added, "But keep the beach house. I heard you used to vacation there in the summer."

"I did. Lots of good memories there of the four of us. Cassandra and Keith were married there." With that thought, she remembered Marty hadn't attended the wedding, only Keith's three girls. Had he not been invited? She prodded, "Were you out of town during the wedding?"

Marty gave an awkward smile as if forced. "No. I wasn't invited. We had had a disagreement, and then Keith decided that he would just keep the wedding small."

Addison knew firsthand about disagreements. "I'm sorry. My last conversation with Cassandra had been an argument. But hey, it looks like you and Keith got that straightened out." She gestured around the office at the company he was to inherit.

"Yes, we did. I don't mind telling you what it was about." He poured himself a glass of water and took a sip, then said, "I was mad at Keith because he had decided not to sign a prenup with Cassandra like he had done with Reba."

Clarity emerged for Addison. Yes, of course he would have been concerned about that. In fact, Addison had been shocked herself when Cassandra had told her Keith's plan. She asked, "Do you know why he chose not to? Cassandra had told me there was no prenup and, honestly, well, I was a little blown away myself."

He shook his head. "He never gave me a straight answer. Just insisted this was different and he loved her, and I was to keep my opinions to myself. It was awkward between us for a few weeks, and then it passed. We never brought it up again. What was done was done, so there was no point." He looked at his watch again and asked, "So, do you know your plans yet?"

"No. Just to survive over the next few weeks and keep it together for my son."

"Well, there's no rush to do anything. Take your time. I hope the lawyer told you that."

"Yes. Mr. Greer has been extremely helpful. I've got a lot to think about. I won't keep you." She stood. "Thank you for your time. I might call on you again and take you up on that offer for financial advice."

His face lit up. "I wish you would. I'd like the chance to get to know you better. See for myself why my brother adored you."

She felt herself blush. "Thank you."

"My pleasure. Let me walk you out."

Remembering Jonas right outside the door, she responded, "That's not necessary. Goodbye, Mr. Rose. It was nice meeting you as well."

"Likewise." He reached into his jacket pocket and pulled out a card. "My mobile phone is listed as well." He squeezed her arm. "Call me anytime and, please, call me Marty."

She took the card and left.

*** 

The ride to Peter O. Knight Airport was quiet. Jonas had asked few questions after Addison had repeatedly told him there was really nothing to discuss. Marty had been a complete gentleman and had laid out her role in the company, which was no role at all.

Once they arrived at the airport, her luggage was removed from the SUV. Jonas stood by the passenger door as she checked to make sure she had everything.

"When you land in Atlanta, give Agent Greene a call. Someone is set to meet you at the airport and escort you home and check things out."

She nodded. "Thank you. I will." She rolled her luggage through a double door and spotted Caleb.

"Ms. Shaw." He nodded. "You ready?"

"Yes." He took her luggage. "Thank you."

She turned and saw Jonas still standing in the small lobby, waiting and watching her. She turned back around and climbed the stairs to board the plane. Within fifteen minutes, she was back in the air heading home. She gripped the armrest as they lifted off.

Jonas picked up his phone. "She's airborne."

"Good," Aiden replied. "I need you back at headquarters. I think we finally found a break with Wayne Keaton."

# CHAPTER 13

*FBI Tampa Field Office*

Aiden was talking on the phone when he spotted Jonas walking down the aisles of desks toward his office. He motioned for him to enter and slid a new folder across his desk for Jonas to view as he quickly ended his phone call.

"We finally got that break."

Jonas looked at the first page in the folder. "Sunshine Properties?"

Aiden smiled and leaned forward, barely able to contain his excitement. "The owner, Isaac Mullins, leased a property to Wayne Keaton six months ago. When the lease came back up, the rent was paid three times."

"Three times?"

"Yep. Went from two thousand dollars a month to six thousand."

Jonas clapped his hands with excitement. "Wow. I've heard of property value increasing, but not by that much."

Aiden stood up from his desk. "You ready to go check it out?"

Jonas read the address. "One hundred and three Washington Street. Where is that?"

Aiden walked around him and pulled his bulletproof vest from a hook behind the door. "On the industrial side, about two blocks from the shipping docks."

"Everything seems to keep pointing back to the shipping channels. Interesting." Jonas shut the door behind him as Aiden unbuttoned his white shirt and suited up. He flipped through the pictures in the file. "Any idea what this business is used for?"

"That's what I was trying to figure out on the phone. I want to tread carefully here. I ask the wrong person enough questions, and we'll most likely stumble upon one of Keaton's rats."

"Yeah, I swear he's got someone in every government agency in Tampa working for him."

Aiden checked his weapons and slid them into his holsters. Then he pulled on a black blazer. "I want to do a drive-by first, access what we're up against, then go from there. You ready now?"

Jonas patted his shirt. "Yeah. Didn't bother taking it off yet. Hot as hell in this thing too."

Aiden nodded. "Better hot than dead, though."

They walked out and decided to take a dark Chevy Tahoe out of storage for their run. The SUV that had been abandoned two months ago in a drug raid was now FBI property. Aiden liked it because the windows were slightly tinted, hiding their profiles. Firing up the engine, he asked, "How did Addison act today? Anything off?"

"Not that I could tell. Looked tired, ready to get back home to her son." Jonas looked both ways as they entered the busy highway during lunch hour traffic. "I really don't think she has any knowledge of Keith's money laundering and ties to Keaton."

Aiden sighed loudly. "I think you're right." Then he gave a quick glance at Jonas before turning onto Lambert Street, which would take them south to the shipping channels. "She's not giving off any weird vibes on my internal radar."

"I know what you mean. I got nothing either, but I spent less than an hour with her total." He looked at his watch. "She should still be in the air. But someone will call."

"The sooner she gets back to her life in Atlanta, the better for everyone."

Jonas laughed. "Yeah, just get back to your old life with fifty million dollars."

"You know what I mean. She can spend her money in Atlanta. No reason for her to come back to Tampa. She has no family down here now."

"Just property and Marty Rose. She liked him."

Aiden frowned. "She'll probably keep the beach house. When we were there, she walked around in a daze looking at photos and staring at the beach."

Jonas adjusted the air and then settled back. "I would keep the beach house and spend my entire summer vacation down here."

Aiden checked his rearview mirror before replying. "Why not? With teaching, she's got her summers off. But she's not going back to work."

"She didn't sound like she was quitting."

Aiden made a right turn at a red light. They were two blocks away. "She will. She's just not admitting it to herself yet."

The Tahoe slowed to the speed limit as they did a drive-by down Washington Street. The building was one of those metal structures that contained small businesses with one door to the public parking area and another at the back. There was only one sign outside the white door with the number *103* posted by the entrance. Aiden cruised by at the same speed. When they were at the end of Washington, he turned left and then made an immediate left again onto Jefferson Street.

He kept the same pace down Jefferson. On the left was the back of the business complex showing each individual address had another white door with a twelve-feet-by-eight-feet opening for receivables. Each were numbered; they all looked the same. Two down from Wayne's business, the receiving door was fully opened: Boxes were being unloaded from a delivery truck inside. Aiden kept driving and looked to his right. An identical metal building lined the street, except the front of its businesses faced the next street over, Biggs Street.

Jonas reviewed the paperwork inside the folder he held. He reached for the printed map that showed Crane Industrial Park, owned by Larry Crane. There were four streets listed: Washington, Jefferson, Biggs, and Lamar. Only Jefferson and Lamar were used as delivery streets, while over thirty businesses could be accessed by Washington and Biggs Streets, each building holding ten stalls each. All were rented except three.

Jonas looked at the names listed on the directory that had been printed from the industrial park's website. Holden's Supply Shop and Hick's Welding Supply Company bordered Wayne's business, which was titled KW shipping. Anyone looking at this directory would have little clue exactly what business was conducted at 103 Washington Street. That information wasn't too suspicious. There were six other businesses in the park that had only initials for their name too.

"I wonder how many drugs go through this park on a monthly basis," Jonas mused as he slid the map back inside the folder.

Aiden drove down another street, closer to the shipping channel. "Nah, too risky to put drugs down here. They hide them in plain sight downtown in skyscrapers."

"You think girls go through here?"

"It's possible. The three units not rented are going anywhere from eighteen hundred to twenty-two hundred. Not six grand. Something's going on here."

Jonas pointed at the corner of a building complex. "Limited cameras. Looks like a cheap, amateur security system. Definitely not adding up. This place isn't worth six thousand a month."

"Exactly." Aiden turned the Tahoe around and headed back toward Washington. "Time to go see what's inside."

He parked the Tahoe directly in front of KW Shipping. Aiden removed his piece strapped to his ankle and turned off the safety. Then returned it to his holster. They exited the Tahoe and walked up to the white door by the one marked *103* and twisted the knob. It was locked. There was a peephole, but it didn't do them any good. Aiden saw a doorbell and pressed the button.

They waited about a minute, and then a lock turned and the door opened. A large woman with a Hispanic accent asked, "Can I help you?"

She was not what they had been expecting. Aiden tried to look past her, but she blocked the door well with her body. Only a portion of a desk with a computer could be seen.

"I'm Jeb Downey with Spartan Supply. Is the owner here?"

She shook her head. "May I take a message?"

A phone began to ring behind her. She looked confused as to what to do: Leave them standing or shut the door and answer the phone. She quickly looked them over and stepped backward. "Give me a minute."

Aiden looked at Jonas with raised eyebrows as she allowed them to enter. The room was small, containing only a desk, chair, computer, and phone. Another door was behind the desk. There was a window on the door, but the blinds were drawn, blocking whatever was behind the small reception area.

She took a seat in the chair and answered the phone. "KW Shipping. How may I help you?"

Aiden and Jonas tried not to stare as she made a few taps on her computer and then replied in Spanish. Both agents tried not to grin as they understood every word spoken: "You dumbass, they arrived yesterday at three. All accounted for. It's on you that you ran out."

She hung up the phone, picked up a pen, and removed a sticky note from her desk. "What's the message?"

"Well, I just had a question about our rent," Aiden said with a boyish smile. "Crane is trying to raise it again. I just wanted to get a feel from everyone else if I'm being screwed." He gave a serious look. "Pardon my language."

She dropped the pen. "Rent is not my business." She sat back in her chair. The phone rang again. She frowned with irritation. "You should go next door. Ask them."

The phone rang again, and she made no move toward it. Aiden got the hint. "Okay, I will. Thanks anyway."

When they opened the door, they heard her voice once again: "KW Shipping . . ."

Aiden closed the door behind him. "That was useless."

"You could have pushed."

"Not with her. They didn't hire her for her looks. She's connected."

"What now?"

"We wait. Follow her home."

***

A little after twelve, Sebastian stepped out of a taxi onto Charleston Drive in Downtown Tampa. The streets were packed with women and men from the corporate world out for lunch. No one would take a second glance at two well-dressed men sitting in a crowded restaurant discussing the trade of women, which was exactly why they had chosen this location.

Wayne had arrived ten minutes ago, making sure the FBI hadn't followed him. He had increasingly become paranoid since the call had been made to take out Keith and the FBI had ramped up their investigation. Now he carefully watched his every move. He chose when he wanted to be seen and followed by the authorities. He had caught their tail earlier and had driven straight to Dolls, parking in his reserved spot in the back. From there, he had walked through the establishment, out the front door, and into a waiting cab.

Sebastian walked into the Red Pine Bar and Pub and scanned the room until he saw Wayne. He smiled at the hostess and explained he was meeting someone. Soon he was sitting across from Wayne.

"How's the food here?"

Wayne checked the front door before replying, "Better than before. I think the new management will be good."

Sebastian nodded, and they first discussed Marty Rose. So far, Marty had been predictable as he adjusted to his new role as CEO of Rose Investment Firm. They hashed out the pros and cons of reaching out to him. The timing had to be just right. Transferring money or closing any account so soon after Keith's passing would warrant an alert. Marty would want to know why the company had lost someone's business.

Then there was the unknown. How much were the FBI watching, and had Keith cut some kind of deal with them? If they were monitoring the accounts, then the FBI were just waiting on them to screw up and follow the money. They decided to wait and not contact Marty. They hedged their bet with the fact that they could always move their money out of the accounts by logging into the secure website and making a transfer. Yes, it would raise a red flag, but at that point, extreme measures would be warranted. Sebastian had accounts all over the world, and a system was in place that would move the money quickly from one account to another with the goal of hiding any money trail. They both silently hoped it would never come to that.

Wayne lifted a menu and slid over a set of keys with an address neatly printed on the key chain. "The house is ready. My guest will arrive promptly just after dark, around eight thirty. Will you be ready?"

Sebastian pocketed the keys. "So far, all is on schedule. I don't foresee any issues. Do you?"

"No. All looks good. Is your wife attending again?" Wayne asked.

A frown appeared. Sebastian didn't like having his wife in the States for these exchanges. It left too much to chance: a car accident, a witness to a gas station robbery or worse, an ugly exchange with the buyers that could lead to murder. "Yes. It's important for the girls that she is here. She will help calm their nerves and prepare them as necessary." He shrugged his broad shoulders. "We can't just have anyone preparing the girls, now, can we?"

Wayne noticed a change in his demeanor and said, "You seem worried. Why?"

"I always worry, and I always plan for the unexpected."

"Like what happened with that girl who jumped off the boat?"

"Well, that won't happen again. I fixed that." Sebastian tossed the menu. "I'm not eating here."

Wayne wasn't surprised. Rarely had they met long enough to share a meal together. "What about Addison Shaw? Is she going to be a problem?"

"Not sure. We can assume the FBI have talked to her by now. Every move we make has to be under their radar. No slipups."

Wayne frowned. "She's going to have an accident as well?"

Sebastian chuckled. "I wish, but I can't exactly right now take everyone out that I suspect. Besides, she'll do everything in her power to protect her son. I expect her back in Atlanta by nightfall."

Wayne looked skeptical. "Nightfall?"

Sebastian took a sip from his water. Then he replied, "She boarded the jet earlier. She's gone." He looked around the crowded room and observed everyone. Then he finished his water. "I'll be in touch after the close of the sale. If things calm down, maybe I'll have something for you in October." Sebastian reached across the table and shook Wayne's hand. Then he stood.

Wayne stood also. "Sounds good."

Sebastian patted him on the shoulder and advised, "Stay alert."

Wayne nodded and watched as Sebastian left through the front doors. Then he took his seat again just as the waitress reappeared. "Just one for lunch now?"

"Yes."

# CHAPTER 14

It was 12:15 p.m. when Maria selected a shop on Ocean Drive. She had just over an hour before her designated pickup at 1:30 p.m. that would take her to Tampa. The drive would take a little over four hours. Then she would have less than two hours to get the remaining girls ready for their appearance at 8 p.m. To her, it wasn't enough time to shop properly, but Sebastian had insisted that little time be spent in public. Less time in a store meant shorter memories if a salesclerk was ever questioned in the future.

The store sold dresses for young women that were suited for clubbing. She declined help as she browsed the racks. The dresses weren't for her; they were for Tatiana and Bianca to wear tonight in Tampa. Every dress she picked suited Tatiana well. She was just shy of six feet and weighed around one hundred and twenty pounds. Bianca was a different story. She was the most beautiful of the five girls. Her Middle Eastern descent was evident in her dark eyes and jet-black hair. Her height of five three and her curvy figure made shopping for her a little more challenging. She thought of them both as she held up the dresses. It was a tough call, which girl would bring in the most cash. Her job was to present them in the best light possible.

An emerald-green dress caught her eye. It was low cut and would show off Bianca's larger-than-average chest. The material held the right amount of spandex to accommodate her well-rounded hips. The length was a little too long, causing Maria to pause with the dress held in midair. She glanced over at the shoe rack, debating how to make this dress work for Bianca. A bell sounded, and two young women walked in and headed directly toward the shoes, blocking her view and concentration.

Maria lowered the dress and clutched it to her body as she stepped toward the women and the shoes. As she neared, the younger one turned and looked directly at Maria. She was pale skinned with red hair and green eyes. Maria immediately saw in her mind Rebecca, her childhood friend. She stopped dead and turned back to the dress rack. She quickly hung the dresses up and fled the store, ignoring the saleswoman's words that sounded jumbled as Maria opened the door and the July heat wrapped around her. Her stomach did a flip-flop, and a clammy coldness spread throughout her body. She was going to be sick.

Across the street was a coffee shop. She ignored the crosswalk and ran across the street and into the café. Few patrons were inside. One person was placing an order, and two more were sitting at small computers along the wall. The sign above advertised internet access with prices listed below in smaller lettering. She then saw the restroom in the back corner with another sign: CUSTOMERS ONLY.

She walked over to the counter and scanned the items for sale. She concentrated on her breathing, trying to settle her nerves. Hopefully, a water and a blueberry muffin would also help. She paid cash and took her items to a table in the corner by the restroom.

As the minutes passed, her stomach relaxed, and she regained her composure. She looked up and around the shop, remembering what Sebastian had always told her. She froze when she saw a small camera aimed at the front door. She had not entered with her head down. She took another deep breath as a man at one of the computers got up and left, leaving the computer still connected to the internet.

She took her bottled water, walked over, and sat at the computer. The time on the bottom corner read *6:48* before the session expired. Maria glanced at the prices above. One needed a credit card to access the computer. Another glance at the time: *6:22.*

She typed *Rebecca O'Malley Boanne Hungary age 24*. A new screen appeared with many search options, mostly soliciting money for finding more information on Rebecca O'Malley. She closed her eyes briefly to think, then she glanced at the remaining time: *5:41*.

She started a new search. The local town paper appeared. She clicked on the Obituary section. A search box appeared on the next screen. She typed in Rebecca's name and glanced at the time as she waited for the search to complete: *5:05*.

Forty-five names appeared, with the names *Rebecca* and *O'Malley* highlighted in each set, each with dates beside them. The one she wanted was at the top: *Rebecca Sierra O'Malley, 1998–2017*. She clicked on the name and waited. The small article appeared without a picture. The time now read *4:02*.

Slowly, she read the brief three paragraphs. The cause of death was complications from an infection. No more information was given. It listed her father, Martin O'Malley, and two sisters, Jillian and Constance, as survivors.

Time stood still as Maria stared at the screen. Memory after memory of her childhood flooded her mind after years of being dormant: walks in the field, whispering behind boys' backs at school. Then another memory slammed her back into reality: Constance whining to her mother that Rebecca and Maria wouldn't let her go with them to the store. When had her mother died? She typed in *Monica O'Malley*.

There were less names, with only twenty-seven given. *Monica F. O'Malley* was at the top. *1976–2017*. She had died the same year as Rebecca. She clicked on the name. Just as the obituary appeared, the screen returned to a desktop, asking for another deposit before continuing, but not before she caught the words *complication* and *infection*.

Maria pushed away from the computer and fled to the restroom with her bottled water and purse.

*\*\*\**

Another hour passed before Aiden saw a car approach and park in front of KW Shipping. A man in his early thirties got out of a black van and opened the door.

"Not locked. She knew he was coming."

Five minutes later, he walked out, carrying a box. Two minutes later, he was pulling away onto Jefferson Street.

Aiden looked at the time. "She probably works till four or five. Let's follow the van. You agree?"

"Yeah, let's go."

The Tahoe, which was parked three businesses away near a machine shop, pulled out onto Jefferson. Traffic was light until they reached an intersection that crossed six lanes. They followed slowly under the green light into heavy traffic and got behind a small sportscar, two lanes over at the next light. They continued following the van until they realized the vehicle was most likely getting onto Interstate 12 up ahead. The Tahoe slowly moved over the two lanes and entered the freeway about five cars behind the van.

Another five minutes passed before the van slowed and signaled for the slow lane to exit. The Tahoe, which was already in the slow lane, followed the van off the exit ramp. The exit led to the south side of Tampa, a lower-economic area known for clubbing, warehouses, and strip joints.

"He's going to Keaton's Chandelier Bar," Aiden stated with confidence.

"How can you be sure it's not the Angels strip club?"

"He would have taken the next exit. It skips two lights."

Jonas nodded. "We spend too much time down here."

Aiden didn't comment as the van slowed and eventually turned right into the parking lot of an outdoor shopping mall. The Chandelier Bar was on the corner. It was painted black and had an all-white sign. Aiden and Jonas had both been in the bar before. Wayne had put a lot of money into the building to give it a classy appearance. Various lighting fixtures dangled from the ceiling at different heights.

Aiden had no desire to go back into the bar and suggested, "Let's get back to the industrial park. This was a waste of time."

"Not really. We know they store booze back at KW Shipping. At least that's what the box that guy was carrying looked like, anyway."

The Tahoe did a legal U-turn at the next intersection and headed back toward the interstate. "If it was liquor, why not have it shipped directly to the clubs like a normal bar?" Aiden wondered.

"Because it's Keaton's bar, that's why. Probably wasn't all liquor. Could be high-end illegal cigars out of Cuba tucked in the bottom."

"Good point. That's something you wouldn't want hanging around in excess if there was ever a raid. We need to search what's being stored at KW Shipping."

Jonas laughed. "There's not a judge left to give us a warrant. All favors concerning Keaton have been called in, remember?"

Aiden cussed softly as he accelerated up the ramp that would take them back to the interstate to the shipping channels. "Let's just see where the woman goes tonight. Maybe she'll get careless and drop her keys."

"We can make that happen."

Aiden tapped his steering wheel, deep in thought. They had to be careful, or they could lose their only lead. He thought about the tail that had been placed on Isaac Mullins. "Call Agent Reid. See what our little real estate agent is up to."

Aiden guided the Tahoe back to the interstate while Jonas made the call, then reported, "He's with two clients, showing a house in Memorial Heights."

"So he's busy. We'll see if he stays busy at nighttime too," Aiden commented.

# CHAPTER 15

At 1 p.m., Maria walked out of a different clothing store from earlier with two bags. One contained two pairs of shoes, and the other held four dresses for her to choose from for tonight. Now she needed perfume, makeup, and hair supplies. She scanned the stores nearby, looking for a drugstore. She saw one across the street and over two blocks. Walking along the sidewalk, her eyes were shielded from the world behind her sunglasses. She did her best to blend in with other tourists out shopping on a warm, busy day in South Beach. Unlike earlier, she was in complete control as she waited with others to cross the street.

Earlier, Maria had broken a rule: She had called Sebastian from her prepaid cell phone from inside the locked single-stall bathroom. She had been a wreck and needed to hear his voice. Although she had expected him to be angry, he was not. Sebastian was calm as he listened to her rant about quitting. Once she finished speaking, he assured her for several minutes that everything was going to be fine. She listened and finally was able to end the call, focused and determined to see this sale through to the end. The end that Sebastian had reminded her would be here in less than seven hours. She could do this. He was counting on her. She could fall apart when they returned to the Caymans. He had promised her a trip, just the two of them, to get away from it all and regroup. He was also open to the idea of quitting the business after she had reminded him once again how much money he made just from furniture sales.

Now composed, Maria entered the drugstore with her head down. Fifteen minutes later, she walked out carrying her purchases with no drama. Maria kept notice of her surroundings as she walked down Collins Street toward her pickup location. At the corner where she was to meet the black van was a bar. She looked at her watch. Ten minutes early. Sebastian had told her not to wait on the sidewalk, as it might draw attention. She scanned the stores near her. She chose the bar instead of more shopping.

Upon entering, she walked up to the bartender and ordered a house wine. She paid with cash and walked over by the window and took a seat in view of the street corner.

The ten minutes it took waiting seemed like eternity as she sipped her wine. She tried her best not to replay the earlier events in her mind. Instead, she focused on Sebastian's words: a trip and that he was open to quitting this nasty business. She took another sip and placed her wineglass on the coaster. For the first time, she noticed the name of the bar: O'Malley's. She was in an Irish bar. Rebecca's family had originally been from Ireland.

She looked back out the window and saw the van appear, driving toward her. For a split moment, she thought of running away from it all. The van came to a stop. Time seemed to freeze but only for a moment.

She shook the thoughts away, grabbed her bags, and left O'Malley's Bar. She headed to the van and to her future with Sebastian and his soft-spoken promises.

*\*\**

It was 4 p.m. when the white door opened, and the woman walked out of KW Shipping and closed the door. She checked the lock. Satisfied it was secure for the night, she walked over to and unlocked a Ford Fusion that sat in the parking lot. Aiden and Jonas had run every tag in the parking lot earlier. The Ford was registered to a Miguel Emmanuel at 1009 Wilson Park Road, an older section of town populated by many Cuban migrants.

After about five minutes of following her, they backed off. As they predicted, the woman appeared to be headed home to her Wilson Park Road address. Miguel was a two-year resident of Tampa with no prior criminal record. He had received a green card eight years ago after moving from Guatemala to Miami. There was no record of a marriage license, and Miguel's paperwork for employment stated he was a cook.

The Tahoe pulled over two streets from Miguel's home. Five minutes later, they turned onto the street and drove past 1009 Wilson Park Road. In front of the gray-painted home of about twelve hundred square feet sat the Ford Fusion. There was no garage, and the stairs leading up to the door weren't covered. Bars covered the windows on the front of the house. They circled the neighborhood, parked a few houses down the street, and waited.

At 5:15 p.m., the front door opened. A man wearing a suit who matched the height and weight description from the DMV records jogged down the stairs and climbed inside the Fusion.

Aiden glanced at the picture he had pulled up on his phone. "It's Miguel. Looks like there's only one vehicle. Let's see where he goes. Dressed like that, something tells me he's no longer a cook."

They were right. The Fusion pulled into the parking lot of Tampa's Wild Things. Aiden also pulled in a parking slot and watched Miguel exit his car. "I don't think he's here for the show."

"No," Jonas said. "Too small for a bouncer. Dressed like that, Keaton has him doing something else. Maybe he just works the front door."

Aiden picked up his phone. "If there's only one car, she won't be going back to work." He placed a call.

After three rings, a male's voice answered. Aiden asked, "You busy tonight?"

"Jeez! Again?"

Aiden ignored his theatrics. "Yes. Meet in twenty minutes?"

"It will take me thirty."

"Thirty it is."

The line went dead. Aiden looked at Jonas. "He's good."

They headed to the designated meeting spot at a secluded park. They were going to meet Eduardo Menveo, a snitch. A few months ago, the Drug Enforcement Administration team had picked him up. One more go-round with the law and Eduardo was doing time. Luckily for them, he would sell out his own mother if it meant avoiding jail. So far, he had been capable in helping out the Human Trafficking Division.

Aiden sat on the park bench next to Eduardo while Jonas staked out the place to make sure Eduardo had not been followed. Eduardo was jumpy. His eyes darted around, and he couldn't keep his right leg still. He finally met Aiden's eyes and asked with dread, "What have I got to do this time? And how many more times, man?"

Aiden smiled. "This will be easy and involves no other people. All I need you to do is take a look around. Get in and get out. I just need to know what's inside, that's all."

For the first time, his leg paused, and Eduardo began to relax. Breaking and entering was easy for him. Aiden showed him the address, and when he nodded after committing it to memory, Aiden stood. In short of two minutes, Eduardo walked away, and Aiden and Jonas were leaving the park.

# CHAPTER 16

At 6:30 p.m., Juan Diego, who had worked for Sebastian Hawks for the last four years, drove a dark van carrying Maria, Tatiana, and Bianca into a quiet golf course community. Juan sent a quick text message to open the garage door to the house. They had passed only a few cars once entering, and so far, they were on schedule.

The mood had greatly changed since last night's boat ride. Once safely in the marina, they had discreetly transferred all five of the girls to a private yacht owned by one of Wayne's associates. Once the girls saw the yacht and were allowed to shower and change, they had become manageable again. Then Maria had presented each of them with a shopping bag with a new dress and matching jewelry. Bill Banks then soon arrived and inspected each girl. Tatiana and Bianca had stayed overnight on the yacht under close watch by Juan while Maria and Gabriel had taken the other three girls to Bill Banks in Downtown Miami. Once the final exchange had been made, Gabriel had dropped Maria off at The Tides to meet Sebastian and returned to help Juan.

The girls were excited to finally be in the United States, and Maria continued to make small talk while she sat between them in the back seat. Once settled in the car, she had showed them her purchases from South Beach, and she had been studying Tatiana closely, looking for any sign of trouble. So far, she had seen none. She began to relax as Bianca made comments about the nice homes they passed.

Finally, the van slowed in front of a house, and Maria saw an open garage door with another car sitting inside. Juan pulled into the driveway and carefully parked beside a black Mercedes.

The garage door closed, securing the van inside, and Juan turned around and faced Maria. He asked, "Are you ready?"

She smiled. "I believe we all are." She looked at Tatiana, who was still holding a blue dress with the highest price tag. "Tatiana, you ready to wear that and look beautiful?"

"I am."

Maria looked at Bianca next. "Well, have you decided on your dress?"

Hesitation filled Bianca's face. "I don't know. I just want to look perfect. I will try them all on."

Maria nodded to Juan. He got out and opened the side door. Bianca stepped out first, then Maria and Tatiana, all carrying their bags. Juan led the way as he opened a door that led to the kitchen. Aroma filled the air. Italian pasta was simmering on the stove. The table was also set for four.

Tatiana's eyes widened at the display. "This is for us?"

"Yes. We will eat first, then get ready."

Bianca walked past the kitchen and into the living room to inspect it. She slowly turned around and faced Maria. "Will this be my home?"

Maria walked toward her. "No. Your home will be much larger and grander." She touched Bianca's arm. "You are a woman with incredible beauty and charm. You will become a princess just like me."

Tatiana picked up a plate and knocked a spoon to the floor, causing them all to turn. Tatiana looked up. "I'm sorry, I'm nervous!"

Maria guided Bianca back to the kitchen and bent down to retrieve the spoon. "Of course you are. Your life will change forever tonight. Now let's eat so our nerves will settle. And how about a little white wine to go with our meal?"

"Oh yes, please," Tatiana said as she placed pasta on her plate from the stovetop.

Juan walked over to the wet bar and pulled a wine bottle out of a bucket of ice. He carefully removed the cork and poured them each a glass.

"You aren't drinking?" Bianca asked Maria.

A hand went to her stomach. "No. I'm with child."

Juan nearly dropped the wine bottle as he set it back down. Maria gave him a look and then turned back to the girls, who were both grinning.

"Wow, you really do have it all, don't you?" Bianca asked.

Maria gave a big smile, then picked up her plate, scooped a small portion of pasta onto it, and then sat between the girls. Just as she picked up her fork, Tatiana offered to say grace.

Maria's heart skipped a beat. She swallowed her guilt. "That would be lovely, Tatiana."

After dinner, each girl was shown to a bedroom with an adjacent bathroom. They were to shower, then Maria would help them with their hair and makeup. When the girls were settled, she left Juan to guard their open doors and returned to the living room and found Sebastian. He immediately embraced her tightly.

"Well done. I heard everything. You handled them like the pro you have become. The line about the baby was very touching."

Maria pulled away from his embrace. "I'm not supposed to drink

157

tonight. What was I supposed to tell them?" She looked at her watch. "We don't have much time."

Sebastian cracked a smile. "Hey, I'm the one who is to worry about such things, not you." He touched her arm and led her over to the couch. "Are you better now?"

She knew he was referring to their phone conversation earlier. "Y-yes, I-I . . ." she stammered. "I don't know what happened. Constance really got into my head last night." He touched her cheek. "Then I had a dream, and I awoke all alone."

He pulled her forward and kissed her tenderly on the lips.

"One more night, and we will be back home in the Caymans. And that little trip I promised you . . ." He paused to watch her face light up. "It's already in the works. We will leave the following day."

Maria closed her eyes in delight and wrapped her arms around him. "Oh Sebastian, thank you. I need this." She pulled away and looked him in the eyes. "*We* need this. We have lots to discuss." She placed a hand on her stomach. "I wish I *was* pregnant. I . . . I want a family." She saw the change in his eyes. "That can't be too much of a surprise, can it, darling?"

He smiled. "No, of course not." He rose and pulled her to her feet. "I must go now. Juan will take care of you tonight. I will see you at home tomorrow, my love."

He kissed her quickly on the lips and left through the kitchen and into the Mercedes in the garage. She heard the garage door open and close. She squeezed her arms around her shoulders, trying to fight off a chill that had just entered the room with his absence. She took another breath and went to prepare the girls.

# CHAPTER 17

Maria sàt in the back seat alone as Juan drove the van, listening to a hip-hop radio station. She hated his music, but the alternative was silence, and that would have been enough to drive her over the edge.

Maria squeezed the armrest as a vision of Tatiana appeared before her. She was dressed in blue. She could have passed as a runway model with her height and looks. Her long hair graced her shoulders with soft curls. The makeup Maria had chosen was light and natural with just enough eyeliner to brighten her eyes. Tatiana was naturally beautiful without makeup. Tonight, her client had desired a natural look, so she had complied.

She poured another glass of wine. She caught Juan's expression in the rearview mirror. "You know I'm not pregnant."

He laughed. "No. I just don't want to make a hundred stops between here and Miami."

She tuned him out and sipped the fine wine as she thought of Bianca. Her look had been completely different. An American of Iranian decent had purchased her. He liked his women showy and well defined. The jewels the man had placed on Bianca's neck and wrist had turned her into a bubbling schoolgirl. The man had found her charming and kept complimenting her. Everything had gone as planned. Tatiana and Bianca had walked out of the home on the arms of two men of their own free will.

A tear slowly rolled down Maria's face. The two men were the same ones who arrived every time. They had been chosen for their looks and age. Both were just under thirty. They wore their designer suits, drove fancy cars, and showered the girls with gifts. Selfies had been snapped as the men sent the photos to their perspective buyers for final approval. After sharing a few drinks and light conversation, Tatiana and Bianca were off, their heads filled with hopes and dreams as they were driven away to a life that was sure to become one of misery.

"Stupid, stupid girls. How can they be so stupid?" The sound of her words caused her to sit up. She hadn't meant to speak aloud.

Juan had a quick answer. "Because you play the role of princess so well, they believe you."

The words were like a sucker punch to her gut. She looked away from his stare in the rearview mirror and rubbed her forehead. "How much longer? I'm tired beyond words."

Juan tossed a small bag to her. "Take two of these. It will put you right to sleep."

The bag hit the floorboard. She retrieved a small bottle of pills from it. "What are these?" she asked with hesitation.

"No clue. Sebastian gave them to me to give to you. He said to take two; they will help you relax."

Maria looked at the bottle of pills. She had spent more time with Gabriel in the Caymans over the years than Juan, whom she only dealt with in America during the exchanges. He was a wanted man who had fled Panama when accused of murder. Wayne had found him, and then Sebastian had met him and given his approval. Both men liked Juan and thought highly of him and his skill sets. Maria, however, didn't much like him due to his eyes. To her, she could see evil. But when she had given her opinion to Sebastian, he had laughed and told Juan to wear sunglasses while around his wife.

She removed the top of the bottle and placed two pills in her palm. She closed the bottle and returned it to the bag. As she rolled the pills around, trying to inspect them, Juan said, "Sebastian said take them only if you need them."

Maria pushed all doubt from her mind and tried to concentrate on the conversation that she had had with Sebastian back at the house. He was going to take her on a vacation. They would leave tomorrow. She smiled at the thought and then popped the pills in her mouth and washed them down with her wine. Ten minutes later, she was slightly snoring in her reclined seat.

Juan removed his sunglasses, picked up his phone, and made a call, saying, "She's out." He listened carefully to further instructions as he continued to drive into the night.

***

Aiden got the call from Jonas at 9:50 p.m. Isaac Mullins, the owner of Sunshine Properties, was leaving his home. His very late dinner was going to have to wait. Aiden grabbed his truck keys off the counter and patted Samantha on the head. "Stay and protect."

Samantha slid to the floor by the front door of the condo. Aiden checked the hallway and then locked up. Isaac lived on the same peninsula just southeast of Tampa. Aiden's condo faced the west, overlooking Hillsborough Bay, and Isaac lived on the east side in a canal home facing Old Tampa Bay. The price difference was substantial.

Climbing in his truck, he connected his phone to Bluetooth and drove east. Aiden pressed Reid's number in his phone. "Jonas called. I'm mobile. Where to?"

Agent Trevor Reid replied as he carefully trailed Isaac, "Memorial Highway North toward the airport, but he has no luggage."

Aiden quickly took a sharp right. He would jump on Interstate 275 to catch up. "Maybe he's meeting someone's flight, a family member."

"I thought of that. They have young kids, so it makes sense the wife would stay behind."

They chatted for the next twenty minutes. Traffic flowed nicely at this time of night. Aiden had made up ground and was only about five miles behind now. Isaac had passed the airport exit; he was continuing north into a large residential area located just west of Downtown Tampa.

"He's getting off at Highway 584. Taking Exit 6A. Turning left," Trevor said.

Silence passed as Trevor followed at a safe distance. Several golf course neighborhoods dotted West Waters Avenue. Finally, Isaac slowed and turned on his right signal.

"Turning. Looks like Sugar Bay Golf Course. Yeah, take the entrance to Sugar Bay."

"Be careful. Can't be too much traffic."

Trevor slowed until he saw Isaac brake and disappeared up ahead as he turned left. Trevor floored it. Just as he turned, he caught Isaac's Mercedes pulling into a driveway. He eased forward and got a glimpse of a garage door closing behind his car.

"He's inside a garage. One thirty-five Sugar Bay Cove. I'm going to circle back and park a few houses down."

"This doesn't make sense. Is he having an affair?" Aiden wondered with skepticism.

"Wouldn't be a complete shocker, but no, I don't think so. Looks like no one's home waiting on him. Only lights that are on are the flood lights."

Aiden remembered seeing Isaac's picture on Sunshine Properties' website. By his side was a beautiful young woman in her early thirties. They were holding two small children, equally as beautiful as their mother. A picture-perfect, all-American family. The exact image Sunshine Properties wanted to project for potential clients.

"I'm parked across the street. All's quiet."

Aiden saw Trevor's car ahead and cut his lights. He eased behind him, turned off the engine, then carefully stepped out of his truck and looked around. They hadn't attracted any attention.

Trevor rolled down his window. "He's turned on very few lights."

Aiden took a longer assessment of the neighborhood. Large trees separated the homes from one another. The setting felt secluded. Aiden noticed a For Sale sign in the yard next to the home Isaac had entered. "Whose realty sign? Can't see it."

"Sunshine Properties."

He looked at Trevor. "That's interesting. So Mullins knows the neighborhood. We know who owns the house yet?"

"Not yet."

Aiden leaned against the car and mumbled, "What are you doing, Mullins? It's too late to be checking on a property."

A light went off and then another.

"He's leaving. You pull out and wait somewhere along the highway."

Aiden jumped back into his truck and pulled forward four houses with his lights still off. Turning his truck around, he saw the light of the garage door and Isaac's Mercedes backing down the driveway. He called Trevor. "We'll tag-team him. You first."

Once Isaac's car made a right and pulled out of sight, Aiden turned his headlights on and followed. He looked closely at the house number as he passed: *135*. It appeared empty. Only the flood lights were still on.

Trevor said, "He turned east on Waters Avenue, heading back the way he came."

Aiden pulled out of the neighborhood and turned left as well. Trevor and Isaac were too far ahead to see them.

Trevor announced, "He's turning into the shopping center on the right."

Aiden recalled a small shopping center with about a half dozen businesses. *What could Isaac possibly be up to?* he thought.

Trevor continued. "He's going through a drive-through—oh, wait. He's parking in the back."

"Be careful." Aiden heard him order a hamburger and a drink. Then he heard a window being raised.

"He's popping the trunk. I've got to move forward."

Aiden turned into the shopping center. Trevor was at the drive-through window, paying for his order. Aiden parked on the other side. Isaac was returning from the large garbage dumpsters located in the back. He quickly looked around, then jumped back into his Mercedes and drove off.

Aiden said, "Meet me in the parking lot. Don't follow him."

A few minutes passed, then Trevor pulled up beside Aiden, sipping his drink. He got out of his car and went to Aiden's driver-side door. "What did he do?"

Aiden pointed to the dumpster. "Got rid of some trash."

A frown immediately appeared on Trevor's face. "Oh joy, and I'm wearing my new shoes."

Aiden looked down at his feet. "Not going to be new anymore."

Trevor was a single twenty-five-year-old who always dressed to impress. He never missed an opportunity to leave a good impression if he met a pretty woman. Aiden tried not to laugh as Trevor jumped into the dumpster and retrieved a white trash bag that Isaac had disposed of. It was easy to spot compared with the other boxes and large black bags the fast-food business had discarded.

Aiden carefully placed the bag in the back of his truck. Wearing gloves, he opened the bag and looked at the contents. Three silver disposable trays smeared with pasta and vegetables appeared. He gently moved them around and saw two cans of hairspray and two makeup kits that had barely been touched. Then at the bottom, they really got lucky: There were two hairbrushes that contained strands of hair.

He looked at Trevor. "You seeing this?"

Trevor smiled. "The house was a drop house."

Aiden returned his smile. "We're getting closer now." He carefully closed the bag. "We need to find out who owns that house."

Trevor looked at his shoes. "Glad it was worth it."

With the trash bag tightly sealed, Aiden left with the trash in the bed of his truck and headed to the FBI Tampa Field Office downtown. He had already called and informed a crime lab tech to be ready. Aiden could feel the pound of his heart racing with adrenaline. This had to be something. Nobody rents a standard building for three times the rent and no successful real estate agent would leave his family at 10 o'clock at night to remove trash from a home.

# CHAPTER 18

*Saturday Morning*

Aiden sat in his truck watching for Eduardo Menveo to enter the park. Three minutes after 7 a.m., he arrived on foot. He looked around, then opened the passenger door and climbed in.

"Where's your car?"

Eduardo looked nervous. "I don't like meeting you; someone could have followed me. The only thing worse than going to jail is being strung up by my balls and getting lynched for being a snitch."

Aiden just nodded. There was no point in arguing facts. "What did you find?"

"Well, there were no dead bodies, thank God. I kept waiting to see one as I flashed the light in the boxes, but nothing."

Aiden chuckled. "That's good. I'd hate for you to drop dead of a heart attack. See any drugs?"

"No. Just boxes and a couple of bar-top tables and chairs."

"Anybody see you?"

Eduardo shook his head and then glanced around, looking for spying eyes. "Security is shit. Nobody was around either."

"Were you able to reset the alarm?"

"Now, about that . . ." Eduardo shrugged. "I couldn't figure it out."

Aiden frowned. "Christ! Must not have been that shitty of an alarm system."

"Hey, I got in, looked around, and no one's the wiser. When they come in tomorrow, it will just be off. They'll just think they forgot to set it." He saw Aiden's look of doubt and added, "It was old. They won't know. Trust me."

Aiden dropped it. "What was in the boxes?"

"Liquor, some illegal cigars, and some sparkly clothes. You know, like costumes for strippers. Feathers and all."

"What about the computer?"

"That was a piece of cake." He handed over a flash drive. "There was a paper calendar on the desk. I took photos. All on the drive."

"Thanks." Aiden started his truck engine.

Eduardo touched the truck handle and paused before getting out. He looked back at Aiden. "Are we done now?"

"Maybe. Stay out of trouble, Eduardo."

He opened the door, mumbling profanity, and slammed the door.

Aiden backed out of the park. He couldn't care less how Eduardo felt.

The drive to the field office was fast for a Saturday morning. He arrived at 7:30 a.m. and signed in at the secured gate. Upstairs in his office, Jonas was waiting on him.

"I was just about to call you. We got the lab work back on the prints found in the garbage." He handed Aiden a sheet of paper. "We got one matching print in our system!"

Aiden took a seat and looked over the paperwork. The image of a black-and-white fingerprint was at the top with notes underneath it. The print matched to an unknown woman who had been seen meeting Wayne back in January. The meeting had lasted for about thirty minutes, until 1 a.m., inside The Chandelier Bar. The glass had been bagged by an insider, a waitress working the club. The woman had yet to be identified. On the next page was a grainy photo of the woman in question: slender with light hair and light skin. It was the best the tech guy could do with the image in a dark nightclub with strobe lights flashing in all directions.

He studied the photo, then laid down the paperwork. "Leftover food, makeup, and bottles of hairspray. That house is being used to traffic women. And this woman is likely connected. We need to find her."

Jonas shook his head. "We have nothing else. No passport with her fingerprints either. What about KW Shipping? Anything?"

"Our snitch came through." He produced the flash drive. "About to check it now. But the place is just storage for his clubs. He did see illegal cigars, but I want Keaton on trafficking. I'm not settling for small fish."

"But selling illegal cigars in his clubs gets up a warrant," Jonas suggested.

They heard a knock at the door. Aiden looked up and saw Wendy, a research specialist, with a file.

"Got the information on 135 Sugar Bay Cove." She walked in and held out the file. As Aiden reached for it, she pulled it back.

"Not so fast." She glanced at Jonas, then looked back at Aiden. "You never called me."

169

Aiden thought back to a few months ago. They had hooked up after work one night. It had been a great night and, no, he hadn't called her the next morning like he had said he would.

"You're right. I didn't. I'm sorry."

She gave him a hard stare, and then the corners of her lips lifted. "Don't sweat it. It was for the best. I'm with Jacobs now." She gave him the file.

"The guy from the sixth floor?"

She nodded. "The very one." She winked and walked back toward the door. When she turned and noticed how he was still watching her, she laughed and closed the door behind her.

Jonas looked at Aiden, dumbfounded. "You hooked up with that fine thing and didn't call?"

Aiden opened the file. "It seems like forever ago." He added for clarification, "Look, I'm not boyfriend material, okay?"

Jonas raised his hands. "Only according to Melody. You've got to move past her and get her out of your head."

Aiden frowned when he thought of his ex-girlfriend. "Melody was right. I'm never around, and if you asked Samantha, she would say the same thing. I need to drop her off in your backyard more to play with the kids."

Jonas shook his head. "Hey, whatever. I'm not judging, but I'm not giving up, and I know Alanis isn't either. She mentioned just the other day that she found someone she'd like you to meet. Wanted me to suggest a double date next weekend when her parents come to town to help with the kids."

"We'll see, but don't hold your breath. Besides, we'll most likely be working."

Aiden opened the file. On the first page was a picture of 135 Sugar Bay Cove. The home was purchased in 2017 by Dr. Jim Marx from Denver, Colorado. Jim, a plastic surgeon, had his Denver home listed as his primary residence. The tax records showed that Sugar Bay Cove was used as a vacation home. Isaac's company, Sunshine Properties, was listed as the property manager.

Aiden smiled. "I think it's time to go pay a little visit to Isaac Mullins."

At 8:45, Aiden and Jonas waltzed into Sunshine Properties, where Georgia immediately gave them a warm greeting. "Good morning. How may I help you gentlemen?"

She was easy on the eyes, and Aiden couldn't help but smile back as he read her name plate on the counter. "Good morning, Ms. Fountain. We're here to see Isaac Mullins."

"Do you have an appointment?" She looked at her computer as she asked the question.

"No, but I saw his Mercedes parked outside and was hoping we could just pop in."

Her smile was forced now. "What are your names?"

"I'm Aiden Greene and this is Jonas Parker."

Georgia paused as she contemplated what to do. Finally, she said, "He's expecting a client in ten minutes. If you want to discuss or view a property, I have Kimberly Bills available. She's very good."

Aiden took a step toward her and leaned down. "Ms. Fountain, I'm sure she's an excellent agent. But this meeting has nothing to do with property." It was a lie, but Aiden wanted to see how she responded. If Isaac was dealing with the likes of Wayne, then maybe this wasn't such an odd request.

Georgia didn't respond. Instead she picked up the phone and said, "There is a Mr. Greene and a Mr. Parker wishing to see you." There was a short pause, then she responded, "Yes, sir." She hung up the phone and stood. "He can only give you five minutes. Follow me, please."

For the first time, Aiden and Jonas got a full view of the lovely Georgia. She gracefully walked down the hall wearing three-inch heels that matched her yellow dress. As they followed, Aiden could smell her fragrance in her wake. She stopped at a door, briefly knocked, and then opened the door. She slid to the side with a forced smile.

Aiden said, "Thank you, Ms. Fountain."

The door closed behind them as Isaac stood behind his desk, extending his hand. "I'm Isaac Mullins. How may I help you gentlemen this morning?"

Aiden shook his hand, followed by Jonas. "I'm Special Agent Aiden Greene, and this is Special Agent Jonas Parker. We're with the FBI Tampa Field Office."

Immediately, Isaac lost his smile. "FBI? Well, I must admit, this is a first in my office." After gesturing toward the seats in front of his desk, he sat apprehensively and then asked, "So, what's this about?"

Aiden saw a framed photo of Isaac's family on his desk. It was identical to the one on Sunshine Properties' website. He picked up the frame and smiled at the beautiful family. Then he placed the frame down. "I want Wayne Keaton, and I think you're just the man to help me get him."

The Adam's apple in Isaac's throat moved as he swallowed over what he just heard. Then Aiden saw his eyes dart to the framed photo. Something in his eyes changed. Then his face turned emotionless. He sat back in his leather chair and stately clearly, "I'm not sure what your intentions are with Mr. Keaton. But as for me, I only rent him property. He's a client, and as you well know, client and contract agreement information are protected by the law."

Aiden tried not to frown. Isaac was going to play innocent. "Tax records show that you rent an office and storage building to Keaton on 103 Washington Street, am I correct?"

"That sounds about right, but I would have to check my files."

"But he only advertises as KW Shipping, which nicely conceals his true identity," Aiden commented.

Isaac gave a small nod. "I was the one who insisted he use initials for his business. It's really not good business renting space that has ties to a bar and strip clubs. I lease all the buildings on that street, and I prefer the neighboring businesses not know he rents there too."

"He listened to your advice? Interesting."

A frown appeared. "Look, the office and space were for lease. I represented that lease. KW Shipping signed it." Isaac sat back in his chair. Then, with a confident voice, he continued. "My job is to lease and sell property. All the proper paperwork was filed. Now, I'm a very busy man, and I'm not quite sure how I can help you gentlemen today."

Aiden searched his eyes and found that Isaac did know how he could help him. He should never play poker and expect to win. "May I see a copy of the lease?"

Isaac raised his hands as if he was helpless. "Sorry, that would infringe on client confidentiality. I can't just hand that over."

Aiden was tired of playing games. They had been chasing Wayne for almost three years now. In his gut, he knew Isaac was the break that he needed to finally nail Wayne on human trafficking.

Aiden picked up the family photo again. "Pretty wife and kids." He traced Demi's smile with his finger. "Tell me, Isaac, how did you land such a beautiful and understanding wife?"

A vein appeared in Isaac's forehead.

173

He continued baiting him. "Does she help you with cleaning houses?"

Isaac reached across the desk and grabbed the photo. "I think it's time for you both to leave."

"No." Aiden leaned forward closer to Isaac. "I think it's time to stop playing games." He leaned back. "Tell me about Dr. Marx's vacation home in Sugar Bay Cove. Did your wife refuse last night to help you clean it, or could you not get a babysitter for the kids?"

Isaac gripped the photo tighter, his eyes darker now with that same vein pulsing. "This conversation is over."

"Oh no, Isaac. It's just beginning," Aiden taunted.

Isaac stood up. "I'm not saying another word without my lawyer present."

Jonas said, "Ah, a lawyer. Now, what's Demi's best friend's name? Isn't she married to a lawyer?"

Aiden snapped his fingers. "That's right, I forgot about the Carsons. Let me call Demi and get their number." He pulled his phone from his jacket.

"Stay away from my wife. Demi has nothing to do with this."

"Oh, but she's going to want to know what's going on. That I can bet on, knowing very well my own wife." Jonas chuckled. "She wants to know everything."

"Does she know about 135 Sugar Bay Cove, or do you keep those little dirty secrets from her?" Aiden smiled. "I know I sure would if this was whom I had waiting on me at home. But I don't have a wife, so everyone is fair game to me."

Isaac's face had turned pale with a touch of green. He tried to speak but no words formed.

"Tsk-tsk. By the look of your face—nah. I don't think your wife would approve of selling young women. Am I right?"

Suddenly, Isaac sat down and reached for the phone. He picked it up and pressed a button.

"Georgia." His voice cracked. He cleared his throat and continued. "I will need someone to cover my next client. Please hold all my calls."

Isaac lowered the phone and missed the cradle. The phone clattered on the desk.

Aiden reached across and put the phone correctly in place. Isaac shifted in his seat.

"You need to pick a side: our side, the FBI; or Wayne Keaton and a damned good lawyer." Aiden looked at his watch and added, "You got five seconds to make up your mind."

He watched as the black hand passed over five tiny hashes on his watch. He stood, followed by Jonas.

Isaac spoke in a broken, panicked voice: "Yours."

Aiden looked at Jonas and smiled. They both sat again.

Isaac never changed his story. He adamantly repeated that he didn't know what went on behind closed doors. He only allowed Wayne to borrow property. What he did there, Isaac didn't ask and didn't want to know. After an hour of heated conversation, Isaac appeared a broken man, not the polished one who had arrived by fancy car wearing an expensive suit to work this clear, sunny morning with high hopes of a profitable Saturday.

"How often does Keaton need property?"

"There's no set routine. I get a day's notice. Sometimes four months will pass before I get another call."

Aiden scrolled through all his options in his head. He couldn't wait another four months. Isaac would never make it that long without having a nervous breakdown. Finally, Aiden formed a plan.

"You need to call Keaton and set up a meeting."

"What . . . Why would I do that?"

"You're going to tell him you no longer are satisfied with the amount of his rent. Too much of a risk. You want an additional two grand."

Isaac's mouth opened to complain, but no words formed. He sat back in his chair. Another moment passed.

"I don't know that I can do this. He'll see right through me; he'll know something's wrong. He's not a stupid man. He's very intuitive," he rambled without taking a breath.

Jonas spoke. "You can do this and you will. You're a salesman, so make the sale. Just think of it as another negotiation. We all know you didn't get where you are today by being weak. Play the role."

Isaac covered his face with his hands and then rubbed his face. He sat up straighter as if trying to build his confidence. His eyes locked in on the photo of his family. He nodded and then looked at both special agents. "I don't have a choice, do I?"

"Of course you do. I can arrest you, and you can call your lawyer," Aiden replied.

Isaac quickly shook his head. "If I do this, I want something in writing that I'm cooperating with your investigation."

Aiden laughed. "Now that's the ole confident Isaac returning."

Isaac frowned. He didn't appreciate the sarcasm.

At 9:30 a.m., the call to Wayne had been placed and the meeting had been set up. Isaac had convinced Wayne to meet him at 137 Sugar Bay Cove, a vacant property that was for sale next to the house Aiden and Jonas had followed Isaac to last night. The meeting was to take place at 2 p.m. Isaac was to report at the house at noon to allow men from a carpet cleaning service inside the home. The carpets would get a good cleaning, and Isaac would be wired by the FBI. Aiden wasn't taking any chances. Wayne could have eyes on Isaac since he made the call.

Aiden stood and held out his hand. "You need to pull this off. Your ass is on the line." This time, Isaac had a limp shake.

Aiden walked away with Jonas following to the door. Then Aiden turned. "In case you think of running, we got eyes on you, Isaac—and your family."

After the special agents left Sunshine Properties, Isaac canceled his appointments for the rest of the day. His plan was to sit in his office undisturbed until 11:30 a.m., then make his way over to 137 Sugar Bay Cove.

Aiden and Jonas returned to the field office around 10 a.m. and met with Trevor. The goal of the day's meeting was to get Wayne on tape divulging something about his role in transporting and selling women. With any luck, a date with a new shipment would be revealed, then they could work on a sting operation. The girls from last night were gone, and Isaac trying to find out any details about them would raise flags. Aiden knew that to move forward in bringing down Wayne, they needed to be patient and wait for the next group of women to arrive. It was disheartening, but last night's girls were gone and there was nothing they could do about it. Aiden knew they had to focus on the next victims—the ones he could save.

A group of four men walked in, the tech guys. They were briefed on what time to arrive at 137 Sugar Bay Cove and whom they would be meeting. Aiden, Jonas, and Trevor would be one street down, listening in another van. The team had few questions; to them, this was just another routine job. They were experts at wiretapping and would get the job done. The only worry Aiden had was Isaac and if he could hold up his end of the deal without tipping off Wayne. The realization of the unknown was getting to Aiden and making him nervous. Never had they had someone this close to Wayne.

Someone knocked on the door and opened it. All the men looked up as Agent Joe Billings, a research specialist who worked on the eighth floor, entered. "I think I've got something you guys are working on."

Aiden stood up. "Tell me."

"We got a hit in our system. It's your case." Joe walked over to Aiden and handed him a printed sheet. "A female murder victim was found early this morning near PortMiami at five a.m. by a fisherman. Her prints were lifted. They match your case on Wayne Keaton. It's still early in the investigation, but I wanted you to have this right away."

Aiden took the paper and read the details. Two pictures showed a fingerprint and a photo of the woman's face. She had been beaten beyond recognition. The coroner had estimated her height to be five feet eight, her weight to be one hundred and twenty pounds, and her age to be between twenty to twenty-eight. Cause of death: strangulation.

Aiden looked at the notes under the fingerprint. It was the print of the same woman who had met with Wayne earlier this year at The Chandelier Bar. Aiden sank in his chair. She would never answer their questions about last night at Sugar Bay Cove.

Aiden addressed Joe. "Thanks for the intel. Yes, this is helpful. Keep me posted if you can find out anything else."

"Sure thing. Take it easy." He waved at everyone and left.

Aiden sat back down at the table. The three men concluded that something had gone terribly wrong last night and this woman had been killed as a result. Theories were hashed out. Had someone seen them follow Isaac? Had they been careless? Did Wayne have eyes on the house, and had they watched as Trevor had lifted the trash from the dumpster?

Aiden looked back at the photo. It made him sick. They were so close, and now doubt filled his mind. If he proceeded with the meeting at 137 Sugar Bay Cove, they could be walking into a trap.

*\*\*\**

Sebastian sat on his balcony and twirled the ice cubes in his glass. The third glass of vodka had been drained quickly. He watched as one wave after the next crashed below on the rocky shore.

Memories of Maria, full of life and hope, haunted his conscience. He closed his eyes and remembered her touch upon his chest. A touch that could melt the coldest and strongest man. He had made the hardest choice in his life when he had made the call to Jayden back at The Tides. No matter how much Maria meant to him, he couldn't risk keeping her alive because Constance, one of the girls who had been left in Miami, had recognized her. In the light of day, it did not escape him that he had chosen greed and power over love.

As he poured another glass, he heard footsteps along the tile from behind. "I said don't disturb me!" He turned slowly and found Gabriel standing before him, wearing shades and dressed in a black suit.

Gabriel apologized. "I'm sorry, but there may be a problem."

Sebastian drained his fourth glass and shouted. "Can't you just fix it yourself this time?"

He didn't respond. He just stood silently, waiting on Sebastian to come to his senses. He looked at the bottle of vodka: almost empty. This behavior was odd for Gabriel to witness. He had only seen his boss in total control. He tried not to frown at the knowledge that a woman like Maria could have such an effect on a man as strong as Sebastian. Never had he seen this in the last twelve years of working for him. This was new territory, and he didn't know how to proceed.

Finally, Sebastian stood and broke the eerie silence that had formed between them. His head had cleared. Now he tuned back into life and heard the ocean below. He took a good look at his surroundings and then the vodka bottle. He walked toward Gabriel and asked in a more controlled voice, "What is the problem?"

"I can't find the blue diamond ring. Everything else is accounted for."

Sebastian immediately recalled an image of slipping the large blue rock on Maria's hand on her birthday. They had been standing in this very spot watching the sunset after a romantic dinner on the patio. She had been in total awe of the ring. He recalled her words: "It's the most beautiful blue I've ever seen, just like the waters of the sea below." She had questioned how he had been able to bottle up the ocean and place it on her finger. He had wrapped her up in his arms, and they had kissed as the sun had set behind them over the ocean. It had been a perfect birthday celebration. An uneasy feeling consumed him, and he sat down.

Several moments passed as Sebastian stared into the ocean. He was trying his damnedest to block out that night and concentrate on last night, the last time he had seen her. Had she been wearing the ring? She should have been. She had never taken it off. But he couldn't remember. "Did you ask Jayden?"

"Yes. He said the only ring on her finger was her wedding ring. He got defensive. I don't think he was lying."

"What about Juan? Does he remember it?"

"He said his focus was on driving safely from Miami to Tampa and then back to Miami. He wasn't paying attention to what each of them was wearing."

Sebastian thought of Jayden. He had paid him very well over the last decade. He would not be so stupid as to steal from Sebastian. He would know the consequences. After all, he was the one who carried out the consequences when Sebastian had been done wrong. No, Jayden hadn't taken the ring.

"Proceed without the ring." He spoke without turning around.

The sound of footsteps resumed and faded into the distance. He was now alone once more. Sebastian closed his eyes and cursed his new predicament.

# CHAPTER 19

Aiden sat in the van one street over from 137 Sugar Bay Cove with Jonas and Trevor. It was nearing 2 p.m., and Wayne had yet to show. After the body of the young woman had been found, they had decided to move forward with Isaac and their plan. The consensus was that they had not been followed last night when tailing Isaac. Something else had happened that had gotten that woman killed. They agreed to place more men around Isaac to protect him just in case Wayne was indeed on to them. Aiden had thought about Wayne killing Isaac in their presence; that would put him away for life. He tried to reassure his conscience that that had always been a risk for Isaac when he had jumped in bed with Wayne.

A voice sounded through the van. "Got an Escalade turning into the neighborhood."

"Copy that," Aiden responded. He looked at the list of vehicles registered to Wayne. A black Escalade was on the list.

Another minute passed. "It's him. Parked right beside Mullins's blue Mercedes," a female voice said. Agent Deborah Wills was walking with Agent Janet Coleman. Both were wearing running gear with ponytails, shades, and hats that covered their earpieces. "He just entered the house. We're walking past now."

"Copy that. Everybody, stay low and focused."

Isaac's voice now filled the van. "Glad you could make it." A door sounded in the background.

"Why the hell did you pick this house?" Wayne spoke with irritation.

On the computer screen where Aiden watched the meeting, Isaac turned around and smiled. "Because I want you to buy it."

"What?"

"Yeah. Last night when I came by to check on things—or, I should say, *clean up*—it dawned on me how quiet this neighborhood is. Most people use it for vacation homes."

"I'm not buying this damned house. Too risky."

Isaac continued into the kitchen, then turned around and faced Wayne. He leaned up against the island with his arms crossed. "So I'm the one to take the risk? Is that how it works?"

Wayne didn't hide his displeasure. "Why didn't you just mention this on the phone? I would have told you no and saved us both the time." He turned and walked back toward the front door.

"You're not paying me enough."

That caused Wayne to stop in his tracks. He laughed, then turned and walked back to Isaac. "Really? You want to go there? Are you blackmailing me?"

Aiden saw on the computer screen that Wayne's words had clearly shaken Isaac. Aiden grew worried along with the other agents inside the van. He said, "Everybody hold your positions. No one moves without my command." He quickly glanced at Jonas and then back at the screen, watching as the events continued to unfold before them.

Isaac ran both hands through his hair. "Look, Wayne, you have no idea the excuses I have to come up with to leave my wife and kids at nine thirty at night. Demi half-joked last night that I was having an affair."

Wayne noticed his body language. "So this is about your wife?"

"Damn it, Wayne, not just her. If the owners from Denver had accidentally shown up last night, we all would have been screwed. Luckily, Dr. Marx didn't notice the security system wasn't working yesterday. I just think if we had a house as a permanent go-to spot, we would have less risk and I wouldn't have to leave at ungodly hours to clean and re-prep the house. And if you didn't notice, this neighborhood doesn't have a gated entrance. That's a bonus."

Wayne walked into the living room and started to check out the house. Aiden felt a sense of relief. Isaac was doing it. He was really selling a good pitch.

Slowly, Wayne turned. "How much for the house?"

"Low eight hundreds."

"What the hell? It's over thirty years old, at least."

Isaac went into real estate mode. "It's all about location, location, location. Plus the neighborhood has a less-than-thirty-day turnaround, so it's easy to unload if needed."

Wayne started shaking his head. "I can't put a house like this in my name."

"No, no, no, of course you wouldn't. Get the Russian to put it in one of his shell companies."

Wayne's face turned hard. "What do you know about him?"

Aiden looked at Jonas. Isaac had never mentioned another partner from Russia.

Isaac quickly backtracked. "Hey, now, I know nothing other than what you told me. When you rented that storage building, you said it was Russian-backed guaranteed, that's all. I just assumed he's the boss that makes all the decisions."

"Don't assume. People get killed for assuming."

"Oh, like Keith Rose? Now who's threatening who?" Isaac threw his hands up. "Look, Wayne, you call me on a moment's notice, and I always deliver. But one day, I'm not going to be able to. What if something wasn't available or, worse yet, I'm out of town on vacation with my family; then what? Who are you going to call? It's not like I can call my secretary and get her involved too."

"You wouldn't!"

Isaac smiled and shook his head. "That's the whole point. Buy this house, we'll put it in a fake business name, and all our risk will become considerably less."

Wayne strolled back into the living room. He started to go down a hall toward the bedrooms.

"Wait; they cleaned the carpet earlier. It's wet. I got someone looking at the house first thing in the morning. Serious buyers too that are very interested." Isaac caught up with him. "It's got four bedrooms and three and half baths. Master suite is on the other side. Split plan."

Wayne turned around. "So not only do you want me to come up with the money, but you want me to buy this place today with wet carpet?"

"I can show you the backyard." Isaac laughed. "Come on, Wayne, I've never steered you wrong. This is a good solution to an unforeseen potential nightmare."

"How fast do we have to close?"

Isaac couldn't help but grin. "The sooner the better. When's the next gig?"

Wayne narrowed his eyes and approached Isaac until he was inches away. "Why do you want to know?"

Isaac took a step back and folded his arms across his chest in a pout. "Good God, Wayne. I could lose my wife, my kids, my license, my business; everything. Even go to jail. And you question my loyalty? Maybe it's time for me to end this."

In a flash, Wayne grabbed Isaac by the neck and pushed him across the living room and pinned him up against the wall. It all happened so quickly. Aiden was just about to make the call when Wayne released him and started laughing. He stepped back. "It's not a bad idea, but not this house."

"What the hell Wayne!" Isaac rubbed his neck and adjusted the collar on his shirt and looked genuinely perplexed. "What's wrong with this house? The neighborhood is perfect."

Wayne walked to the window by the front door and looked out. "Nothing, but this drop didn't go as planned. The next drop won't be in Tampa or Miami."

"You leaving Florida?"

Wayne replied angrily, "Hell no."

"So where does that leave me?"

"No clue. But don't worry, I'm sure your services will still be needed. I'll be in touch." He looked at the time and then walked out the front door.

Isaac walked straight over to the small camera mounted by a novel in the bookcase. He looked into the camera and gave the agents the finger.

"Escalade pulling out of the neighborhood," reported Deborah, who was still walking with Janet.

"Copy that." Aiden relaxed slightly. He turned to Jonas. "Did I hear that right? Did he just confirm the murder in Miami and the hit on Keith Rose?"

Jonas grinned. "Sure sounded like it when he stated the drop didn't go as planned."

Aiden spoke into the radio: "Keep Keaton in sight. Do not lose him, and make sure Isaac stays protected. They could be cleaning house." He looked at Jonas again. "Let's get back to the field office and update Aikens. Maybe, just maybe, we might have enough on Keaton to finally bring him in."

"If not, we still got those boxes of illegal cigars," Jonas joked, trying to lighten the tension in the van that had formed over the last few hours.

It was nearing 6 p.m. when Aiden returned to the field office. After he had met with their boss, Supervisory Special Agent Quincy Aikens, and he had listened to the tape, their team had been instructed to continue to watch Wayne. Everything had to be carefully pieced together before handing it over to the judge. Waiting was the hardest part for Aiden, so he decided to review the flash drive from KW Shipping again. The computer files turned up nothing illegal. KW Shipping was a reputable business designed for storage and shipping items for Wayne's nightclubs. The files would never be seen by a judge. The only evidence they could use was the excessive rent. Something Aiden held in his back pocket to nail Isaac.

Aiden was now reviewing the tape from Sugar Bay Cove again and checking his notes. Who was the Russian, and why hadn't Isaac mentioned him earlier today? He thought of calling Isaac but knew the risk involved in doing so. Isaac had left Sugar Bay Cove and gone home to his wife and kids. Two agents were watching him closely. They didn't think Wayne suspected anything, but they weren't willing to bet two small children and their mother's life on it. Wayne had been followed back to one of his clubs. With it being a Saturday, routinely speaking, he wouldn't leave till closing time around 3 a.m.

Aiden noted the time. It had been a busy Saturday. It was time to call it a day. He stood and heard his phone vibrate. It was Jonas.

"What's up?"

"Where are you?"

"Just reviewing the tape with the tech geeks."

All four technicians stopped and looked at him. He smiled.

"Come downstairs. I'll meet you in your office."

"Okay, leaving now."

Aiden hung up and shrugged his shoulders. "You guys are the best computer geeks I know. It's a compliment, okay?" He left before they had a chance to respond.

Aiden took the stairs because they were closer than the elevator and jogged down two flights. When he was down the hallway, he rounded the corner and saw Jonas's grin, along with Trevor waiting on him. This looked like good news. He jogged over. "What happened?"

Jonas smiled and handed over a sheet of paper to Aiden. He grabbed it and looked. It was a picture of a silver ring with a very large blue stone. "Where did this come from?"

"Down at PortMiami. The woman found dead this morning, the one who matched the print? Well, they found this ring near her body."

"They think it's hers?"

"Yes."

"But someone stripped her of her clothing and jewelry. You think whoever did that would have missed a rock like this?"

Trevor shook his head. "Their theory is she might have struggled, and it came off and she landed on it, pushing it into the mud beneath her."

"The ring is a perfect fit for her index finger on her right hand. There's even an indention with a tan line from wearing the ring," Jonas added.

"It's a big rock. What is it, a topaz?"

Jonas answered, "No. Actually, it's a diamond. A rare, blue diamond. Three and a half karats with a specially designed silver band. I got our jewelry and gem theft team on it now. There's a good chance a rare diamond of this size was registered."

Aiden walked into his office and took a seat. "We've been working on Wayne Keaton close to three years, and we get two breaks within twelve hours?" he asked with an incredulous expression.

Jonas took a seat. "Hey, sometimes it falls like that."

"Yeah, don't question it," Trevor said. "Look, I got a call coming in. Call me if something comes up."

Trevor left, and Jonas picked up the picture once again, studying it.

Aiden asked, "What are you thinking?"

"She was a well-kept woman—maybe the daughter?"

"Or the wife . . ." Aiden's words trailed off.

"What?" Jonas asked but answered his own question. "She would be a young wife. Maybe her keeper married a teenage bride."

"We need to call them down in Miami. This the number?" Aiden asked.

Jonas replied, "Yeah. Her case file has already been transferred to Agent Josh Brown out of the Miami FBI office."

"Good. I like Josh. We can work together on this." Aiden picked up his desk phone, put in on speaker, and placed the call. Josh was in an interview, so their call got passed on. It took two transfers before Aiden was finally speaking to someone at the field office who had the latest information on their victim.

Aiden asked about other ring indentions. It turned out it was suspected she had been wearing a wedding ring as well. When asked about her ethnicity, they were told they had a rush on her DNA. Her blonde hair and porcelain skin was leaning in the direction of European descent. Then they threw the bombshell: She had been four weeks pregnant. Probably hadn't even known it yet. No signs of rape, and she hadn't borne any children. They hadn't gotten her tox screening in yet; that would take a little longer.

Aiden continued to listen to the agent's theories, and they tossed around ideas. The agent said they would call with anything new. Soon he ended the call and made some notes.

Looking at Jonas, he stated, "So, she was pregnant. She sure pissed off the wrong person."

"They were trying to make her unrecognizable with that beating. We got lucky with that print in Keaton's Chandelier Bar. With the damage they did to her face, it would have been impossible to re-create it. At least we have a picture of our Jane Doe." He picked up the photo taken in January. "Even in a bad photo, you can tell she was a looker." Aiden opened another file and pulled out notes he had taken after interviewing the waitress who had served her and Wayne. "She was polished, spoke with an accent, beautiful, a wedding ring on her hand, and now she's dead."

"It wasn't Keaton. We had eyes on him all night at his club."

"Maybe the Russian," Aiden replied.

"Yeah, what was that today? Mullins has got some questions to answer when we see him."

"He does, but we can't risk calling on him now. If Keaton is the least bit suspicious, he's got eyes on Mullins. But whoever killed her, it wasn't Keaton." Aiden snapped his fingers. "We need to pull Customs' entry and exit logs and take a closer look." He wrote on a piece of paper: *Male traveling with a Russian passport. Names that sound Russian. Any male traveling in and out of the country in a 48- to 72-hour window.*

Aiden picked up his desk phone, called US Customs and Border Protection, and made his request for Miami and Tampa. Then he hung up. "We won't get it till morning. They're gonna pull photos as well for the last forty-eight hours, then expand out to seventy-two."

Jonas frowned. "Her prints aren't in the system. How did she get into the country?"

"Probably the same way as the girls: by boat. I'll get our Joe Billings on it. We need to check the shipping logs over the last two days and cross-reference the companies with the time frame when our Jane Doe was last in the country."

"Sounds like a long shot and a hell of an undertaking with the amount of shipments coming into the States on a daily basis."

"I know." Aiden stood. "Let's call it a day. There's nothing left for us to do."

Jonas smirked. "My wife won't know what to think." As he walked to the doorway, he turned. "Why don't you join us for dinner tonight? I'll grill my famous steaks."

Aiden was about to decline until he felt his stomach rumble. "Can I bring Sam?"

"The kids would love that. Yeah, bring the furry beast."

# CHAPTER 20

*Saturday Night*

The garage door opened, and Addison pulled Cassandra's Lexus inside. She checked her rearview mirror. Seeing no one, she pressed the remote button, closing the door behind her. She popped the trunk and retrieved only her large suitcase. The suitcase felt extra heavier than before. Nothing had been added; she was just dead tired.

She dragged the suitcase up a flight of stairs to the second floor. She unlocked the door and entered Riley's birthday into the alarm system. Then she quickly poured a glass of wine from one of the bottles she had brought with her.

Leaving her suitcase in the kitchen, she opened the balcony door and felt the ocean breeze. She closed her eyes, smelled the salty air, and tried to take in the last few day's events.

Everything had been set in motion early that morning when she had called Owen at seven thirty to tell him that she was flying him, Kristy, and Riley to Orlando, Florida, to visit Disney World for the next several days. He had asked a dozen questions about the police showing up, along with expressing concern for Riley and Kristy. She had done her best to downplay the danger, saying that it had just been another crazy person who had picked up the story online. He hadn't believed her.

Once they had landed in Orlando, the four of them had taken a limo that she had arranged to a five-star resort where Addison had used her credit card to pay for two rooms with an all-inclusive package. When everyone had gotten settled, she had said her goodbyes and paid a taxi driver double fare to take her to Tampa, eighty-five miles away. She paid cash. She had spent only twenty minutes at the canal home on Davis Island. Addison had loaded up three boxes of Cassandra's personal items from the closet and two bottles of wine, then reset the alarm. An hour later, she was back at the beach house.

She looked at the skyline and listened to the waves below, hoping they would bring her some peace and strength to finish what she had started. They did not. She left the balcony and closed the door, locking it.

Walking over to her bag, she grabbed Keith's letter and reread it. Dread washed over her. She had no clue what she was going to find. She wished it was a hoax of some kind. Just another internet fan of the Rose tragedy getting their jollies off at her expense. Deep down, though, she knew that was not the case. A bank had sent the letter. She took a deep breath; she couldn't put this off any longer. Riley had been threatened, and she had to know why.

Addison put the letter down and made her way to the second staircase that led to the master bedroom and slowly climbed the stairs. She flipped on the light, and the master bedroom came into view. Following the directions from the letter, she walked straight to the nightstand, opened the top drawer, reached in, and gently ran her hand over the back of the drawer. She felt an object secured by tape. She carefully removed and unwrapped the object, revealing a key. She turned, and her eyes swept the room, scanning for anything that seemed out of place. It appeared no one had been to the beach house except the cleaning staff. Cassandra had never left clothing behind; she had explained that Keith had sometimes allowed clients to stay.

Taking the key, she returned downstairs and retrieved her glass of wine. She opened the balcony door again, took a seat on a cushion, and listened to the sound of waves crashing below. As she sipped her wine, she thought about everything Marty had told her. Keith was careful.

196

Always locking everything up at the office. Then there was the fact that Keith had left him the company. She had no role except to just take the money and be happy. She smirked. But where had the money come from, and what would she find in the lockbox at the bank?

With the FBI sharing no information with her, she could only guess who could be behind the boat explosion. Someone on the board at Rose Investment Firm? Marty and maybe a few of the board members? Was he conspiring with someone? It would only take two members to have a majority rule. Was that what everything had been about—money?

Then a brief image of Reba entered her mind. Had Marty been implying that she was unstable? Could she have killed them in a fit of jealousy? She shook her head. No. The FBI weren't stupid. And Cassandra had always told her that Reba was a walking idiot. No way could she pull off a double homicide, set a boat on fire, and fool the FBI. She rolled her eyes at the absurdity of those thoughts.

She set the wineglass down, picked up the key and Keith's letter, and reread it. She had read it so many times she had it memorized. There was nothing in it that pertained to anything regarding guilt. Just a letter in the event of Keith's death with directions to where the key to the lockbox could be found. Yeah, right. The key had been hidden, and he hadn't told his lawyer.

She set the letter and key down and grabbed her phone. There was no point speculating anymore. She was going to drive herself insane. She typed in the bank address. The bank was less than three miles from the beach house. Now she just had to wait till Monday.

She picked up her glass of wine and tried to relax. Riley would be safe with Owen in the middle of an amusement park flooded with summer visitors. She would use this time to figure out what was going on. A ping of guilt tugged on her conscience. Should she call Special Agent Greene? Should she really do this alone? Well, she would just sleep on that again.

A light flashed below across the sand. A chill ran down her spine as she sat up to take a closer look. Another light flashed as well. Then she heard children's voices. It was a young family looking for sand crabs. She sat back once again and took another sip. The family was laughing below, but she felt uneasy sitting there alone. Looking out at the moonlit sea, she imagined the boat explosion. A tear slid down her cheek. She wiped it away, hoping Cassandra and Keith hadn't suffered.

Special Agent Greene's words reentered her mind. Keith was the target. Suddenly, she was filled with anger. She stood and walked over to the balcony. How could Keith have been involved in something illegal and Cassandra not know? Yes, she had been busy, but still. Several more minutes passed as no new insight came to her mind bringing clarity. Finally, she pushed away from the railing and went back down to the car to retrieve her other items.

She climbed two flights of stairs again, then walked into the master bathroom and set a bag on the counter. She had made one stop at a drugstore before arriving. She pulled out a hair color box and looked at it: platinum blonde, just like Cassandra's hair.

Seeing her reflection staring back at her, she second-guessed her decision. She had contemplated what color to buy for ten minutes as she had examined all the shades in the aisle at the drugstore. She touched her red hair and saw the dark roots. The red hadn't suited her. She looked best as a brunette. Now a blonde? She tried to picture what she would look like. She couldn't; she had never been blonde before. With the courage of alcohol, she stopped second-guessing and tore open the box.

\*\*\*

*Miami*

She saw an open door and ran. She didn't think as she pushed one foot in front of the other. Her head was pounding from the drugs, but her will to survive was stronger. *Get out! Go now!* her mind yelled.

The doorway led to another hall with a door at the end. She turned the knob and pushed. It was stuck. She twisted the knob again and rammed it with her shoulder, sending her flying forward. She landed on the hot pavement, dazed.

It took her a moment to gather her wits. She was in an alley between two buildings. She looked up at the dark sky and then in both directions until she saw light.

Her body began to betray her as she tried to run but stumbled to the ground. She heard voices ahead, and she willed herself to work through the fog in her drug-induced brain to move. To move meant to live.

She closed her eyes and pictured her mother's sweet face. She heard her say, "Don't cry. Get up. You're going to be okay. Shake it off, my little tough one."

She opened her eyes and bolted forward. With a new sense of energy, she ran.

***

Jayden looked at his watch. The girl had been in the sex room for an hour now. The older man in his early fifties had exited five minutes ago with a smile on his face. Enough time, in his opinion, to enter.

Jayden looked around and saw no more patrons in the poorly lit hallways. By design, no one wanted to be identified in this shithole. He turned the knob, but the door was locked. Trying to control his frustration, he tapped lightly on the door and waited. Constance didn't answer.

He tapped again. Nothing.

Taking a quick look over his shoulder, he twisted the knob and pushed with his shoulder, breaking the cheap restraint.

The room was empty. Another door across the room stood wide open. He ran and soon found himself down another hallway. He checked all the doors; some had patrons and some were empty. The door at the end opened to the back alley. He examined the door; it was meant only for exit.

His eyes scanned the alley, and something shiny caught his attention. On the ground was a red feather attached to a small stitch of lace with a few sequins. Constance. He had seen her enter the room earlier wearing a red lace piece that matched the fabric on the ground.

He checked his watch. Seven minutes since the man had left the room. He ran down the alley in pursuit.

*** 

The alley seemed to run into eternity with no end in sight. Constance willed herself to keep moving, and with each step, the noise became louder. She continued.

The laughter from the people and the brighter light from the street now guiding her. She made it to the corner and leaned up against the building, trying to catch her breath. Constance reached out to a couple for help, but they balked and hurried away. She looked at the street. Cars were flying by with few people standing around. If she walked into the street, a car was sure to hit her instead of stopping to help.

Hearing a noise behind her, she turned and saw Jayden running toward her. She quickly pushed off the brick wall and turned left toward the busy intersection.

The light was green, and the cars were moving fast as a group of people eagerly waited to cross the street. She joined them and tried to push her way through to the middle to hide herself. Finally, the light turned yellow, and the traffic began to slow. She moved with the crowd.

A woman holding a man's hand sneered, "I think you're heading the wrong way, sister; the clubs are back that way."

Constance pushed past them and ran ahead onto the sidewalk. She heard laughter but didn't stop. A cab was parked up ahead. She ran faster. Jerking open the back door, she climbed inside.

"Go, please," she said.

The cabbie turned around. "I'm waiting on someone. You need to get out. I'm not for hire, you trashy whore."

Tears welled up and spilled out. "Please, I have to get out of here. Please!"

A tap on the passenger window sounded. The cabbie lowered the window. "Are you Frank?" he asked.

"Yes," a man in his late twenties replied. He opened the back door and jumped in. Constance quickly slid over, making room.

"Well, hello there." Frank looked at the cabbie. "Is this a shared ride or what?"

"No. She just climbed in. I'm waiting on her to get out."

Constance turned around to look at where she had just come from and saw Jayden running their way. She screamed.

Frank turned to see what she was looking at. He saw an angry man running toward them. He stammered to the cabbie, "G-g-go, d-d-dude! Go, now!"

The cabbie cursed, threw the cab into drive, and accelerated just as Jayden reached out and slammed a hand on the trunk. Constance was still screaming.

The light ahead turned red. The cabbie didn't have to be told to run it. With no other traffic in sight, he dropped the hammer, leaving Jayden behind.

Frank finally turned back around and looked at Constance. "Did he hurt you?"

Crying hysterically, she nodded and lunged at him, hanging on him for dear life. Frank, dressed and ready for a fun night out with his buddies, hesitated slightly before wrapping his arms around her to comfort her. It was then that he saw the bruises. "How old are you?"

"Fifteen," she sniffled.

Frank sighed. "Geez." He commanded the cabbie, "Go to the police station. This girl needs help."

"I'll drop you off, but I'm not going in. No way. Nope. I'm not getting involved."

Frank shook his head. "Fine, whatever. Just get us there, fast." He took out his cell phone and gently pulled away from Constance. "I've got to make a call." With his free hand, he pressed a few buttons, then spoke. "Hey, look, something's come up. I'm not going to make it tonight. You guys go on without me." He paused to listen, then replied. "Yeah, later."

Frank ended his call and looked at the girl. His night out with the guys had just taken an awkward turn.

# CHAPTER 21

The Miami police station was packed as usual on Saturday night. Every green plastic chair was filled with either a drunk, a prostitute, or a drug dealer, all with their hands cuffed and ready to be booked. Frank, a twenty-nine-year-old financial planner who worked for his family's business, looked totally out of place standing beside a teenager wearing feathers and sequins attached to barely enough fabric to cover his own right hand.

He awkwardly rocked back and forth with his hands on his hips. He saw the time on his watch and cursed, then guided Constance to the officer behind the counter again to plead his case.

"Excuse me, but we've been waiting now for over an hour. Someone was trying to hurt this girl. She's only fifteen, for crying out loud. How long do we have to wait out here like some common criminals?"

The large woman slid her glasses down from her eyes, which scanned Constance again. "Hmm, fifteen? Starting younger and younger these days."

Frank was about to explode when a voice spoke from behind. "Frank Jackson?"

He spun around and found a young female officer holding a clipboard with a look of genuine concern on her face.

"Yes. Thank you. I thought someone had forgotten about us."

She looked over at the full waiting room with all the lawbreakers that needed to be booked tonight and then back at Frank. She smiled. "I saw you earlier. I took the liberty to pull your name ahead of the others. Follow me."

She turned and swiped her card through a reader, and the door leaving the waiting area buzzed. She opened the unlocked door and stepped aside for them to enter. The door closed behind them. "Second door on your left."

Frank followed her commands and walked into a small empty room with one table and four chairs. He looked at the walls and heard her laugh.

"Yep, just like in all the TV shows." She motioned for them to take a seat. "I'm going to get her a blanket and some water for the two of you."

The officer reappeared less than a minute later. Constance quickly grabbed the offered blanket and water. Frank thanked her as she sat across from them. He watched as she noted the time on her watch on the paperwork. Then she spoke.

"My name is Officer Julia Stephenson, and the time is eleven thirty-five p.m. The date is Saturday, July eighteenth. This conversation is being recorded. A lawyer is not present, and a lawyer has not been requested. Before me is Mr. Frank Jackson, white male aged twenty-nine, and a fifteen-year-old female who have entered the police station of their own free will." She paused and scanned the paperwork before continuing. "Mr. Jackson, can you please explain why you are here?"

Frank looked over at Constance, who hadn't said much since the cab ride over no matter how hard he had tried to get her to relax and open up with at least her name. When it became apparent she wasn't going to say anything, he slightly frowned and turned his attention back to Julia. "I called for a cab around nine o'clock. When I—"

She interrupted. "Street name?"

"It's my address listed: 45 Macon Avenue."

She made another note. "Continue, please."

"When the cab arrived, I opened the door, and she was sitting inside, trembling and scared out of her mind. The cab driver informed me she had just opened the back door and jumped in. Then she screamed, and that was when we realized someone was chasing her. He looked like a really bad dude, so we got the hell out of there. When I noticed the bruises on her wrists, I asked her age, and she told me fifteen. Well, that's when I told the cabbie to drive straight to here."

"And the cab driver, where is he?"

Frank shrugged. "Refused to come in."

She smiled again. "Of course he did." She made a note and then looked directly at Constance. She leaned over the table and spoke in a much gentler voice, "Okay, miss, I know you're scared, but I need some information from you. Did Mr. Jackson here help you tonight?"

A look of disbelief filled Frank's face. It wasn't until that very moment he realized how he must look with a bruised and scantily dressed minor sitting beside him. He was about to interject when Julia held up a finger to him but never broke eye contact with Constance. He slumped back in his chair and looked over at the girl, begging with his eyes for her to confirm he was telling the truth.

Finally, after what seemed like forever, she nodded.

"And your name," Julia prodded.

She whispered, "Con-Constance."

"That's a pretty name." Julia filled out the name on her paperwork. "What country are you from?

"Hungary."

The officer nodded. "How long have you been in Miami?"

Constance looked down and saw that she had completely torn off the label on the water bottle and had been slowly ripping it to shreds. She stopped and placed the bottle on the table. "I'm not sure. Two or three days. What is today?"

Even though she had already stated the date and time for the recorder, Julia politely responded, "It's Saturday night. So possibly Thursday night?"

Constance looked as if she was trying to complete a logic problem in her head as her eyes darted from side to side while she concentrated. She slowly nodded to confirm.

"Did you arrive by boat?"

"Yes."

Julia looked at Frank. "Mr. Jackson, could you follow me, please?"

They stepped out of the room, leaving Constance alone. In the hallway, Julia said, "I appreciate you helping her tonight. Do you mind working with a police artist?"

"No, not at all. Anything to help."

Julia smiled. "Thank you. It will help and hopefully be enough to catch the bastard who smuggled her in and has been abusing her."

A sad expression formed on Frank's face. "Human trafficking, isn't it?"

She nodded.

"Yeah, yeah, of course. Damn. You hear about it, but never would anyone dream they would come face-to-face with it."

"It's an ugly and dark world out there. Trust me, I know. I see it nightly."

She motioned him to follow her down another hallway that opened into offices. She found Nick Carter, their police artist, and made a quick introduction. With Frank now in good hands, she went to the office of Detective James Prince, her supervisor. She tapped on the open door.

He looked up. "Officer Stephenson, come in."

"We got a human trafficking case." She handed over the paperwork and highlighted the key facts.

A few moments passed as he scanned the paperwork. "Stay with her. I'll call the FBI."

***

"Good morning. At this time, we would like to welcome our first-class customers to board," a young, perky flight attendant announced.

Sebastian stood and walked over with his passport and ticket.

"Welcome, Mr. Gates," she said with a smile.

He nodded and continued down the narrow hallway onto the jet bridge and was greeted again by another flight attendant. This one was older and didn't seem as happy at 5:35 a.m. "Something to drink before takeoff?"

"Screwdriver."

Once his luggage was stored above him and he was settled in his seat, she paused boarding to quickly deliver his drink.

"Thank you."

"My pleasure."

He felt a vibration inside his coat pocket. Sebastian reached for his phone. A text message from Juan appeared:

*She's in plain sight.*

Sebastian pocketed his phone and took a long sip. He had debated whether to use Juan to take care of Addison. He would have preferred to use Jayden, but Jayden couldn't be in two places at once. Constance and Addison needed to be eliminated immediately. If he waited on Jayden to finish in Miami, then it might be a missed opportunity in Tampa with Addison.

He rolled his drink in his hands, thinking of Juan. He wondered where this doubt was coming from and reminded himself that Juan had completed all the jobs for him correctly for the last four years. Maybe it was just Maria's death and he was now being haunted by her words, when she had said she could see evil in him. He took another sip. Maybe it was also the missing ring and the fact that Juan was unpredictable, because Maria had been right about one thing: Juan had no soul, no conscience. He was truly evil. Regardless, he had had no choice but to use Juan.

He took another sip and pushed the doubt away, refocusing his thoughts on Addison. He smirked. She had thought she had outsmarted everyone with her little trip down to Disney World. Little did she know that he had eyes and ears everywhere. Anyone could be bought if the price was right—even the pilot who had worked for Keith Rose.

Sebastian had known something was wrong when Addison had taken a taxi back to Tampa instead of the jet. Somehow, Keith had gotten to her from the grave. He remembered once again Keith's threat to Wayne if anything should happen to him. He had claimed that he wouldn't be the only one to go down; others would too. Whatever Addison was up to, it wasn't good. She had sealed her own fate by returning to Tampa. Now Juan just needed to find the perfect opportunity and then get out. Tampa was no longer a welcoming city for him—or Sebastian, for that matter.

Sebastian caught the eye of the stewardess and raised his glass. She brought him a refill.

He took a long sip, trying to relax. If only he would hear back from Jayden before takeoff. He rechecked his phone. Nothing. He again reminded himself that Jayden was the best and just because he hadn't heard from him since 9 p.m. last night that it didn't mean he had failed to take care of Constance. Jayden knew the rules of communication, and he trusted Jayden explicitly to take care of business. So why was he worried?

"Boarding is now complete for American Airlines Flight 459 to Madrid, Spain. If this is not your intended destination, please proceed to the front of the plane to deplane." The flight attendant gave a little laugh and then continued with the plane's safety instructions.

Sebastian drained his second drink. He checked his phone and, after seeing nothing again, he silenced it. Then he picked up his head-phones to drown out the noise. He desperately needed sleep because the last week had truly been exhausting. He closed his eyes and cleared his mind, determined to get some rest before landing in Madrid and making his next move.

# CHAPTER 22

Aiden pulled his black truck into the FBI parking lot at 7 a.m. He opened his door just as Jonas pulled into a slot two cars down. They met up with each other, and Aiden asked, "Alanis and the kids going to church today?"

"Yes. She reminded me that this is week four as a no-show."

"Well, I wish I could say you'll be home for Sunday lunch, but I think there's a better chance of snow today." Aiden chuckled as he opened the door and began the scan process to enter the building.

Their small talk continued as they made their way upstairs to a briefing room that had been set up yesterday. The discovery of the drop house on 135 Sugar Bay Cove had been just enough for Quincy Aikens to open a special room and add two more team members: Agents John Fisher and Brock Glen. Both were waiting on Aiden and Jonas when they entered.

"Good morning. Thanks for joining us so early on a Sunday morning." Aiden shook hands, followed by Jonas.

Brock replied, "No problem. The change of scenery from the terrorism unit is welcome."

"He's right. I don't look at anyone on the street the same anymore," added John.

Aiden responded, "I bet. Welcome. We appreciate all the extra hands on this case. We're getting close." He grabbed a cinnamon doughnut off the table and took a seat.

A few more pleasantries were exchanged. John had been working in the Tampa office for three years now after transferring from the New York City Field Office. He had been working with the FBI Counterterrorism Division since 9/11. Brock was younger and had just started two years ago when he had been paired with John. Aiden immediately picked up on Brock's young, enthusiastic personality. He was still green but eager to help in any way possible, which was music to Aiden's ears. Since he had been working on this case almost three years now, it was nice to have a set of new eyes reading intel for the first time.

Aiden asked, "Did Aikens brief you about our case on Wayne Keaton yet?"

"Yes. We met earlier. Some case you got here." John picked up his second doughnut and retook a seat.

Trevor entered. "Great, the gang's all here. I heard the boss man gave us extra help." He grinned as he stuck out his hand and brief introductions were again given. Then he continued. "Well, we had a busy night last night." Trevor passed out a document, and they all got settled.

Trevor said, "First page, we got a list of a hundred and twenty-eight men entering the country via Miami and Tampa that could possibly fit our mystery man's profile. The data team is focusing on a two- to three-day round-trip window first. Then they will widen it to just entry only in case he's still here—"

Brock interrupted, "Anything over an eight-hour flight time on such a short trip already raises a red flag with Homeland Security."

"And chances are, the Russian knows that. We need to look at the Caribbean first and then maybe Mexico or Central America." Aiden read the list and scanned the countries listed by flights: "Cuba, the Dominican Republic, Puerto Rico, and the Caymans."

Trevor added, "Hope to know more soon. I saved the best for last: the second page."

Everyone eagerly flipped through the document.

Trevor said, "Josh out of the Miami field office called. Miami PD called about a fifteen-year-old girl named Constance who claims to have arrived in Miami by boat a few days ago. After working with a sketch artist, it matched the woman found beaten and dead thanks to our photo of her with Keaton at the club. Said it was the woman who had dropped her off at a Miami strip club where she had been used as a sex toy ever since."

"Poor girl. Sure looks like we found our connection though." Jonas stated.

Aiden listed the facts. "Young girl connected to dead woman, dead woman seen with Keaton at The Chandelier Bar, and dead woman's print from the drop house with a recording of Keaton and Isaac. We're getting close, everyone!"

Trevor continued. "Constance said there were five girls total who came in by boat with the woman in the sketch. Unfortunately, she was drugged and couldn't remember much about the man who chased her, but the good Samaritan who brought her in did and he helped with the sketch. They are working on a plan to draw out the suspect."

Jonas asked, "How about that ring search? Anything yet?"

"They didn't have the manpower last night, but someone should be working on it now," Trevor replied.

"Thanks, Trevor. Get on home now and get some sleep. I'll see you tomorrow." Aiden picked up the poster board chart and laid it on the table. He grabbed a pen and wrote *Timeline*. Then he addressed his team. "Alright, let's get to work on creating a foolproof timeline. We can't have any holes that Keaton can worm his way out of this time."

\*\*\*

Addison awoke to sunshine beaming into the master bedroom overlooking the beautiful Florida coastline. She wanted so hard to forget the circumstances of why she was there. Instead, she just wanted to pretend that it was time to wake up Riley and go down for a quick walk on the beach before breakfast.

She looked at the time: It was 7:30 a.m., and Sunday. The bank didn't open till tomorrow. She had the whole day ahead of her. She lay there contemplating what to do to make the day go by faster. She turned and looked back out the window at the view. She was alive to see this. Cassandra was not.

She jerked off the covers and got out of bed. She would have coffee first and then think of what to do. But one thing was for sure: It wouldn't be moping in bed all day waiting on Monday morning to roll around.

Walking into the bathroom, she stopped suddenly when she saw her reflection in the mirror. She had forgotten about the blonde hair. Reality quickly set in. She leaned closer to the mirror and inspected her work. It wasn't bad, but it wasn't salon-quality either.

She frowned as she took a brush and untangled her hair from her night's sleep. When she was done, she stared at her image for some time. A chill rose on her neck. She favored her sister now. Addison slowly pushed away from the counter and headed downstairs for coffee.

Downstairs, she retrieved one of the boxes from the hallway and took it outside to the balcony. As she sipped her coffee, she reread the label on the box: *Cassandra's office*. Putting her coffee down, she picked up the box and opened it. Inside was another box. The mailing address stated it had been sent from Memorial General Hospital. She picked it up and noticed the seal had yet to be broken. She checked the date: a week after the accident. Her hands shook with anticipation as she broke the tape.

The box was full. On top were Cassandra's framed diplomas and medical certifications. She gently picked each one up and read it, then raked a finger across the glass over Cassandra's name before placing each one on the coffee table beside her coffee. Three lab coats were neatly folded. Each bore her name and specialty.

She clutched the coats to her chest and took a deep breath. There was no fragrance. She studied them. They had been washed. Under the coats were her stethoscope and a few other shiny metal instruments Addison couldn't name. On the very bottom was a leather-bound book. Opening the page, she smiled at the realization it was a calendar. It started with the month of December. She set it aside and repacked the box.

Addison refilled her coffee cup and then took the calendar to a lounge chair. She stretched out and eagerly began reading. The first month only confirmed what she already knew: Cassandra had been busy. It wasn't until the beginning of March that she noticed patterns. Cassandra had a standing hair appointment every six weeks, which wasn't unusual because she had to cover her dark roots.

Cassandra also had met with a personal shopper every three months, coordinated with the seasons. A laugh escaped her. There weren't really four seasons in Tampa. A flashback of standing in Cassandra's closet during a summer visit filled her mind, Addison asking, "Where do you wear all these clothes?" Cassandra had answered matter-of-factly, "To work, dinner parties, and little getaways with Keith." She searched every weekend, looking for one of those little getaways. She didn't find any until the weekend of the accident.

She flipped back to December and studied Cassandra's schedule. Her days had been long, and she had been on call most weekends.

In May, she noticed the name *Stanley* written on her calendar on a Wednesday at 12:30. She flipped over to June and saw that it had been added every other week at 12:30.

*Stanley?* She tried to think if she had ever heard Cassandra mention that name. Looking at the hour, it couldn't be a patient. It was mostly likely an appointment she had kept over lunch. Was he a doctor? Or could it be the last name of a girlfriend? Funny, she couldn't remember anyone with that last name at the memorial service. But again, she barely recalled that day. But still, if it was a close girlfriend, she thought she would have heard of her with their passing conversations. She flipped through each month, finding the name repeated up until August. Nothing had been beyond then except Riley's birthday on October 10.

She flipped back to April and studied each entry. On the last Thursday of the month, Cassandra had written *Keith's meeting*. She turned the page to May. Every week, there was an entry for Keith's meeting. Different days and different times, but all at night. In June, the meetings increased: There were two a week; some had a question mark beside them. No meetings were written past the weekend of the accident, but the name *Stanley* had been. Why had Cassandra started keeping track of Keith's meetings?

Addison closed the calendar and finished the last of her coffee. Her mind was racing. She couldn't figure out what was worse: learning her sister had been having an affair or the fact that she had been keeping track of her husband's meetings because she suspected him of having an affair. Aiden's words echoed in her head: Keith was the target.

Addison grabbed her phone and began to search the hospital directory.

# CHAPTER 23

A man who looked like Frank Jackson exited a locked gate from a condo complex carrying a small duffel bag. He walked down the street, unlocked a navy Ford Explorer, and got in.

Jayden smiled as he started his car and pulled out to follow. His source at the police department had provided Frank's address and vehicle registration. They had also said that the young girl he had brought into the station had barely talked and then left on her own alongside Frank.

Following a few cars back, he patiently drove about five miles before Frank pulled into a roadside motel. Jayden continued and then quickly turned around and made his way back to the motel just in time to see Frank walk to a room and knock on the door. He parked a few slots over as the door opened and Frank walked in.

Jayden took his knife from the glove box and debated the need to take out Frank as well. He could stage it where it looked like Frank had roughed up Constance and, when the girl fought back, she had cut a major artery. Then in despair, she slit her own wrist. It could work. He had done it before, and no one had questioned his work.

He thought of calling Sebastian. Last night, he hadn't given him an update. He struggled to figure out why. He had worked for Sebastian for many years now, and a level of trust had developed, something

Jayden had thought would never happen with anyone in this line of work. He figured that the reason why he was good and eluded the authorities was because he didn't trust or lean on anyone. He was a loner and preferred to work that way. And he didn't fail. Last night had felt like a failure, and he couldn't bring himself to call Sebastian until the mission was complete. He pushed the thoughts away and refocused on the present.

The two-story, *L*-shaped motel was of the lowest budget and didn't have security cameras. A few cars were parked in the parking lot, but no one was loitering around. After the one cleaning lady on duty entered a room on the other side, it was finally time to act. During the five minutes that had passed since Frank had entered, Jayden had decided to take them both out. It had been dark, but Frank had seen his face last night. All it would take was one police lineup, and he would be caught. Jayden had made a mistake, and now Frank would be the one to pay for it.

Glancing around one final time, he exited his vehicle, concealing his knife. He casually walked straight to the door and knocked.

"Who's there?" a male voice asked from behind the door.

"Manager. There's an issue with the payment."

The door opened without hesitation. Frank stood right in front of him. This was going to be too easy.

Jayden took one step, and suddenly, a gun was pressed to the side of his face.

"FBI! Freeze!"

Jayden quickly scanned the room and saw at least five men. There was no Constance in sight. Shock and disbelief registered across his face at the knowledge that he had indeed been set up.

\*\*\*

Agent Josh Brown out of the Miami FBI office called Supervisory Special Agent Aikens and shared the good news. He in turn told Aiden and his team in the conference room that the decision to issue the warrant was no longer in question. If they didn't act fast, someone or something could tip Wayne off that Jayden had been arrested, and Wayne would run. The warrant was now on its way to a judge to be signed.

Aiden told the team, "I don't want Keaton taking a piss without us knowing. We need all eyes on him till we get the green light."

Joe entered the conference room and saw their happy faces. "I got more good news for you guys."

Jonas stated, "Now I know why they call you the legend."

They shared a laugh. Joe said, "Well, when you've been here as long as I have, you've sorta seen it all."

"Well, don't keep us waiting. We're on a roll now," Aiden replied.

Joe complied. "We got a hit on the jewelry store that sold the blue diamond ring."

Aiden high-fived Jonas, then asked, "What's the location?"

"Roscoe Fine Jewelry Store located on 268 Main Street," Joe read from a sheet of paper.

Jonas spoke first. "Never heard of them."

"Not Tampa, boys. The Grand Cayman Islands," Joe replied with a smile.

He handed Aiden a copy of the report. Aiden read it, then explained to the team, "Looks like the registry picked up four blue diamonds between 3.6 and 3.85 carats. From there, the picture from the Caymans is an exact match to the photo, it's on a silver band instead of gold like the others. There's a number and we're in luck: they're open on Sundays."

Aiden called the number, and after the fifth ring, someone finally answered, "Good afternoon, Roscoe Fine Jewelry. How may I help you?"

Aiden pushed a button to connect to speaker. "Good afternoon. I'm FBI Special Agent Aiden Greene out of the Tampa Field Office. Is your manager there?"

"Speaking; I'm Emily Roscoe."

"We came across a ring that is listed on your registry. I need to ask some questions."

"Well, I'll try to help. I'm not too familiar with the system. This is my father's business, and he passed last month."

Aiden frowned. It would have been nice to talk to the man who had sold the ring. For a ring of that value, the store owner would have been fully aware of the purchase and backstory on who had bought it. He pressed on anyway.

"The ring is between 3.6 and 3.85 carats. A blue diamond on a silver band. A picture was also uploaded into the data base, but there was no name listed for the owner, just Roscoe Fine Jewelry."

"Well, that is odd. A ring of that value, you would expect the owner to document it for insurance purposes. What happened to the ring? Has it been stolen?"

"Sorry, ma'am, I'm not at liberty to say, but I can have a warrant delivered within an hour, if needed."

"Oh, I don't think that's necessary. I was just curious. It's not every day one gets a call from the FBI. Let me just place you on a brief hold, and I can get to the computer."

Joe was in no hurry to leave to get back upstairs to his research. He was curious what they would find. He asked, "I never read the value. What's something like that cost?"

Aiden looked back over the paperwork and found the value listed. "Somewhere between one hundred fifty and two hundred thousand dollars."

"Shewhiz!" Jonas whistled. "And no individual name was given in the registry. That should have raised a red flag itself."

Emily said, "Okay, I'm back. So, I got the program opened, and it looks like I can just search by the diamond's color and size. Sorry; bear with me. I'm not used to working with the program. My assistant is, but she just ran across the street to get coffee." A moment passed before she spoke again. "Oh, there it is!" she exclaimed in an excited voice. "Sold on April twenty-ninth in 2019, but no name was given as the purchaser."

"Does it say who sold it in your store?" Aiden asked.

"Let's see . . . oh, there's a note section. I'll just click on that."

Aiden looked at Joe, who was the most tech-savvy in the room. He was visually cringing as time ticked away waiting on Emily to figure out how to use the registry system. Aiden smiled at Joe, who just shook his head in disbelief.

"Okay . . . yes, the notes section says, 'Sold by Gregory Roscoe.'" Then she explained, "He's my father."

"We'll need to speak with anyone who was there that day your father sold the ring," Aiden pressed.

"Well, of course. I should know something within the hour. Would you like to call back then?"

"Yes. Thank you. I'll be in touch." Aiden hung up.

Joe announced, "Well, that was fun. I hope you get something, boys."

"Thanks again," Aiden said.

As Joe left the room, Aiden pondered their next move. Finally, he looked at Jonas and said, "Call Alanis and tell her to pack you a bag. This can't wait. We're going to the Caymans right now."

# CHAPTER 24

With the help of the Lexus's navigation system, Addison pulled into the valet parking lane outside Nordstrom department store without one wrong turn. She stepped out, dropped her keys with the attendant, and retrieved a ticket, saying, "Thank you." A security guard opened the door for her.

Looking around, she was immediately reminded that this wasn't a typical department store. A well-dressed woman approached her.

"May I assist you today?"

Addison smiled. "I have an appointment with your spa."

"Oh, how lovely."

Addison couldn't help but notice how the woman's eyes did a quick inventory of her appearance. She forced a smile. "My first time. Could you point me in the right direction?"

The smile appeared again. "Of course. Take the elevator straight ahead. Third floor."

"Thank you."

Addison moved forward, adjusting her worn handbag over her shoulder. The lockbox key was safely hidden inside a zipped pocket.

She got on the elevator. When the elevator door opened, a woman behind the counter welcomed her. Addison walked forward and gave her name. Another woman who had just appeared beside her offered a glass of wine. "Sounds great, thank you!" Addison said.

Addison was directed toward a chair, and her wine was brought to her. She sipped. The wine was heaven on her tongue. This was exactly what she needed. She couldn't stay another minute in that beach house alone. She also couldn't shake the feeling that she was being watched. Here at the department store, she felt like she could relax for a few hours while hiding from the outside world.

"Addison Shaw, Cassandra's sister? I'm Aileene Nell, her personal shopper." Spoke a third woman who appeared from a hallway.

Addison saw moisture in her eyes and tried to fight her own tears. "Nice to meet you. I'm very thankful you were able to squeeze me in today."

She touched Addison's hair and then studied her dress, shoes, and handbag. "Come on back, dear." As the door closed behind them separating them from the waiting room, she turned. "You were very lucky. I had a last-minute cancellation."

Addison followed Aileene down the hallway and through a door marked number three. Inside was a large room filled with beauty supplies. A hairstylist was organizing her desk. She quickly turned with a big smile on her face. She clasped her hands together and walked forward.

"I'm Lauri Jo, Cassandra's hairdresser. So you're her sister, Addison?"

Addison nodded.

Lauri Jo's hands immediately went to Addison's hair. "Is this new?"

Addison blushed. "Just a crazy decision I made last night after a couple of glasses of wine." She looked at the glass she was holding. *Oh dear God! What am I becoming?*

"Well, don't worry. We can fix it." Lauri Jo looked at Aileene. "Can't we?"

Aileene said, "In three hours, you will walk out of here a new woman. Trust us. Now first things first. I need a few measurements, and then you'll be in Lauri Jo's hands as I find you a new wardrobe."

Addison complied with all the instructions as her measurements were taken. Then she undressed behind a screen and put on a white robe and slippers. She emerged carrying her purse and was directed to the stylist's chair.

***

Aiden was sitting alongside Jonas in a private jet owned by the FBI when the pilot announced their arrival at Owen Roberts International Airport, George Town, Cayman Islands. Mary Ann, the long-time assistant to the late Gregory Roscoe, had been very informative when they spoke just before takeoff. The day after the diamond had been sold, she had realized immediately that it was gone when she had opened the store. When she had inquired, Gregory had reminded her that he didn't partake in idle gossip, so she had dropped it. But later that night, when he had shared her bed, he had confided that it was the wealthy local furniture man who had bought it for his young wife and discretion was requested.

It had only taken forty-five minutes to figure out the owner of Premier Design and make the cross-references on flight records to reveal the man who bought the blue diamond found on the dead woman had been Sebastian Hawks. A DMV record listed his driver's license number with an age of fifty-six and a home located at 2355 Coral Parkway, Grand Cayman.

From there, it had been easy to locate his passport number and travel records. Sebastian had been on a flight to Miami last Thursday and had stayed at The Tides hotel in South Beach for one night. He had flown out of Miami on a red-eye late Friday night. There was no doubt in Aiden's mind that he was the Russian. It was no surprise to find little on his wife. According to their marriage certificate, her name was Maria Zurich, age seventeen from Hungary. With the age difference, it appeared Sebastian had married one of his child brides he had taken from Eastern Europe. When he had left Tampa, Joe had promised Aiden he would keep digging.

The pilot soon appeared and opened the cabin door. Heat immediately consumed the small jet cabin. A young man on the ground was rolling a staircase their way. Aiden grabbed a small bag above his head and deplaned with Jonas behind him.

On the ground, a man in his late fifties dressed in a navy suit purposefully walked their way. He wore dark shades and had the determined look on his face of someone who meant business. With a firm handshake, he announced, "Christian Meadows, chief of police."

"FBI Special Agent Aiden Greene, and this is Special Agent Jonas Parker. Thanks for meeting us on such short notice."

After the customary greetings and handshakes, Christian got straight to the point. "So, Sebastian Hawks. What do you want with one of our most respected residents on the island?"

Aiden was briefly taken back. "Respected? How so?"

"He donates large amounts of money to the community and has been named businessman of the year by the Chamber of Commerce."

"Great. Nice to know he gives back to the community after selling young women into sex slavery," Aiden replied.

Christian removed his dark shades and pointed at the agents. "You sure about that?"

Aiden nodded. "Pretty confident."

The police chief sighed. "Great. Just what I needed today. Follow me. Let's get out of this damned heat and catch up in the car."

They piled into a black SUV with Christian behind the wheel and Aiden riding shotgun. Christian started the engine and then turned to speak. "I knew something was off about him."

"How so?" Jonas asked from the back seat.

"His wife. I only met her one time. Young thing; she barely spoke two words. I asked myself, 'How does a man at his age land someone so young and beautiful?'" He looked at both of the agents. "I guess it really is always about money, isn't it?"

Aiden pulled out a folder from his backpack. "We think she's dead." He opened it and removed two photos, one from the meeting with Wayne at the nightclub and the other one of her lying in a morgue. "I should warn you, they are gruesome. She was brutally beaten." He handed both to Christian "Is this his wife, Maria Zurich Hawks?"

The agents patiently waited as he examined both photos. Slowly, he nodded. "I can't tell anything from this one." He shoved the picture from the morgue away. "But this one, yes. That looks like the woman he introduced as his wife." He looked at Aiden and asked, "Who killed her?"

"We don't know. But we suspect her of handling the girls at a drop house. Then, a few hours later, she was found dead in PortMiami." Aiden returned the folder to his backpack. "What can you tell us about his estate on Coral Parkway?"

"Large and gated. He also has it manned by a security guard." Christian grabbed a folder off the dash. "Got a satellite image of the estate." He removed a picture and handed it over to Aiden.

Aiden viewed the image of a white stucco home sitting atop a bluff surrounded by a thick concrete wall. Inside the walls were three structures: the main house, a separate guesthouse, and garage. A pool hung over the bluff with each end attached to the concrete wall. Aiden thought about how the Caymans were known for money, so it wasn't unusual to hear of an estate of that size housing an on-site security guard. He handed the picture over to Jonas. "He's well protected and will know we're coming the moment we drive up to the gate."

"His furniture store is on Main Street. We can call and see if he's at work." Christian pulled out a page with details about Premier Design. "Here's the number."

Aiden pulled out his phone and dialed. On the second ring, a female voice answered. "Premier Design."

"Mr. Hawks please."

"I'm sorry, but Mr. Hawks isn't in today. May I take a message?"

"No, that's not necessary. I have his cell number." Aiden looked at a number written down in his folder. "I've got 606-432-8970. Is that correct?"

After a brief pause, she finally confirmed and then asked, "May I ask who is calling?"

"Of course. This is Pierce. I met him at a reception, and he told me to call him personally when I was ready to outfit my new beach home."

"Well, yes, that sounds like Mr. Hawks. I'm Vivian, his floor manager. He isn't expected in this week. I would be happy to set up an appointment with you."

"Not in town, is he? Well, I'll have my wife, Megan, call and make an appointment then. She returns from the States on Thursday."

"I'll look forward to it." Vivian spoke in a cheerful voice.

"Thank you, ma'am. You have a good day."

Aiden ended the call and looked at Jonas. "If he's not at the house packing, he's gone."

"Shit! He killed his wife and is cutting all ties," Jonas responded in frustration. "If he's running, what about Keaton?"

Aiden replied, "Call Trevor and find out the status of the warrant."

Christian put the SUV into drive. "Let's get to the house. I'll request backup and get us a warrant to enter."

"Is it that easy?" Aiden inquired.

Christian smirked. "It is when the judge is my aunt."

It took forty-five minutes to obtain a signed warrant and drive to 2355 Coral Parkway. A security guard met them at the entrance and informed them the Hawks were not at home. When two squad cars arrived shortly afterward, followed by a crime lab van, they produced the warrant, gaining entrance to the property. The security guard opened the gate, and they drove through. They immediately were greeted by a muscular, tall man in his thirties wearing a black shirt with black slacks. His head was closely shaved, and his eyes were hidden behind his dark shades.

Christian held up the warrant. "I have a warrant to search the property. We were told Sebastian Hawks is not here. Who are you?"

No hand was extended for any type of greeting. Instead, the man's hands rested by his sides. "Gabriel Hoffman. I'm Mr. Hawks's foreman. What on earth do you want with Mr. Hawks? What is all of this?"

Aiden stepped forward. "I'm FBI Special Agent Aiden Greene, and this is Special Agent Jonas Parker. Where can we find Mr. Hawks?"

Gabriel's lips parted in a slight grin. "He's out of the country on holiday."

Aiden stepped forward. "Where?"

Gabriel smiled. "He did not share his plans."

Aiden wanted to slam his fist into his face but took a deep breath instead. "Mr. Hoffman, may we go inside? We'd like to talk to you more about your boss."

Gabriel looked at all the men and nodded, then turned around. "Of course. Follow me."

During the next four hours while the house was processed, Gabriel never changed his story no matter how hard Aiden or Jonas pressed. "Mr. and Mrs. Hawks left the country for an extended vacation that was well overdue. I got the call Friday afternoon that I was to arrive today to prepare the house for a short vacancy." When asked when the last time was that he had seen Sebastian, he responded, "At Premier Design, before his scheduled trip to Miami on Thursday." Vivian Birch, the floor manager at Premier Design, backed up his story when they called again. There was no doubt of Gabriel's loyalty. He wouldn't give them anything.

They left Gabriel in the kitchen and walked through the estate with Christian. The guesthouse was empty: no furniture, no clothing, nothing. Hoffman had said that Mrs. Hawks was planning on remodeling when she returned. Another statement Vivian was able to collaborate. In the main house, the master closet had been stripped of all of Maria's clothing. According to Gabriel, Maria had taken all her clothes because they would be traveling for several months. When asked about the security footage for the last week, the response: "Aw, the system broke down on Thursday. We just got it repaired yesterday. Sorry, no videos."

Aiden and Jonas had seen enough and made their way out to the pool area. Aiden stated, "I've never in my career seen a house this clean."

Jonas replied, "Yeah and that is not a normal guesthouse design. What do you think spooked him? The girl in Miami didn't run away from that strip club until after Maria was killed."

"I don't know. Maybe he knew we found Keith Rose and made the connection to Keaton. Or hell, maybe his wife was going to betray him, and he killed her and cut all ties." Frustrated, Aiden gazed out into the blue water below. "Where the hell did you go, Sebastian?"

Jonas placed a hand on Aiden's shoulder. "We got enough on Keaton to hang him now. Let's just get back home and nail his ass."

"But Sebastian will start all over again," Aiden countered.

"Maybe, maybe not. At his age, he's probably been at this a long time. Look, Aiden, I know you're pissed and so am I, but we've got to look at what we have. If we get Keaton, we close his entire US operation, and that's a win."

Aiden was listening to Jonas, and he knew he was right. In this line of work, you had to celebrate the wins or you experienced career burnout way too soon. He broke his fixation from the blue water and turned to face Jonas. After a long silence, he finally replied, "Yeah, I know you're right, buddy. Let's get out of here and go home and finish Wayne Keaton."

# CHAPTER 25

Addison returned to Rolling Tides after 5 p.m. She unpacked all her new clothing from Nordstrom that Aileene had picked out for her. Bright summer colors filled the master bedroom as she laid the items out across the king-size bed and the couches, the price tags still visible. Aileene had gushed at the bargains she had gotten since all summer clothing was on clearance to make room for the fall collection. The thought of only signing a sheet of paper was all that was needed to walk out the store was still astonishing. No way her credit card would have covered the amount with her $15,000 limit. She had already charged so much this month.

Addison had almost fainted at the total price of her well-thought-out plan. The purpose of the appointment had been to hide out for a few hours and uncover information, not spend a fortune. But it had paid off. Every woman she knew talked too much to their hairdresser. Addison had learned that at Cassandra's last appointment, she had been distracted and hadn't talked much, stating she was tired. Lauri Jo had also hinted that Keith and Cassandra might have been having some problems because Cassandra had shared that Keith was working more at night. She thought of the calendar with Keith's nightly meetings that Cassandra had recorded.

Addison picked up Cassandra's calendar again and flipped back through the entries. She saw Stanley's name. They had all been made during lunch hours. Addison noted the time again. She still had a lot of time to fill before the bank opened tomorrow. Finally, she stopped second-guessing herself and picked up her cell phone. It was time to call James Stanley. It hadn't been that hard to find him. He was a doctor at Cassandra's hospital.

She lifted her phone and realized it was dead. She sighed. Definitely time to upgrade her phone. She plugged it into the wall, then used the house phone. He answered on the third ring.

"Hello?"

She heard the alarm in his voice. Then she immediately realized her mistake. Cassandra's name would have appeared on his phone.

"My name is Addison Shaw. I'm Cassandra Rose's sister." She heard him exhale deeply. "Dr. Stanley, I'm sorry for the surprise, but I would really like to see you."

"Her sister?"

"Yes. Are you available tonight to talk?"

There was a long pause before he finally replied, "Why?"

"I really don't want to discuss it over the phone, but it's important. Please?" Addison begged.

"I can give you thirty minutes. That's all."

Addison was relieved. "Okay. Thank you so much."

"You're at the beach house, correct?" James asked.

"Yes."

"I'm in the city. I can meet you halfway. Got a pen?'

Addison looked around the room and finally found a pen with a notepad in a drawer. "Yes."

"Fifth Street Coffee Shop. It's at the corner of Davis and Fifth Street, just off Highway 60 before the bridge."

Addison confirmed, "I can find it."

"One hour."

"Thank you," she said, and then the line went dead.

Addison hung up the house phone and looked at all the clothing. There were too many choices. Finally, she settled on a blue halter dress and cut the tags off. She picked it up and carried it to the bathroom. Once again, she was startled by her image reflected at her in the mirror. Never had she noticed before how similar she looked to her sister. Now with the same hair color and the weight loss, the only real difference was their height and eye color. It was a little unnerving. She shook it off and began to undress.

***

Juan kept a safe distance as he followed Cassandra's Lexus after it pulled away from the beach house. His orders from Sebastian were clear: Tonight would be Addison Shaw's last night on this earth.

Early in life, Juan had been accused of not having a conscience. He couldn't care less who paid him. If the money was right, the job would be done. He had no loyalty to anyone. When he had left Panama five years ago, he had arrived with nothing but the clothing on his back. After various jobs, Wayne had hired him to exclusively work for him and Sebastian. He had accepted the deal but still did contracts on the side that neither of them knew about. His number one priority in this life was only Juan Diego.

As traffic picked up, he was able to stay a few cars back. He knew she had been extra cautious lately, as he watched her double-check the doors at night and do full sweeps of the house. She was now making this much easier by leaving the beach house with its state-of-the-art security system. He looked at his map app and noticed a shopping and dining district up ahead. If she parked and left the Lexus unattended, it would take only a moment to set the trap for her car.

He stopped at a red light as the Lexus braked ahead. He smiled as the car completed a near perfect parallel park along a side street. He looked around as he waited for the light. He spotted two couples: one heading away from their car and walking into a shop and another walking down the street, laughing and holding hands. Neither paid him any attention.

Passing the Lexus, he saw Addison applying lipstick with the visor pulled down. He continued on and parked in an open spot a few cars away. He pondered his options. He picked up his phone and made a call. Five minutes later, a decision had been made. Now he just needed to be patient and find the right moment. He settled back, relaxed, and waited.

# CHAPTER 26

Addison was proud of her parallel parking and wondered how she could ever go back to her car that lacked the driving assistance that the Lexus offered. She hit the Power Off button, and her smile slowly disappeared. Once again, she was reminded that she had inherited Cassandra's car because she was dead.

Pulling the visor down, she flipped open the lighted mirror. The transformation was incredible. She had never considered herself beautiful until today. Funny how a new hair color, makeup, and fancy clothes could do that. Taking a deep breath, she got out of the Lexus.

The Fifth Street Coffee Shop was full inside, with the time nearing 7 p.m. Addison checked for traffic and then crossed the two-lane street at the light. Opening the door, she stopped at the hostess stand and looked around for James, trying to find the man who looked like the picture on Memorial General Hospital's website. She recognized him about the same time he saw her. He looked startled.

He stood as she waved off the hostess that she had found whom she was meeting. She asked, "Dr. Stanley?"

He looked her over and stated, "I can't get over how much you look like your sister."

"Thank you. I'll take that as a compliment."

He slowly sat down and gestured for her to do the same. "I'm curious as to why you called. I was so shocked to see her name appear on the caller ID."

Addison noticed a wedding band upon his finger. He was married! Oh dear God! What had her sister been doing? Then she remembered Lauri Jo's hinting about Keith and Cassandra having problems. Addison chose her words carefully. "My sister was close to you."

The doctor's eyes quickly scanned the café. "What makes you think that?"

James was younger than Keith. He appeared to be in his mid- to late thirties. Good looking and fit with piercing blue eyes that gave one the impression that he was a good, honest man. He appeared confident and strong. Add that to the fact that he was a doctor with much in common with Cassandra and, well, yes, he could be someone she could definitely see her sister accidentally falling in love with.

Addison stared directly back into his eyes and lied, "Cassandra told me she was in love with you. She said it was complicated."

He laughed. "I'm sorry, I don't understand. I'm a happily married man. I was Cassandra's doctor and colleague, nothing more."

"What? I found her calendar. She had so many meetings with you over lunch."

He leaned toward her. "And you just assumed we were having an affair?"

Addison felt her cheeks warm as embarrassment consumed her. What was she doing? She grabbed her purse from the booth. "I've been very foolish. I'm so sorry for wasting your time."

James gave her a look of sympathy. "Wait—stay."

Addison hesitated briefly, then set her purse back down. "I'm sorry, but if you weren't having an affair, then why did she write down so many appointments with you? Was she sick?"

He asked, "Did you bother to read my specialty when you looked me up? Unfortunately, I really can't disclose anything, but no, she was not sick."

Clarity slowly emerged as Addison remembered his specialty listed on Memorial General Hospital's website. He was a fertility doctor. "Wait! Was Cassandra trying to get pregnant?"

Sadness filled his face. "I'm sorry, but I really can't say. Look, Ms. Shaw, I considered Cassandra a friend as well. Why are you digging through her calendar?"

She sat back, not sure what to tell this man. Finally, she answered, "I honestly don't know. It's just the accident seems too far-fetched. What are the odds of being killed in a boat explosion right outside your beach house?"

He shook his head. "I know. Her death was a great shock to many who knew Cassandra. Please know that she was very well liked at Memorial General and considered a great surgeon by many in her field."

Addison sat lost in thought. If Cassandra had been trying to get pregnant, then surely he had met Keith at his office during one of their appointments. She decided to ask him. "So how well did you know her husband?"

"Not really. I never met him. She was always alone for our appointments. She said he was a very busy man, just like her."

Addison sighed. This kind man was not going to be able to help her. "Okay, well, I'm sorry I took up your time this evening. Thank you, though, for meeting me. I might follow up and try to get her records, but honestly, what does it matter now if she was pregnant?"

James reached across the table and squeezed her hand. "I'm sorry for your loss, and I'm sorry I can't be of any help to you. Allow yourself more time to grieve. We don't always get all the answers we want when life is suddenly cut short."

Addison gave a faint smile, then grabbed her purse to stand. "I'll try. Thanks again for meeting me."

She watched him signal for a waitress, and Addison turned to leave. Once outside the shop, Addison still couldn't get her phone to turn on. Earlier, she had tried charging it, but the battery wouldn't hold. She glanced around the street, saw a phone store, and walked that way.

***

Aiden and Jonas returned to the FBI Tampa Field Office exhausted after the daytrip to the Caymans. Over the last two hours while traveling, they had continued to work on finding everything possible about Sebastian and his late wife. Then they had created another timeline and tried merging it with the one they had on Wayne. Some gaps had been filled in thanks to Constance, the young woman in Miami who had luckily escaped.

Aiden found Trevor and asked, "Do we know what's taking the judge so long to sign the damned warrant for Keaton?"

"No clue. But we're watching Keaton's every move. Tonight, he's at The Chandelier Bar playing poker in the back room. He's not going to get away, Aiden."

"What about the man they arrested in Miami? Is he talking yet?"

Trevor shook his head. "Hasn't said a word."

Aiden was tired, and the waiting game with Wayne was starting to wear him thin. Hopefully tomorrow, they would have their signed warrant and Wayne would be behind bars by this time tomorrow night.

Jonas and Aiden entered the conference room and found Joe sitting in a chair waiting on them.

"This has got to be good if you're waiting on me, right?" Aiden asked.

Joe stood. "Yes, I just got here. We got an alert from the Rose beach house. Someone used the landline."

"The house has a landline?" Jonas asked in disbelief.

Joe said, "Yeah, it's actually quite common along the coast, you know. When a storm hits, you might not be able to count on cell phone towers."

"When was the call made?" Aiden asked.

Joe replied as he handed over the report with the time stamp, "It was made at five forty-five."

Aiden looked at his watch. It was just after 7 p.m. "Who the hell is at the beach house?"

"I took the liberty of sending over a car immediately. No one answered the door or seems to be there."

"Can we trace it?" Jonas asked.

Joe shook his head. "Sorry, too short to trace."

He pulled up the tracking system on the computer of all the vehicles registered to Keith and Cassandra. All were parked at the canal home except the Lexus. Aiden frowned as he wrote down the location of the parked Lexus.

"Addison Shaw? You think she came back from Disney World?" Jonas asked.

"Maybe, maybe not," Aiden said. He quickly unplugged his laptop and thanked Joe. Five minutes later, he was pulling out of the FBI Tampa Field Office parking lot, heading west, Jonas by his side.

"Any chance it could be our missing, presumed dead couple?" Jonas mused as he texted Alanis explaining he wasn't coming home as planned.

"If Keith and Cassandra faked their deaths and disappeared with the five million, then they are making a colossal mistake."

"Yeah, they would never step foot in Tampa or that beach house again."

"So if it is Addison, why did she come back and what is she up to?"

Aiden made a sharp turn onto the interstate. Traffic was heavy due to it being a Sunday night. Aiden tried to remember to use his turn signal with each change of the lanes, but his mind was reeling with all the possibilities.

Jonas directed him to merge right onto I-65; it would lead them straight to the parked Lexus. Aiden checked his rearview mirror at the sound of a car horn. He had inadvertently cut someone off.

"She's not answering her phone," Jonas reported.

\*\*\*

Addison returned to the phone store and continued to wait for an available associate. Earlier, she had written her name down on a list and then had returned to the coffee shop for a coffee to go. Now she was back in the store, and another ten minutes had passed. She looked at the time again. At this rate, they would close before she had time to get a new phone.

After getting the attention of a saleslady, she was given her options, and she bought a battery for her phone. It would have to do until she placed an order. The phone was powering up when Addison paid with a credit card. After she finished the transaction with the salesclerk, her phone immediately sounded with several notifications. She had a missed call from Special Agent Greene and several text messages.

Leaving the store, Addison didn't pay attention to anything or anyone around her as she walked out into the hot summer evening while staring at her phone. The text messages were from Owen, who had promised to send pictures and update her regularly. She opened a few, and her heart warmed at the last picture of Riley standing beside Donald Duck with a big smile on his face. She relaxed, knowing she had made the right decision sending them to Disney World. Now it was time to return Agent Greene's call. She wondered if he had an update for her.

She opened the door of the Lexus and slid inside. After pressing the button to turn on the ignition, she punched the air-conditioning button, then settled in her seat. Addison glanced in her rearview mirror and screamed.

# CHAPTER 27

Aiden and Jonas were less than one mile away sitting at a traffic light behind several cars when the red light on the laptop computer started flashing again with an alert sound.

"The Lexus is on the move again," Jonas announced.

Aiden cursed their luck. "Is she coming this way?"

"No. She's heading east toward the bay."

Aiden hit the horn when the light turned green. No one seemed to care and gave him no room to move ahead.

"Take a right up here. We can cut through a few streets," Jonas suggested.

Now Aiden heard from his fellow drivers. One honked as he cut them off, quickly braking and sharply taking the turn. He yelled in frustration, "Oh, you'll get over it!"

Jonas didn't hide his smile. "They didn't issue you a vehicle for a reason."

"What?!" Aiden asked in disbelief. "Well, I got news for you: It was my choice. I don't want one."

"She's getting farther away. Must be making the lights."

Aiden accelerated hard and swerved in between traffic. "What road is that?"

"Harbor Lane. But it ends at a *T*. She'll have to stop and go north or south onto Cove Bay."

Safely clearing another car and seeing no red lights ahead, Aiden stole another glance at the computer screen just in time to see the red dot flashing over the blue water and disappearing from the screen. A new icon appeared with an alert sound and a message: *Tracking lost.*

Jonas shouted, "Aw, shit! She's in the water! Hurry; take a right on Pelican and then a left on Cove Bay. She's three miles away." Then he called for backup and gave the address.

Following Jonas' directions, Aiden pounded on the steering wheel, urging his truck to go faster. Once on Cove Bay, a STOP sign appeared ahead. There were two cars parked, and people were outside of them, shouting. One was on a phone, presumably calling 911.

"There!" Jonas yelled. A car was half-engulfed in the water.

Aiden braked and came to a screeching halt. They jumped out, hurriedly removed their gear and boots, and jumped in the water. As Aiden swam closer, the trunk was all that was barely visible. It was only a matter of time before the car was dragged down by the swift current.

Jonas came up for air. "It's too dark! I can't see anything."

Aiden took a deep breath and went under. It took three tries to finally get the door open. With his lungs exploding, he pushed ahead and found the front seat empty. He felt the car shift suddenly, and he started swimming back as the car continued dropping to the bottom of the bay. He felt Jonas grab him and pull him upward against the pull of the current. They both broke the surface and gasped for air.

They made one more attempt but couldn't find the car. Exhausted, they swam back to the seawall. Ladders had been built into the concrete about twenty yards apart. Aiden swam to the nearest one and began to climb. A uniformed officer was at the top and pulled him up.

Aiden mumbled, "Thanks, I'm FBI. Badge in the truck."

He sat on the ground trying to catch his breath while Jonas was helped up behind him. A few moments passed, then both were able to stand again.

The officer looked at the water. "It's a recovery mission now. You boys tried your best."

Aiden and Jonas changed into clean T-shirts thanks to a gym bag Aiden kept in his truck. Their jeans slowly air-dried as they waited on a nearby crane. They had gotten lucky when they had learned that heavy equipment was nearby due to active dredging along the waterway on Cove Bay. They had also called Trevor, who was heading to Fifth Street where the Lexus had been parked earlier. He would call with an update.

Just as the last rays of the sun faded away, the crane was finally able to hook to the Lexus, which had come to rest on the bottom with the strong current pressing it against a large rock. They waited patiently as the crane lifted it out of the water and slowly swung it over land. A crowd along with media was behind a barricade with Tampa's finest holding everyone back. It was a total circus.

Finally, the car was lifted to the edge and hung just above the ground. Aiden and Jonas neared the mangled car to take a closer look as a helicopter above flashed a light across the Lexus. Everyone was expecting to find someone dead inside. When the car turned on the swinging cord, they saw the broken windshield. The car was gently lowered till it touched the pavement. They took another step and checked the back seat. The Lexus was empty.

Aiden's eyes couldn't help but shift to the rough water below. The wind had picked up in the last hour, and lightning appeared in the distance. Their time was fading fast before another summer storm rolled to shore. Aiden's gaze shifted back to the street, looking for any sign of brake marks along the dark asphalt. The only visible markings were a tire-stained sidewalk that had taken a blow as the Lexus had bumped it just before crashing into the bay.

Aiden removed the tracking system from the Lexus and placed it in a bag. He handed it to an officer. Then he saw the officer who had helped him up the ladder heading toward him. He asked, "Anyone see anything?"

The officer nodded. "We got one couple who were walking their dog about a quarter of a mile down Harbor Lane." Aiden looked to where he was pointing. "They gave me their address. Couldn't stay, said something about getting the baby down to sleep." The officer wrote down the address and handed it to Aiden. "Young couple. Probably still up."

"Thanks." Aiden walked back to Jonas, who was still closely inspecting the Lexus.

Jonas turned around. "I can't believe there's no bag, purse, nothing."

"At that speed, everything would have flown toward the front on impact and then washed out. We'll know more when they get it back to the lab. Hopefully, they'll tell us how exactly the windshield got busted." Aiden looked at a text message. "They found some security film on Fifth Street. Let's head over." They thanked the officers for their help and left the scene.

At that time of evening, parking was easy because most businesses along the shopping strip were now closed. Trevor was waiting outside by his vehicle. He informed them that they had gotten a credit card hit from Addison making a purchase at the phone store. The saleslady had said she had been holding a coffee cup from the café across the street. When asked about security footage, she had said the manager would have to see a warrant. Trevor then explained the café owner had been more helpful. She had given permission for them to view her security footage.

Upon entering the café, they were met by a woman who introduced herself as Sally Moore, the owner. She escorted them to a back room and pointed them toward a small office tucked away behind the kitchen.

She said, "Can you tell me anything that is going on? Agent Reid assured me that my customers were not in any real danger."

Aiden had counted five customers when he had walked in the door. "If you watch the news tonight, it will report that a car drove off into the bay just a few miles from here. We believe the driver was one of your customers right before the accident."

"Oh dear Lord! That's horrible."

Aiden said, "Thank you for cooperating with us. Time is of the essence."

Sally motioned them to her computer, and they all watched as she pulled up the camera feed. She stood back and said, "I'll let you look."

Trevor sat down and rewound in thirty-minute increments. He started playing the tape at 6:30 p.m. and slowly fast-forwarded.

"Stop," Jonas directed. "Blue dress at the counter."

Trevor rewound by fifteen seconds, and they all watched the footage. The camera caught the woman's face as she walked by, heading toward the counter.

"Is that Cassandra?" Jonas asked.

Aiden instructed, "Rewind and enlarge that."

Trevor did so. At the correct moment, he hit the Pause button and enlarged the footage. They all studied the blonde woman carefully.

"Can you get it any larger?" Aiden asked.

Trevor tapped on a button and then enlarged the screen again. It became too blurry. He reduced the screen for clarity.

Aiden looked at Sally. "Is the waitress still here that this woman talked to?"

"Yes, that's Tamara. I'll go get her." Sally walked out.

After Sally left, Aiden stated, "If Addison is who made the credit card purchase, then why the hell did she change her appearance to look like Cassandra?"

Jonas asked, "Could it be Cassandra using Addison's credit card?"

Aiden shook his head with uncertainty. "Maybe the lab can enhance it."

Tamara, a nineteen-year-old college student home on summer break, timidly entered the small office. "Hi."

Aiden smiled and introduced himself, then motioned toward the computer screen. "Do you remember waiting on this woman earlier this evening around seven?"

Tamara viewed the screen and nodded. "Oh yeah, vaguely. She didn't stay long. She met a man. They chatted and then she left."

"Show me the man on the tape," Aiden directed.

Trevor rewound the video until Tamara instructed him to stop. "That's the man. Honestly, I just thought they were meeting up from some online dating service. They didn't leave together, so it must have not worked out. But then she showed back up, and I thought she changed her mind."

"Wait—she left and came back into the shop?" Aiden asked.

"Yeah, a few minutes later. That's when I waited on her. She ordered a coffee to go. Dropped a ten-dollar bill, which was a nice tip. I remember thinking that didn't fit her mood."

"Her mood?" Jonas asked.

"Yeah, she looked frustrated. I assumed it was because the man had left and the date hadn't gone as planned. I appreciated the tip, though." Tamara smiled.

Trevor didn't have to be told to forward the tape again. Five minutes after leaving the coffee shop, the woman in the blue dress reappeared. This time, she turned away from the counter and stared directly at the camera while waiting for her to-go cup. Trevor enlarged the footage.

"Look at the necklace," Aiden instructed. "Isn't that the gold necklace with the *R* that Addison wore proudly every day she was in town?"

Jonas studied it. "Yeah, it looks like it."

Aiden pulled out his phone and showed Tamara a picture of Addison. "Try to focus on the face, not her hair. Is this the woman you saw tonight?"

Tamara studied the photo carefully. Finally, she nodded. "Yeah. I'm pretty sure that's her."

Aiden then swiped to a photo of Cassandra. "Could it have been this woman instead?"

Tamara took the phone from him to get a closer look. Then she slowly shook her head. "It was the other woman, not her."

Aiden thanked her for her time and asked to get a receipt from the mystery man's purchase. Soon they were disappointed to find out from Sally that he had paid cash. For now, there was no record of him except for the footage. Aiden thanked Sally as Trevor made a copy of the tape.

Once outside, Jonas called Owen Shaw and got his voicemail. He left a message and instructed him to call as soon as possible.

Trevor pointed out the businesses that had cameras. They would have to send a team in the morning to start fresh when the stores opened. Something had happened here that had caused the Lexus to plunge over the seawall and crash into the bay. With nothing more to do on Fifth Street, Aiden decided to send Trevor to the beach house and gain access. He told Jonas they would return to Harbor Lane to talk to the witnesses and then meet with Trevor at the beach house when they finished. It was going to be a long night after a very long day.

# CHAPTER 28

The young couple lived in a cottage-style home one block from Harbor Lane, where they had been walking their dog a couple of hours earlier. The front porch light was on, as well as a few inside, as if they had been anticipating visitors. Remembering the mention of a baby, Aiden forwent the doorbell and tapped lightly on the wooden door just below the beach-themed *Welcome* wreath.

A barking dog and voices were immediately heard. About twenty seconds passed before a young man in his mid-twenties opened the door, wearing swim shorts and a T-shirt and holding a yappy little dog that he was trying to stop from barking.

Aiden quickly handed over his badge for inspection and announced who they were. The young man, Robby Wentwood, handed the credentials back and invited them in. Robby introduced them to his wife, Casey, who had suddenly appeared, trying to quiet the dog.

Aiden saw no baby in sight. The only evidence was a stroller parked by the front door. Then he heard a cry from a baby monitor sitting on a coffee table in the next room. Casey pointed at the dog and yelled, "You! What am I going to do with you, Zoey!"

Robby spoke to her back as she ran up the staircase. "Don't get him up. Just try patting his back."

Casey stopped dead in her tracks and looked at her husband as if he had no clue what he was talking about.

Robby looked back at the agents and gave a slight grin. "Welcome to our world."

Jonas asked, "How old is he?"

"Four weeks tomorrow. Tonight was Spencer's first night out for a stroll."

They all took a seat. Aiden said, "Well, we all know why we're here, so we'll be quick and let you get back to your family."

Robby shook his head. "Man, that was crazy!" He sat Zoey down beside him on the couch and instructed him to stay. The dog obediently stopped barking and settled down. He placed his furry little face on the edge of the couch, his eyes still trained on the visitors.

Robby continued. "That car had to be going close to eighty when it passed us. Really shook us up with the baby and all. It's supposed to be thirty-five through here, and for good reason. Mostly people go around forty-five—hell, been guilty of that myself—but eighty!" He looked incredulous as he talked.

"So, what do you remember about the car?" Jonas asked.

"Dark color. No idea of the make, but it looked expensive."

"Do you remember if the car was swerving any or driving a straight line?"

"Pretty straight. Just fast. Which is really odd, considering the stop sign would be coming up. But hey, maybe they didn't notice that and that's why they ended up in the water."

"You said 'they.' Do you think there were any passengers in the car?" Aiden asked.

Robby looked deep in thought, then shook his head. "Sorry, I couldn't tell. It just seems like it happened so fast, you know? I just remember the sound of a fast-approaching car and steering the stroller into the grass, pushing Casey and Zoey along with me. Then the car passed without ever touching its brakes. Like they never even saw us walking on the sidewalk. Which is even crazier since it was still daylight."

Aiden prodded, "What about any screeching sounds in the distance?"

Robby shook his head again. "Nothing. Didn't even hear it land in the water."

"And how far away do you think you were from the STOP sign?"

Robby pondered before answering, "About a half a mile away at the most."

"And did you see any other cars?"

"None that stood out or made any impression. Our eyes were mainly on Spencer."

Noise was heard on the staircase, and they all looked up and saw Casey. She smiled at Robby. "He went back to sleep." She stopped in front of Zoey, picked him up, cuddled him in her arms, and took a seat.

*Apparently, the dog is now forgiven,* Aiden thought. He asked Casey the same questions and was pleased when she concluded something different about their encounter with the speeding Lexus.

"Yes, I saw more than one person. There were definitely two heads in the car. Near each other." She nodded, deep in thought. "Yes, there were two."

"Did you hear any noise once the car was out of sight? Like a screeching sound or a crash?" Aiden asked with hope in his voice.

She thought for a moment. "Yes. I . . . I can't describe it."

Robby looked at her. "Really?"

She smiled back at him and then looked at the agents. "Robby is retired military. His hearing sucks."

"Oh, I didn't know. Well, thank you for your service, Mr. Wentwood." Aiden stuck out his hand. Robby shook it. Jonas did the same.

"I was stationed all over the Middle East. Occasionally, we took on a lot of fire. But she's right. My hearing will never be the same. It's mainly why I'm retired now."

Aiden looked back at Casey. "Try to describe the sound."

Everyone could see her struggling with the memory. Aiden suggested, "Close your eyes, and try replaying the scene in your head. Sometimes that helps."

She looked skeptical but gave it a try. Almost a full minute passed, and Casey opened her eyes. "Two people were in the car. I'm sure of it. I was straining to see if they were teenagers and if I would recognize them to call their parents. But the heads were just two blobs. And the noise . . . well, it sounded like a backfire, not a crash."

Jonas and Aiden looked at each other, both thinking about the busted windshield. "Could it have been a gunshot?" Jonas asked.

Casey tilted her head. "I don't know." She looked at Robby. "I would know the difference, right?"

"Maybe." He looked at the agents. "I take her to the gun range a lot. It's important to me she knows how to handle a gun if the time was ever needed."

"What about any other cars along the street—anything stand out?"

"No. Just that car. But I do remember looking around to see if anyone else had just seen what we saw. Again, I wanted to know who they were and if they lived in the neighborhood."

Aiden stood and pulled out his card. "Please call anytime if you remember anything else. I really appreciate you both speaking with us tonight."

They said their goodbyes, and Jonas and Aiden got inside the truck. Aiden looked at his watch: 10:15 p.m. "You think she's right about seeing two people?"

"I do. I think her maternal instincts were in high gear. She was pissed at the car for driving so fast down her street so close to her newborn," Jonas replied.

"Yeah, I do too. Hopefully, the lab should be able to tell us if the windshield was shot out. Let's get to the beach house and see what Trevor has turned up."

# CHAPTER 29

Aiden ended his call with Owen, who was still at a hotel in Disney World. He confirmed that Addison had taken a cab back to Tampa. Addison had been vague, and he was just as perplexed as to why she had left. Aiden then gave him the unfortunate news about the vehicle accident. He said they had every reason to believe she was the driver but would keep him posted if anything else came up in the investigation. Owen was devastated.

Now it was 11 p.m., and Aiden and Jonas were back at the beach house. Aiden cut the engine to his truck and looked up at Rolling Tides. Only a few lights were on. They climbed one of the double staircases to the main level and were met by Trevor. With no body found in the Lexus, it hadn't been hard to gain access to the house. The law office of Greer & Cruz had even stepped up with the security code.

Trevor said, "I only got the house open five minutes ago. Come to the bedroom upstairs."

They followed him up another set of stairs that led to a large master suite with a wall of windows facing the Gulf of Mexico. Clothing and shopping bags were scattered over the entire room. A large suitcase in the corner caught Jonas' eye. "Addison's bag."

Trevor nodded. "Yeah. And look what I found in the bathroom trash bag."

Aiden and Jonas followed him inside the oversize bath and found a L'Oréal hair color box that evidently had been used. It was now in a clear Ziploc bag labeled as evidence.

Aiden looked at Jonas. "Why did she change her hair to look like Cassandra?"

Trevor said, "She'd been busy, that's for sure. I also just bagged a receipt from Nordstrom department store signed by Addison. She'd been shopping and went to their salon."

Aiden mumbled, "Damn it, Addison. Why the hell didn't you stay with your son in Disney World?"

No one answered as he walked out of the bathroom and scanned the room again. A box was open on a side table. He walked over and carefully peered inside. It was Cassandra's personal items from Memorial General Hospital. A calendar was lying on top.

Aiden flipped through the calendar. He noticed the latest entries and showed them to Jonas. "Looks like she was keeping track of Keith's meetings. Why would she do that in her work calendar?"

Jonas answered, "My guess would be because it's where Keith wouldn't know she had been keeping tabs."

Aiden studied the calendar some more. "Wait! Look—here's a name that's circled. Stanley. Looks like Addison was doing her own damned investigation."

They flipped through the calendar and noted that Stanley's name had been circled in each entry. Then they searched the room and found a small notepad on the bed under some clothing that appeared to be notes Addison had made. The name *Dr. James Stanley* was written, along with the address of the Fifth Street Coffee Shop.

Jonas pulled up the website of Memorial General Hospital on

his phone and typed in *Dr. James Stanley*. A picture appeared. Jonas turned his phone around. "Just found our mystery man."

Aiden replied, "Let's go pay him a visit."

\*\*\*

Aiden pulled his truck into the driveway of a two-story stucco home and cut the engine. "Nice place."

"I wouldn't have expected anything less," Jonas said, laughing.

"Yeah, this is going to be fun. He got one kid or two?"

"Twins: one boy and one girl, age three."

They got out of the truck and walked up the stone walkway. Aiden was about to knock and then, at the last moment, rang the bell instead.

Jonas grinned. "Cruel."

Lights started to come on inside, then a flood light and the front porch light. It took about two minutes before the front door finally opened. A man stood before them that looked like the doctor from the website.

Aiden said, "FBI." He showed his badge and continued. "Are you Dr. James Stanley?"

"Yes," James replied anxiously. "What's this about?"

"I'm Special Agent Aiden Greene, and this is Special Agent Jonas Parker. We need to speak with you about a meeting you had with a woman tonight around seven p.m."

It was clear that James wasn't happy to have opened the door after midnight to two FBI agents. He pulled his robe tighter with his belt and looked behind him as a woman's voice was heard. "It's just work, dear; go back to bed." He slowly turned back around. "We can talk in my study. Please quietly follow me."

They walked into the study off the foyer. James flipped a light switch and waited till they entered before closing the double glass doors behind him. Jonas and Aiden took a seat in front of a massive oak desk. The doctor rubbed his eyes and ran his hands through his hair as he took a seat in his leather chair. Then he sighed. "What do you need to know?"

Aiden studied him a moment, trying to read him. He seemed agitated and more frightened than annoyed by the late-night visit. "For starters, who was she?"

James looked at each of them. "You don't know?"

"We suspect but would rather hear the story from you," Aiden replied, slightly irritated.

"She . . . wait, do I need a lawyer?"

Jonas answered, "Only if you have something to hide."

James stood and walked over to a minibar. He poured a glass of scotch in a small tumbler and returned to his desk. He took a swallow and then another, finishing it off. "The lady I met tonight was Addison Shaw, the sister of one of my late colleagues from the hospital."

"Who called who?" Aiden asked, even though he knew the answer from the call log.

"She called me. I almost didn't answer because the name that appeared on my caller ID was Dr. Rose and, well, she and her husband died a couple of weeks ago." He paused slightly, waiting for another question, then continued. "She asked to meet me, and I agreed."

Aiden asked, "What did you talk about?"

James looked at the double glass doors behind them, then asked, "Can this stay between us?"

Jonas said, "We can't make any promises, but we'll try."

His face registered defeat. "Hell, it's probably going to come out anyway." He sighed loudly, then added, "Cassandra was my patient. She was pregnant."

Aiden couldn't hide his surprise. "Cassandra Rose was pregnant?"

James nodded.

Aiden asked, "How far along?"

"Look, I really don't feel comfortable saying anything else. I told Ms. Shaw that she would have to go the legal route to obtain Cassandra's records."

"Why do you think Addison wanted to meet you? Was it just curiosity?" Aiden asked.

"At first, that was what I thought, but then she told me about Cassandra's calendar. She thought I was having an affair with her sister. That's when I steered her questioning toward my profession. Then she put two and two together. I never broke my doctor-patient contract. But, like I said, she'll get the records anyway."

"What else did she ask?" Aiden prodded.

"She asked about Keith Rose. She stated that Keith's name was written in the calendar too and that Cassandra had noted his meetings. She was curious about Keith and why Cassandra was keeping tabs."

"What do you make of that?" Aiden asked.

"Of Cassandra keeping tabs on her husband? I have no clue. If she had doubts about her marriage or her pregnancy, she didn't share them with me."

Aiden decided to shift gears. "How did you leave things at the café with Addison?"

"Well, I felt sorry for her, and I apologized that I couldn't tell her anything else she wanted to know." Suddenly, clarity took hold of him. "Wait—why are you here asking questions about Addison at this time of night? Did something happen to her?"

"Yes. The car she was driving went into the bay. As of now, no body has been found."

"What?" James asked with a surprised voice.

Aiden noted his sincerity and genuine shock. He asked, "Did you happen to see her outside when she got in her car?"

"No. She left first and then I paid. I never saw her again. Did she commit suicide?"

"Why do you ask that?"

"Because she looked so sad, and she seemed to really be struggling with the grieving process. After all, she did falsely accuse me of an affair." He hung his head. "I feel awful. I should have talked longer with her."

Jonas looked at Aiden, and he nodded. They were finished. They were not going to learn anything new from James. They stood.

James looked up and stood too. Then he shook his head. "This is all very sad."

Jonas walked over and opened the glass double doors. Aiden informed James that if he remembered anything else to give them a call.

A brief goodbye was exchanged, and then they were back on the front porch with the sound of a dead bolt turning behind them.

Both agents stayed silent until they got into the truck. Aiden commented, "I didn't see that coming. I didn't make the connection earlier when I read his bio on the website, did you?"

Jonas shook his head and then laughed. "It's been a long day. So no, I didn't think of Cassandra possibly trying to get pregnant and visiting a fertility doctor. Hell, I thought what Addison thought, that they were having an affair."

Aiden nodded. "Yeah. Me too. That's why I was an ass and rang the doorbell." Then he pulled out of the driveway and stated, "Let's go home. There's nothing more to do tonight."

# CHAPTER 30

Aiden was on his fourth cup of coffee in the conference room when Jonas walked in and announced, "Judge said yes to the warrant."

"It's about damned time!" Aiden shouted.

In a matter of minutes, the call was made to pick up Wayne Keaton. A team of four were currently in place, as they had actively been monitoring Wayne for the last two hours after relieving the night shift. Aiden, along with Jonas, Trevor, and Agent Brock Glen, waited on pins and needles until they got the call that Wayne had indeed been picked up and was in the back seat of an FBI SUV headed to Tampa County lockup to get booked. It was hard not to celebrate despite the somber mood from last night.

As of this morning, no bodies had been found in the bay. The coast guard said they would keep looking but mentioned that the storm and the strong currents had hampered their search. A team had worked on the Lexus overnight and discovered that the car had suffered mechanical failure. But they had failed to determine what had caused the front windshield to break and if it had occurred before or after the car crashed into the bay. It all appeared that Sebastian Hawks was cleaning house. First, he had taken out Keith and Cassandra, then Maria, then Addison. Aiden frowned. If only Addison had listened, she might still be alive.

The investigation would now focus on finding Sebastian, and he had already made two mistakes. One, the man he had sent to kill Constance had been arrested, and two, Maria's ring had been left behind, exposing him to the authorities. Aiden thought of Addison's accident. If they could find the person responsible for the mechanical failure, then they might be able to lead the FBI straight to Sebastian.

Aiden had no clue just how many people worked for Sebastian, but it had to be at least a half dozen to pull off the transatlantic human trafficking exchange. The man who had been arrested in Miami had finally been identified overnight as Jayden Hart. He still wasn't talking, and the FBI had recovered nothing more on his identity. They assumed that he was an illegal immigrant. Constance's testimony was enough to hold him without bail until a trial. Aiden hoped that a few more weeks in prison might convince Jayden to start singing and they could cast a wider net for Sebastian.

Aiden was working on more intel on Sebastian when Quincy walked into the room. All chatter ceased among the men.

Quincy smiled. "Proud of the work you guys have done with the arrest of Wayne Keaton. It's been a long three years. Now, I know you're all eager to find Sebastian Hawks, but for the rest of today and all day tomorrow, you are officially off duty. So go home, get some rest, and recharge. We will start at eight a.m. on Wednesday."

After a few handshakes, pats on the back, and thank-you were exchanged, it took only three minutes for the room to clear.

\*\*\*

Isaac Mullins was sitting on a lounge chair watching Demi in the swimming pool with their two children when he got a call from an unknown number. He cringed as he got up and walked out of range from their hearing. He answered, "Hello."

A voice said, "It's time for plan C." Then the phone went dead.

Isaac looked at his phone in disbelief. *No, no, no!*

He ran into the house and then into the study. He quickly opened the wood shutters to see if the FBI still had a car down the street. It was there.

He opened a locked safe and retrieved his family's passports, cash, and a small notebook. Last, he grabbed his computer. He was back outside in two minutes.

Demi, who had noticed his sudden departure, was already out of the pool with the kids and drying off when she saw him. She noticed his backpack and the look on his face. In a scared voice, she asked, "What's wrong?"

"Everything." He walked over and placed both hands on her arms. In case the house was bugged, he whispered in her ear, "Get the kids dressed and down to the boat. We leave in five minutes, tops."

He saw her tear up as clarity of their situation started to form. He kissed her on the lips and then nodded, pulling away. He walked away down to the boat dock as Demi frantically began pulling the kids into the house to get dressed.

Yesterday, Isaac had come clean to his wife of seven years. Her first response had been to laugh at the outrageous story she had thought he was spinning for her. Then when he had pointed to the FBI agents parked down the road, she had slapped him across the face and burst into tears. It had taken Isaac four hours to get her to calm down and not walk out the door with their two kids to her mother's house in St. Augustine. He had had to tell her the ugly truth that if she ran, she would be putting not only her life in danger, but that of the kids and her parents. He didn't see the point of including him in the narrative. Finally, after the shock had worn off and the tears had resided, she had started packing each person a go bag. When he had told her that his was already on the boat, she had slapped him again.

Last night, after dark, Isaac had taken their three bags down to the boat and hidden them with his bag. When the time came, they had to be ready. He just hadn't thought it would happen a day after telling

Demi. He knew it was too soon and she was an emotional wreck. They had slept in separate beds last night, and she had still avoided all conversation with him today.

Isaac guided their small yacht out of the dock eight minutes after receiving the phone call. Demi avoided looking at him as she quickly got the kids settled down below. Once they were safely out of the bay, they could talk, but for now, he just needed to get them across the bay to a marina. From there, they would get in a car and drive straight to a vacant vacation home in Miami. They would change their appearances, and Demi would fly out with Annabelle to Costa Rica under a new name. Then Isaac would fly out the next day with Oliver to Aruba, with a different name.

Isaac looked back at their house. No one was standing on their dock watching. So far, they had left unnoticed, but he knew it was only a matter of time before the FBI realized they had fled. He looked again out into the bay and asked himself, *where did it all go wrong?*

***

The ten o'clock news was on, and Aiden was watching with Samantha by his side. Somehow the media had been able to summarize a nearly three-year investigation into Wayne Keaton into an eight-minute top news story. It started with an FBI press conference that applauded the efforts of FBI agents for busting a major human trafficking ring from Miami to Tampa. A picture of Sebastian Hawks, who was still at large, was plastered on the screen with a number to call. Then the newscaster recounted the tragic boat explosion that had killed Keith and Cassandra Rose and how heiress Addison Shaw was now missing and feared dead. Rose Investment Firm was suspected of money laundering, and a full investigation was underway into the company's finances. Aiden's favorite highlight was Wayne's mug shot. The newscaster wrapped up by stating the horrors of human trafficking and providing a number for anyone who needed help or if they wanted to report something suspicious.

During the commercial break, Aiden got up and grabbed a beer. Leaning against the counter, he took a long swig, then he headed toward his study. He flipped on the light and saw his research spread out before him. He slowly walked over to the wall and removed the picture of Wayne. He ripped it to shreds, releasing some of the tension that had built over the last several days as the investigation had intensified. In three minutes, he had a blank canvas to start his next investigation.

Opening a folder, he pulled out a picture of Sebastian and stapled it to the wall. He studied his face for a solid minute, then left the room and closed the door behind him. His boss was right. It would and could wait till Wednesday.

Tomorrow, Aiden planned to spend the morning playing with Samantha at the local dog-friendly beach. Then he would return and hit the gym, followed by a nice seafood dinner at his favorite restaurant. He even contemplated taking up Jonas on the offer of a double date. Aiden drained the rest of his beer and turned to Samantha. "Let's hit the sack, buddy. We got a big day planned tomorrow."

Aiden felt his phone vibrate. He picked it up and saw Jonas's name. He skipped the introductions and asked, "I thought you were taking Alanis out?"

"Hey, Aiden. Yeah, I did, and as soon as we got home, I got bad news."

Aiden cringed. "Keaton escape or something?"

"No, not Keaton—Isaac Mullins and his family."

"You've got to be kidding me. When did this happen?"

"Agent Jones, who was watching the house, reached out to me. Apparently, Isaac pulled a fast one over them. His boat is missing, and they're not answering the door or phone. Agent Jones is calling Aikens now."

"What the hell? When did we last have eyes on them?"

"Around noon. They were out by the pool."

"So how did that happen?" Aiden looked at his watch and added, "They could be anywhere by now."

"Isaac must have used an app to turn the lights on and off, as well as the TV and music. During the next round to check on the family, the agents assumed they went back inside to put the kids down for a nap. The boat is accessed by a walkway from their backyard. They just missed it. They weren't watching the boat."

"Aw, shit! Doesn't he know that he just put his wife and kids in danger? Selfish bastard!"

Jonas replied, "I know. We can't protect him now."

"Hold on. I'm getting a text from Aikens."

"Yeah, me too."

Aiden read the message. They were told not to return to the office until Wednesday as planned. They would have others working on retrieving Isaac.

"Well, looks like the boss still wants us to recharge and rest."

"Yeah, I see that. Later, Aiden. See you on Wednesday."

"Take it easy, Jonas. See you Wednesday."

# CHAPTER 31

Addison sat in a chair and stared at her sister while she slept. The events of yesterday evening were starting to settle in, and Addison now had more questions than answers.

Cassandra had climbed in the back seat of the Lexus and waited for Addison to finish shopping. Addison didn't know how she didn't go into cardiac arrest when she had seen her presumed dead sister now alive.

Cassandra had quickly explained how a man was watching her and had done something to the car. Addison, still in shock, hadn't said much as she had listened to Cassandra tell her what to do. There had been little time to argue because someone was trying to kill Addison. In total confusion about what was transpiring, Addison had agreed to get in the old, used car that Cassandra had been using and drive to a meeting point five miles down the road. Cassandra had refused to argue, claiming that everything was her fault and she had to be the one driving the car.

After Addison had reached the meeting spot, it had taken Cassandra thirty more minutes to get there on foot. Cassandra had looked disoriented, saying she had hit her head. Addison took her back to the low budget hotel where Cassandra had been hiding. Once there, Cassandra had lain down, diagnosing herself with a mild concussion. She had explained to Addison that it was fine to let her sleep but to call 911 if she started throwing up or appeared to be hallucinating.

Later last night, while Cassandra had slept, Addison had watched the ten o'clock news in disbelief. The Lexus had been pulled out of the bay. To make matters worse, Special Agents Greene and Parker had jumped in, trying to save the driver. Both of the agents had been good to her, and she would have never forgiven herself if something had happened to them. Then the most horrible news had flashed across the screen: the driver was missing and presumed dead. She immediately thought of Owen and Riley.

Addison got up from the chair and started pacing. She was still trying to process in her altered state of mind all that Cassandra had divulged. She honestly didn't know what to believe or if Cassandra had indeed been hallucinating. It had been sometime early in the morning when Cassandra had woken up in tears saying someone had killed Keith on the boat and she had escaped. She explained that she had gone home and searched his study, finding a file that looked suspicious. Keith kept all important work documents at the office. But she had found a file that listed what appeared to be accounts with dollar amounts beside them. So she had taken the file along with some cash, and for the last several weeks, she had been hiding. She had yet to figure out what everything in Keith's file meant. She just knew if she came forward to reveal that she was alive, she would be next.

Addison then had showed her Keith's letter and told her about the key to the lockbox. Cassandra had begged her not to call anyone just yet. They were still in danger, and she needed a little more time to figure out what to do. Addison continued to patiently wait for Cassandra to awaken and monitor the news for anything else that had been reported about the accident with the Lexus.

As time continued to tick by, Addison was second-guessing her decision and was about to call Special Agent Greene when Cassandra finally started to stir. Addison walked over and sat beside her. "Hey there. How you feeling? Better?"

Cassandra replied, "Help me sit up and I'll soon tell you."

Addison grabbed her under her arms and pulled as Cassandra slowly pushed upward. "Do you need water?"

"Yes. A whole bottle if you have it."

Addison quickly produced one, then sat on the edge of the standard queen-size bed found in every hotel room. "I keep replaying last night over and over in my head. What the hell happened after you drove off? The news reported that the Lexus was pulled out of the bottom of the bay."

Cassandra took a sip of the water. "I'm sorry. Everything is a mess. When I saw him following you and then saw him pop the hood, I knew he was trying to kill you. I couldn't let you get in the car. It had to be me. This is my doing, not yours."

Addison let some of her anger go, feeling empathetic. "No, it's not. It's Keith's doing." She tilted her head. "And tomorrow, I'm going to the bank to check the lockbox."

"I swear I didn't know what Keith had been up to. I just knew something was off and he was hiding something from me. I never dreamed he could be involved in something illegal, and someone would try and kill us."

"And that is why you were keeping tabs on Keith's meetings in your calendar?"

"My calendar. Oh yes. I kept it at work. So you read it?"

Addison replied, "I did. Memorial General Hospital sent it with some other personal items. When I saw Stanley's name written during lunch hours, I thought you and Dr. Stanley were having an affair. Boy was I wrong."

Cassandra looked at Addison. "Did you say you called him?"

"So you do remember some of our conversation. And you confirmed earlier that you're pregnant." Addison squeezed her hand. "Do you think the baby is okay?"

Cassandra instinctively touched her stomach. "Miraculously, I think so." She sighed. "I'm tired of running. What is the news saying?"

"That I'm presumed dead since no body has been found . . . Oh my poor Riley! What are they going to tell him if they haven't already?"

Tears rolled down Cassandra's face. "I'm so sorry, sis. I promise you, I will fix this."

Addison had studied the file on the table. None of the numbers had made any sense to her. She walked over and picked it up. "I know you aren't well, but I need you to tell me more about the accident."

Cassandra slowly opened her eyes and nodded. She took another sip of water and then began.

"I was using the weekend getaway to figure out what was going on with Keith. He was traveling more and he started having meetings at night, not during business hours. There had been something bothering him for months, and I felt him pulling away. I tried multiple times to get him to open up, but he just said nothing was wrong. Then I thought he was having second thoughts about having a baby."

"Dr. Stanley told me Keith never came to your appointments."

Cassandra nodded. "Keith was always too busy with work to get away during the day. I wanted to believe it was just that, not that he was having second thoughts." She paused to drink some more. "The trip started as I had hoped. Keith was loving and attentive, but everything changed again when that boat arrived—"

"What kind of boat?" Addison interrupted.

Cassandra shook her head. "I really don't remember. I heard it when I was downstairs getting us a drink. When I heard the motor cut off and then voices, I knew we were going to have company. At first, I thought it was some friends. Then . . . then . . . I . . ." She covered her face and began to cry.

Addison placed a hand on her shoulder. "I need to know what you remember. I know it's hard, but please."

Cassandra slowly lifted her face from her hands and wiped her eyes. "I started climbing the stairs, and that's when I saw men carrying large guns. They were pointed at Keith. I slowly crept back down the stairs and ran to our bedroom. There's a release hatch for emergencies. I lifted the handle and climbed out. They couldn't see me as I slid over to the edge and dropped down into the dingy. From there, I slipped into the water and started swimming backward toward the direction of the beach."

"Wait, are you sure they didn't see you in the water?"

"They were focused on Keith. I saw." She paused to wipe the tears from her eyes. "They hit Keith with the gun, and he fell down on the deck. And that's when I went under the water and started swimming. I swam and swam." The tears were turning into sobs.

Addison hugged her tightly. Through her tears, she kept trying to talk. "I heard the explosion, and I thought I was going to die. Keith is gone. He's gone!" she sobbed.

Addison didn't push her any more to relive the accident. Instead, she pulled back from their embrace and lifted the files again. "I've been reading these files over and over. Nothing makes sense. The news is saying Keith laundered money. Did he?"

Cassandra replied, "I honestly don't know. How could I've been married to someone who engaged in criminal activity and not know about it?" A brief silence passed between them. Then Cassandra added, "Maybe Marty is involved? Maybe, just maybe, Keith came across something at work and he's trying to cover for his brother."

"Maybe. Hopefully whatever is in the lockbox will tell us," Addison offered.

Cassandra pushed off the covers and tried to stand. "Oh, that's right. You said you have a key. Well, let's go now. I need to see if I can clear his name and—"

Addison stopped her. "No. Stop. I'll go tomorrow, first thing in the morning. You need to rest."

Cassandra sank back down into the pillows. She looked up at Addison in defeat. "I'm so sorry. I don't know how I didn't see this."

She squeezed her sister's hand. "How could you? You were so busy taking care of me and working God only knows how many hours at the hospital."

Cassandra squeezed her hand back. "Why are you so good to me after everything I have put you through? And Riley—poor Riley. How can we fix that?"

Addison pulled her hand back and stood. "I honestly don't know, but I will figure something out. You just need to rest for the baby's sake and let me take care of you for once. Okay?"

A tear rolled down Cassandra's cheek. "I'm so tired and so damn tired of hiding." She slowly nodded. "Okay. Do what you need to do."

# CHAPTER 32

Sebastian had safely made it to Mykonos, one of many Greek islands, in less than twenty-four hours. He had gone by air, boat, and train, using his various names that would never be used again. Mykonos was always a good choice when wanting to get lost for a few weeks. It was such a heavily traveled tourist spot, it made it easy to blend in. Also, it was known for its nightlife bringing in thousands of people every summer.

Once settled in and unpacked, the quietness of his rental house got to Sebastian. He needed to be surrounded by people and noise, something that would drown out his thoughts of Maria. He was startled how much the decision to cut her loose was affecting him. Yes, he knew he loved her, but to still be consumed with grief after her passing had caught him off guard. It was a new experience.

He had thought of everything for when he knew this time would finally come. The only difference was he had thought Maria would be with him. Killing his wife had never crossed his mind. He had never even considered that someone from her country might recognize her. But they had, and Sebastian's former life had died the same night as Maria. Now he had to move on and redesign what he wanted his new life to look like, just unfortunately without her.

There was enough money spread among various accounts to live out the rest of his life as a very wealthy man. He also had three sets of identification that he hadn't used yet. He looked at the three names and finally chose one. He would now become Roberto Riveria, a retired millionaire from Lisbon, Portugal. He had no plans to use the other identities unless forced to. After packing a backpack with essentials, he locked up the house and left for Paradise Beach.

His first choice was Paradise Beach Club Mykonos, which had multiple restaurants and beach bars and was known as having the largest nightclub on the island. Since it was just 3 p.m., he made his way down to the beach and requested the largest cabana closest to the water. The young hostess wearing a red bikini showed him the way. Once he was settled, a waitress came over. Sebastian handed her a credit card with his new name and was given a menu. "I'll start with a bucket of Mythos."

"Certainly, and would you like to add a Greek mezze platter?"

For the first time since leaving the Caymans, Sebastian suddenly felt famished. His appetite had seemed to vanish once he had lost Maria. "That would be lovely, thank you."

Sebastian looked around the crowded beach and began to relax. He had chosen well. In a sea of people, no one would suspect he was one of the most wanted men in America. Clean-shaven, wearing sunglasses and a hat, he looked nothing like his photo that was circulating around the world. He had also darkened his hair from the salt-and-pepper look he had sported the last ten years.

Soon the beer and food arrived, and Sebastian settled in. Now he just needed to find someone who looked nothing like Maria to share them with.

***

*Tuesday Morning*

Addison arrived at Rolling Tides at 7:30 a.m. to retrieve the key. She had rehidden it in the original spot when she had returned from her visit at Nordstrom. She looked around the master bedroom. She could tell the FBI had looked through her things. She blocked it out of her mind. She was on a mission. The bank was three and a half miles away, and it would take just under ten minutes to get there.

She quickly changed her clothing and left the house, locking and setting the alarm behind her. Pulling out of the gated community in Cassandra's used car, she glanced around for any cars that looked familiar from her drive over. Nothing. As far as she could tell, no one was following her.

The National Bank of Clearwater was a two-story building located in the middle of a shopping center that was set to open at 8 a.m. Addison parked and checked her surroundings once again. Feeling anxious, she reminded herself what was on the line. She flipped the visor and found a mirror. Quickly she checked her face and applied some lipstick. Then she ran her hand over her hair, calming some loose strands that had fallen from her hair clip. She got out of the car and entered the bank. Soon she was greeted by a middle-aged man wearing a suit.

He smiled and asked, "May I help you?"

She returned the smile and kept her answer short. "I need access to my lockbox, please."

"Absolutely. If you will sign in over here, please. I will need to check your license."

She followed and quickly removed her license from her purse. He recorded her name and then asked her to sign on the line. She noticed her hand was slightly shaking. She looked up and tried her best to smile with confidence.

He asked, "You have the key?"

"Yes."

"This way, please."

They walked down a hallway and stopped at a door. He unlocked the door and gestured for her to come inside. "Take your time. I'll be outside if you need any assistance."

"Thank you."

She waited till he closed the door before walking toward the lock-box labeled *18*. Her hand began to shake again as she tried to insert the key. She had to use both hands to insert it. The key turned and the lockbox slid out of the wall cabinet. Inside was a white envelope.

She carefully turned, placed the box on a table, and removed the envelope. She flipped it over and found it sealed. There was no writing on the envelope. She debated whether to open it now or wait. She chose now. She broke the seal, cautiously peered inside, and found a flash drive. Her gut clenched at the thought of what it could possibly contain. Whatever it was, she knew it couldn't be good.

Addison left the bank in a hurry. She got in the car and drove back to Rolling Tides. She parked her car in the garage and let the garage door close behind her. She exited the car and climbed the stairs.

***

Juan parked his car down the road from the beach house. Then he casually walked on the sidewalk, tossing his keys in the air. When he was two houses down from Rolling Tides, he took the path to the beach. He removed his shoes and kept strolling, trying to blend in with all the other beach walkers. When he was satisfied that no one was watching him, he crossed over a dune and entered the balcony to the beach house.

Juan picked the lock on the window and slowly raised it. Then he carefully opened the wood blinds to see inside. He saw no one. He carefully pushed the shutters forward and then stepped inside. There he listened and heard a noise from the kitchen. He quietly walked across the floor and peered around the corner, where he came face-to-face with Aiden. He quickly turned, but Jonas took him down.

They searched Juan and found a knife, a 9mm Ruger, and a cheap burner phone that didn't require an ID to open. Looking at the text message thread on the phone, they had some time before planning a trap. They quietly loaded Juan in the car that was hidden in the garage, and Trevor and Brock drove him to the FBI Tampa Field Office for interrogation.

Aiden finally called for Addison to come downstairs. "You did good, Addison. Cassandra has already been moved to a safe house and is being checked out as we speak."

"I want to see what's on the flash drive," Addison said, adding, "It was part of our agreement, remember?"

Aiden pulled the flash drive out of his pocket and opened his computer he had retrieved from the car. He, Jonas, and Addison watched as the drive opened to reveal one video and one Word document. The video was titled *Open First*. Aiden opened the video and hit Play.

The video showed Keith sitting at an office desk, adjusting the mounted camera on his computer. When he was satisfied with the angle, he began.

"My dearest Cassandra, if you're watching this, then I'm dead. I don't even know where to begin, so I guess I'll begin at the beginning.

"Before I had the heart attack and met you, I made a mistake. A big mistake. I was offered an opportunity to make a lot of money, and I took it. At the time, I was going through the divorce, and Reba was trying to take everything from me. I know that's not an excuse. Looking back on it, that's probably why Wayne Keaton approached me. Somehow, he heard I was going through an ugly divorce and struggling financially.

"Time went by and the money grew. The money gave me the confidence to start more projects that were legitimate. When I realized that I was going to be just fine, I wanted out. I tried; I really did, but it was too late. You can't do business with the devil and expect to leave alive.

"When you said you would marry me, I was so happy and I tried to get out again. This time, they threatened you and your sister and nephew. I know I should have walked away from you right then, but I loved you too much. That was so selfish on my part. Now you have to live with the disgrace of being married to a crook. Not only a crook but someone . . ."

Keith's voice cracked and he looked away. He wiped his eyes and looked back into the camera.

"This is so hard, but I will not let you hear this from someone else. I laundered money. The people I was helping were bringing young girls into the country. I . . ."

He looked away again and broke down with both hands over his face. Then he slowly composed himself and looked back into the camera.

"You remember when I told you there would be no prenup? I knew then I didn't deserve you. My lawyer was livid when I refused to have you sign one. Oh Cassandra, I'm so sorry. Please, please find it in your heart to forgive me, even though I don't deserve it."

Keith paused and looked down. He grabbed a sheet of paper and held it up to the camera.

"On this flash drive is also this Word document. When you open it, it won't make any sense to you. But if you take this to the FBI in Tampa, they will know what to do with it."

He placed the paper down and looked away as more tears formed. Slowly, he reached up, and the video ended.

Aiden opened the Word document next. It contained names, account numbers, and balances. Aiden and Jonas cheered as they recognized what they were seeing. Aiden quickly made a copy and sent a secure email to their boss, Joe, and the team working the Wayne Keaton case.

Addison looked at Aiden and asked, "What's next? Will everyone see that video?"

"Only the people who need to. I want everyone involved put away for life," Aiden replied.

Addison nodded. "If Keith was alive today, I don't think I could look him in the eye. It's so hard to believe he was capable of something like this. My poor sister. Can you take me to her? I want to be with her."

"Yes, as soon as we drop this off at the field office, we'll take you to the safe house. Both of you will have to stay hidden until all of this is over. I'm sorry, Addison, but no one can know you're alive. Not even Riley and Owen. No one. Do you understand?"

Addison nodded, then touched her necklace and thought of Riley. This nightmare couldn't end fast enough.

# CHAPTER 33

It was 3 p.m., and they now had their suspect's full name—Juan Pedro Diego—but the team working the case doubted it was his real name. After Juan had been processed, they had him sitting in an eight-foot-by-eight-foot FBI holding cell in handcuffs for two hours and forty-five minutes. The air was set at eighty-four degrees. He had not spoken a single word since lying on the floor when they had slapped the cuffs on him back at Rolling Tides at 9:15 a.m.

The burner phone was analyzed and dusted for prints. It appeared the phone had only been used to communicate with another untraceable burner phone. There was only one active text thread. Ideas were tossed around about what response would be appropriate or if they should wait on another message to come through. After much debate, they decided to send a text. But first, Aiden wanted a shot at Juan.

Aiden walked into the room where Juan was being held, identified himself, and took the seat across from him. Juan returned his stare without saying a word.

Aiden lifted a printout and read: "Juan Pedro Diego, 3821 Baker Street, Tampa. Green card issued in 2019. Employment: cook. No wife. No known children."

He set the paper down and waited on Juan to say something. A full minute passed before Aiden asked, "Do you know the prison sentence for trying to kill an FBI officer?"

Juan smirked but gave no response.

"Life." Aiden held his poker face. He wanted Juan to correct him and say that he was there to kill Addison and he had no idea the FBI were there.

"I want a lawyer."

Aiden smiled. "Oh, you do talk? That's good." He picked up a pen and wrote down on the front of a file: *Requested lawyer at 3:05 p.m.* "We have the right to hold you for twenty-four hours first before you can ask for a lawyer, and then it might be a challenge. Lawyers are pretty hesitant about who they represent when going up against the FBI. So, in the meanwhile, make yourself comfortable."

"Bullshit! I don't believe you! Now you write that down." Juan snarled.

Aiden laughed. He sat back in his chair smugly, enjoying the baiting.

Juan screamed, "You can't just keep me here! I want a lawyer now!"

Aiden just shook his head. "You are so clueless. Everyone watches these TV shows about crime and asking for their lawyers and such. Really, it just doesn't work that way when you try to kill an FBI agent."

Juan tried to push away from the table, but his hands were cuffed. "What the hell do you want from me?"

Aiden leaned forward and looked him in his dark eyes, not backing away for a second. "I want your damned supplier. Where can I find Sebastian Hawks?"

It was Juan's turn to laugh. "You'll never find him."

Aiden stood. "Then I guess you'll never see the light of day again."

He left Juan screaming profanity at him. Aiden thought, *Let him stew over what I said. See if he still has the same tune this time tomorrow.*

He met the team on the other side of the glass window. All had watched the exchange. "What are your thoughts?" Aiden asked.

Jonas spoke first. "Something tells me he's pretty hardcore. He's not going to snitch anytime soon."

Agent John Fisher, the oldest in the room with the most experience, nodded. "I hate to say it, but I think Jonas is right. If we wait, then whoever is on the receiving end of these text messages is going to question the timetable.

Trevor added, "And let's not forget that Keaton's arrest has made national news, so chances are, Sebastian knows and he's just gotten even more spooked since running."

"It's a crapshoot, really. We've just got to go with something and make it happen," Jonas offered.

"Okay. Thanks, guys." Aiden opened the door and walked back in. He said to Juan, "I'm only going to make this offer one time: You help us find Sebastian Hawks, and we'll give you a reduced sentence. You don't help us, and I will do everything in my power to see you get the needle."

Juan sat back in his chair. "I'll take my chances."

Aiden nodded. "Okay. I'll see you in court."

He closed the door behind him and again addressed his team, who were still watching the interrogation room. "Well, I'm not surprised, but at least now we have a feel for his personality. Let's send the text."

Five minutes later, they used Juan's phone to send a text message to the untraceable cell. Since there was only one thread, all they could do was send a response to the previous text. Aiden typed the message: *Finished. Got a flash drive.*

They all looked at one another as they waited patiently for a response. Jonas suddenly asked in all seriousness, "So, who do ya'll think is going to win the Super Bowl this year?"

And just like that, the tension was broken. They chatted about Tampa's chances and who was going to be their hardest opponent. Then they saw the phone light up with a response, and all chatter ceased.

Aiden pressed the notification and read aloud: "Can you get to Europe? He looked at his team. "He's not coming back. Looks like we've got to go to him."

***

Addison sat on the back porch of the safe house, lost in thought. School was starting soon, and she no longer had a choice about whether or not to attend. A sadness washed over her. She truly loved teaching and didn't like that the choice was no longer in her hands. With everything going on, she no longer had a job. Hell, they thought she was dead.

"Hey, you. Are you okay?" Cassandra asked as she stepped onto the porch.

Addison turned around. "I don't know. Really, I don't know. I feel like my entire world has turned upside down."

Cassandra placed a hand on her shoulder and then gave her a hug. "I know. I feel it too. How can I ever set foot again in Memorial General? Everyone would look at me and think of the monster I married."

Addison pulled away from her embrace. "Right now, it looks pretty bleak." She gave a small laugh. "But we'll persevere. Isn't that what our parents always said?"

Cassandra nodded. "Yes. They did. They really were our biggest fans. I'm glad they're not alive to see the mess that I'm in." More tears formed, and she wiped them away.

"Look, I'm sure I'll pick up a job somewhere when all of this is over, and so will you. It will just be uncomfortable for a while. We might even have to live together," Addison offered.

Cassandra gave her a quizzical look. "Oh my God, you're worried about money. Oh Addison! Keith placed five million in an offshore bank account for me."

"What?" Addison asked in shock.

"Yes. He did it on the morning of our weekend boat trip. I can access it whenever I want."

"And you don't question the timing of that?"

Cassandra pursed her lips, then spoke. "Yes! I question everything every day since the boat exploded and I ran for my life."

Addison nodded and backed off. It would do neither of them any good to fight. No matter the circumstances, they were stuck here in this safe house. From now on, Addison would watch what she said. She had to, or she would slowly lose her mind waiting for this nightmare to end.

She looked back into the living room at the TV. "Let's watch a movie. I can't even remember the last time we've done that together."

Cassandra smiled. "I'll make the popcorn."

# CHAPTER 34

*Thursday Morning*

Agent Louis Ruiz was the agent they found on short notice who looked most like Juan. With the help of Homeland Security, Louis was able to cruise through all the security checkpoints from Miami to Athens, Greece. They had gotten lucky and found a Delta flight with an empty seat leaving around noon on Wednesday. It would take almost fourteen hours to get to Athens via a layover at John F. Kennedy International Airport. Once landing, the plan was for Louis to blend in as a tourist. Then after making sure he hadn't been followed, he would use the burner phone to send a text that he had arrived.

The work behind the scenes had taken a toll on everyone. Aiden, Jonas, and Trevor had immediately jumped on a plane Tuesday night. As soon as they had landed, they had been on the phone nonstop with Athens authorities finalizing the plans that Joe and the others had worked on while they were in flight. Everyone was on high alert. Officer Carmen Thatcher would be the lead official from Athens law enforcement assisting them with anything they needed.

In addition to the burner phone, Louis carried an FBI-issued satellite phone and a tracker on his clothing. They had debated about luggage and finally decided on a backpack and one suitcase on wheels. They wanted him to look like every other tourist entering Greece.

At 9:45 a.m., wearing a hat that looked like the one Juan had worn to Rolling Tides, Louis walked into a Starbucks at the airport and got in line. While hiding among the crowd, he surveyed his surroundings. He saw no one who looked like the photos of Sebastian. Pulling out the burner phone, he texted *Arrived* and shoved the phone back in his pocket.

He slowly made his way to the front of the line and felt the phone vibrate. He waited in case anyone was watching. He ordered, then casually slid behind the line and leaned up against a wall. When no one seemed to give him a second glance, he pulled out the phone to read the text.

*Take the rail to Metro Chalandri. Text when you arrive.*

Louis shoved the phone back in his pocket and waited on his coffee. Five minutes later, he walked into a stall in the men's restroom. He called Aiden on the satellite phone. After updating him with all the details since landing, he asked, "Do you all have eyes on me?"

"Yes."

"Do you think I'm being followed?"

"We've seen nothing suspicious and no sign of anyone who looks like Hawks."

Louis relaxed. "Okay. Tell me how to get to Metro Chalandri."

Aiden's team had already pulled a map of the international airport. "Follow the signs to transportation and look for Athens Metro. Routes will appear on a board. Stay low, just like Juan would do. Remember, he's a man on the run."

Louis found the underground subway, checked the board, and got on the correct train. He took a seat and watched as people boarded and disembarked along the way. Everyone was in a hurry and too preoccupied with their own travels to give him any notice. Finally, it was announced that their next stop was Chalandri. He stood and waited for the door to open, then followed the crowd, as there was only one exit, and took the escalator up. As he rode, he pulled out the burner and texted *Arrived alone.*

Again, he stuck the phone in his pocket and waited till he found the men's restroom to answer. Behind the bathroom stall, he read: *Go to luggage storage. Number 29. Code 179350#. Take the money and leave the phone and flash drive.*

Louis relayed the information to Aiden.

"He's smart. But we're smarter. As soon as you make the exchange, get on the rail and go back to the airport. That's what Juan would do: take the money and run. Go to the designated hotel at the airport, and someone will meet you. We'll call if we need you. Stay safe. And Louis, you did good."

Louis ended the call and stepped back into the station. He checked the signs for luggage storage and followed the directions. It was a busy place. There were rows of storage lockers all numbered with signs above. He found *21–40* and walked down the aisle. He was partially hidden between ten lockers on each side. He found number twenty-nine and typed in the code.

As the locker opened, he heard a noise. It was a couple walking his way empty-handed. He smiled as they stopped at number twenty-five. They were far enough away. He turned back around and unzipped the backpack in the locker. It was filled with American cash.

He rezipped it and took the bag. He pulled the flash drive from his pocket and placed it inside the locker along with the burner phone and closed the door. He waited until the couple retrieved their bags and then followed them. Keeping his head down, he retreated to the subway.

At noon, a large group of French students converged in the station hall. They were loud, typical teenagers excited about being away from home. They entered the luggage storage area and swarmed several of the aisles to retrieve their belongings.

Five minutes later, an alarm sounded, and the transmitter in the flash drive started beeping. They watched from a screen as a dot moved along the station and then out to street level.

Trevor, who was monitoring the transmission while sitting at a café drinking coffee, saw the French students emerge on the street. He spoke into his headpiece. "They are boarding a white Charter Line private bus. Maybe thirty to forty kids. Four to five adults. Hard to tell."

Carmen viewed the street camera from police headquarters. "I got them. It's one of those school-sponsored trips. It's a private charter popular for carrying school groups. My man on the ground sees no one looking like our guy."

"Copy that. Apparently, our mark has paid a kid," Aiden replied.

Ten minutes later, the bus pulled away from the curb and headed south. Trevor waited fifteen minutes before shutting down his computer and catching up with their tag-team efforts. Carmen continued to update them at each street crossing with their city camera system. Soon they learned the bus was headed to the harbor. The bus came to a stop at a large, busy ferry terminal and delivered the passengers.

A uniformed Athens police officer had eyes on the kids. He spoke into his radio that was on speaker phone at the command center at police headquarters for all to hear. "It appears they have prepaid tickets, and they are headed to Blue Star Ferries. From there, they can board several different ferries. Do I need to hold them?"

Aiden replied, "Tell him no. Just watch and let us know which ferry the kids get on. The exchange could happen there."

It took thirty minutes before the students could board a ferry. In the meantime, Homeland Security confirmed the school name along with the name of each student and chaperone. There were thirty-eight in the group. They boarded a ferry to Mykonos, and so did the flash drive transmission.

The ferry held over four hundred passengers and would take an estimated two hours and thirty-five minutes to reach Mykonos. Carmen had informed Aiden that Mykonos would be tricky with the amount of tourists that arrived daily by boat, but the long distance would help buy them some time to get set up. Aiden, Jonas, and Trevor boarded a chopper and would be met on the ground by law enforcement. Carmen was turning over the mission to Officer Derran Borgue, who was set to pick them up.

By the time the ferry arrived at the Mykonos harbor, a total of fifteen people were set at various checkpoints. The decision had been to wait and not stop the student group. They would all be questioned later at some point and, hopefully, a good sketch could be produced. Aiden hoped it was one of the chaperones who had taken the bribe and not one of the students.

The students emerged with everyone carrying their bags and belongings. The adults looked tired; the kids looked wired and ready to go. They stood in a group and seemed to be listening to their lead instructor. Five minutes later, they began walking in the direction of a long line of buses for passenger pickup.

"Transmission stopped moving," Jonas announced.

"There's a brown lunch sack sitting on a bench," a nearby officer announced.

Aiden commanded, "Hold your positions."

One minute later, a man walked up, grabbed the brown sack, and headed toward a line of cars. He opened the door to a black SUV and climbed in the back seat. The car pulled away into traffic.

"Transmission still moving," Jonas reported.

"We follow the car," Aiden directed.

Jonas replied, "I got a good look at him. He looks a lot like Gabriel Hoffman."

"Sebastian's foreman in the Caymans. Let's get Homeland working on his flight pattern he took from the Caymans. I want to know the alias he's using."

"Copy that," Trevor replied.

The car was harder to follow due to there being less security cameras on the island, and they had to rely heavily on the transmission tracker guiding them through the city. The SUV continued into the outskirts of town and soon headed toward a residential area. Thirty minutes later, it stopped.

An address was pulled for the location, and the team converged. As soon as the flash drive was connected to a computer, the computer would be embedded with a tracker as it infested the hard drive. They had copied everything on the flash drive exactly as it was. They wanted Sebastian Hawks to know without a shadow of a doubt that Juan had indeed delivered the goods left behind by Keith Rose.

# CHAPTER 35

At the base of the Profitis Ilias stood a four-bedroom villa with a private pool. Inside, Sebastian paced as he waited on Gabriel to arrive. He had decided once arriving in Europe that he would cut ties with everyone including Gabriel, his trusted foreman for over a decade. Too many days had gone by without hearing from Jayden. Something must have gone terribly wrong for Jayden not to have reached out by now. After today, his burner phone, Jayden's only connection to him, would be destroyed. Now he just needed Gabriel to make this last drop, and then they would part ways as well.

The black car pulled up along the driveway, and Sebastian watched as Gabriel exited. The car sat idling.

Sebastian greeted him with, "Were you followed?"

Gabriel spoke with confidence. "No. Everything went as planned. I still can't believe how you coordinated with the teacher to help with the drop."

Sebastian smiled. "I know many people, and we got lucky Juan left when he did. Another day and the drop would have been much different. Now let's see it."

Gabriel pulled the flash drive from his pocket along with the phone. Sebastian motioned over to the table in the kitchen where his computer was set up. They took a seat and opened the flash drive. They watched the video first.

"Son of a bitch! I knew he couldn't be trusted!" Sebastian cried. "Rot in hell, Keith!"

He closed the video and opened the file. He read over all the account numbers and amounts, then looked at Gabriel. "If anyone had found this, I would have lost everything."

"Yeah, I can't believe Juan pulled through. I mean, I would have always put money on Jayden getting the job done over Juan."

An eerie silence formed as Sebastian sat deep in thought. "You think Juan saw this and made a copy?"

"You mean try to blackmail you or go steal the money?" Gabriel asked.

Sebastian frowned, and then he closed the flash drive and logged on to one of his overseas accounts. As he waited, he reminded himself how all the money had still been there as of last night. Finally, the account opened, and he saw his balance appeared intact. He smiled with relief.

"I'll move the majority of this today, but first, let me make a transfer to you." Sebastian tapped a few buttons, typed in the amount of $2 million, and looked at Gabriel before pressing the Send button.

Gabriel looked at him in shock. "Two million? I . . . I don't know what to say."

"No, Gabriel, it's me who does not know what to say. Thank you for your loyalty." He reached out and gave Gabriel a big hug, then returned his attention to the computer. He pressed Send. A confirmation was immediately given. "Once you collect the money, change your name and move somewhere far away from the Caymans, and you will be safe."

"I will, Sebastian. I was thinking of the—"

He cut Gabriel off. "No! Don't tell me. I don't want to know. From here on out, we go our separate ways."

Gabriel's eyes showed sadness, but he still nodded in agreement. "Well, Sebastian, it's been a pleasure to know and serve you over the years. Stay safe, my dear friend."

Sebastian patted him on the shoulder but spoke no more. He was a little choked up himself with Gabriel calling him *friend*. Slowly, they made their way to the front door. When it appeared no one was lurking around, Sebastian opened the door. Gabriel walked down the sidewalk and entered the back seat of the waiting car, which soon pulled away.

***

The FBI monitored all the accounts listed on the flash drive that Keith had left behind. Sebastian was moving money around again to protect his identity. Little did he know that when he moved the money, it was immediately frozen. Earlier, when Louis had gone to the hotel to meet local law enforcement, they had emptied the contents of the backpack. Sebastian had paid Juan $200,000. Also, there was a handwritten note inside: *Take care of Isaac Mullins, and I will place $300,000 in the account. Don't try to reach me. I will know when it's done. Thank you for your loyalty.* The intel had been passed on to the FBI and Homeland Security about the threat to Isaac and his family, but there was only so much that could be done to protect them when they were missing and evading authorities.

Five minutes ago, Gabriel had been taking into custody. Now they had everything they needed on Sebastian. The only thing left was to pick him up. Jonas, Trevor, and Aiden, along with a dozen law enforcement officers, set a perimeter around Sebastian's rental home. There they monitored Sebastian as he walked around the property unaware of their presence. Most of the day, he was on the computer creating new bank accounts, and then he made a dinner reservation at one of the finest restaurants in Mykonos. They watched as he sorted through his closet and then took clothing still on hangers to the bath-room. Thirty-five minutes later, he emerged dressed for the evening.

The car was easy to intercept on the way up the small mountain to the home. The driver had confirmed the name and address of his pickup. They asked for him to patiently wait in another vehicle while his was used to do the pickup. He would be compensated for his time. Aiden stepped in behind the wheel and borrowed the man's cap and jacket.

Five minutes later, Sebastian walked out of his rented villa and into the back seat of the car. When he closed the door, Aiden turned around with a gun.

"Hands up, Sebastian Hawks. Game over."

# CHAPTER 36

Agent John Fisher walked into the safe house and informed Addison and Cassandra that he had good and bad news to share. The good news was that Sebastian Hawks had been taken into custody and Addison had been given the green light to contact Owen and Riley. The bad news was he couldn't guarantee Cassandra's safety if the world knew she was alive. Tears and hugs were shared as John allowed them time to process the information.

Once the women's emotions were in check, he loaded them in his vehicle and took them to the FBI Tampa Field Office. Addison stayed with John, who got in touch with Owen and helped her explain what had happened over the last week. She would soon be on her way to Atlanta to see her son. For now, there was no need to make this information public, but he warned it was inevitable. They would have their time to reunite, and then the FBI were going to help Addison. She wouldn't be in the witness protection program but would have a new name and be relocated to a new city that would give her a fresh start after all the media attention she had gotten over the last month. John intentionally let it slip that it was Aiden who had made the request to help with a new identity for Addison and Riley.

Meanwhile, Joe explained the witness protection program to Cassandra and what exactly that meant. She had to cut all ties to her old life. Whether it would be permanent depended on the outcome of the trials of Sebastian and Wayne, who were both at least a year away from trial. Then there was the discussion of the $5 million. The Feds had informed Cassandra that they were not interested in pursuing the money if she would forfeit all rights to Keith's estate. Under the circumstances, it was a deal she could not turn down. The agreement also gave her a new name and a practicing doctor's license. Now they just needed to find a small town in America where Cassandra could practice medicine.

When both sisters were finished, they were given time in a conference room to talk.

Cassandra spoke first. "I hope you'll find it in your heart to forgive me."

Addison nodded. "Oh Cassandra, none of this is your fault. You fell in love with a man who wasn't who he claimed to be. In fact, he fooled me too. He was always so kind and generous and treated me and Riley like we were truly family. I would have never believed in a thousand years he had been involved with crooks and money laundering if I hadn't seen the video he made. I never saw a broken Keith before, only the confident and generous man who adored and doted on you."

"I was so scared I was going to lose you," Cassandra said as she wiped a tear. "The Feds are going to let me keep the five million if I drop all claims to Keith's estate."

Addison couldn't hide her displeasure. "You want the money after knowing where it came from?"

Cassandra frowned. "It's not that straightforward, Addison. I made money too, and all our accounts are frozen. I have no access to money." When she didn't respond, Cassandra added, "I'd like to give you some money to make up for the loss of income from your job."

Addison replied, "I don't know. Look, as long as the FBI can help me find a new job and housing, I will be fine."

Cassandra seemed hurt. She walked forward and placed a hand on Addison's shoulder. "You know, why don't we go grab Riley and disappear? We have enough money to do that, you know. We could run away together, and I'll help you raise Riley."

Addison stepped back. "Don't say things like that. You know I can't do that. No matter how mad I am at Owen, I would never deny Riley his father. And besides, regardless of how much money you made, I will still look at it as tainted."

The door opened, and John and Joe walked in. "I'm sorry, ladies, but this is all the time we can give you. We need to move Cassandra now, and Addison, you need to leave as soon as possible before the media finds out that you're still alive."

Timidly, Cassandra stepped forward and gave Addison a tight hug. "I love you, and this is not goodbye."

Addison smiled. "I think you're going to look great as a brunette." She touched Cassandra's hair. "I love you too, and no, this is not goodbye."

Cassandra turned away and walked out the door with Joe.

***

One week later, there was a big party in the backyard of Jonas and Alanis's house on Saturday evening. All the agents who had worked on the case relaxed and enjoyed one another's banter as the wives mingled and the kids played in the swimming pool. Even Samantha, Aiden's loving German shepherd was invited, and she was playing catch in the pool. Aiden thought of the ear infection soon to follow but didn't have the heart not to let her continue. There had been so many long nights with this case, and she had missed a lot of running and playing time with Aiden.

"Did you look at our next case?" asked Jonas, who was flipping burgers.

Aiden laughed. "Hell no! I wouldn't be able to relax for the next week. How about you?"

"Same. I owe it to Alanis and the kids to truly take a week off. Besides, I have a mile-long to-do list." He grinned as he looked at his wife serving more margaritas to the other ladies.

Aiden followed his gaze. "You're a damned lucky man, Jonas Parker, so don't screw it up."

"I don't plan to. Hey, if you get bored, you can come and help with my to-do list."

"You know I would. Just ask."

Jonas lifted a plate and handed it to Aiden. "Hold this while I get the burgers off." He carefully moved about twenty hamburgers and a dozen hotdogs without dropping any. Then he yelled, "Okay, everyone, come and get it!"

Aiden placed the platter on the table by all the side dishes and condiments. Then turned back to Jonas and lifted his beer. "Need a refill?"

"Absolutely. Let's go grab one."

They walked over to the cooler. Aiden skillfully removed the bottle tops, and then Jonas placed the limes in each. They settled into chairs and were content relaxing while everyone else went through the line for food first.

"The only thing I have to worry about over the next week is Alanis making me fat with her cooking." Jonas grinned as he rubbed his belly.

Aiden laughed. "Well, I can always come over if she makes too much."

Jonas changed the subject by asking, "Do you still think about the case?"

"It's hard not to. It was so time-consuming."

Jonas took a swig of his beer and then commented, "Yeah, it was. Three damned years!" He reached out and toasted his beer to Aiden's with a "Cheers." Then he asked, "You ever think of Addison Shaw?"

Aiden gave him a look. "Maybe."

Jonas grinned. "You know, you can reach out. The world knows she's alive now."

"It's not that. It's just . . . you know, complicated," Aiden offered.

"Complicated, my ass! She's divorced and living in Atlanta with her son. Well, at least for now until she moves," Jonas teased.

Aiden thought back to last week. Addison had been allowed to return to Atlanta with her son. The FBI had helped her change her name to Lydia Smith and will help move her to a town in South Carolina, not too far from Owen in Atlanta. Her teaching job wouldn't start till after Labor Day. Cassandra was in the witness protection program and was residing in a small Montana town as an ER doctor. Her file was sealed, and even he didn't know her new name.

There was something he kept tossing around in his head, and he brought it up to Jonas. "What do you think about the Feds allowing Cassandra to keep the five million?"

Jonas gave it some thought before speaking. "A little unusual."

"Yeah. As I understood it, they didn't want to fight with her over Keith's estate. It would have been a legal nightmare." Aiden took another swig of his beer. "Also, Cassandra claimed she would never be

307

a financial strain on the system, and she promised to continue working for the good of others."

Jonas chuckled. "Making good money too."

Aiden looked out at the crowd of people all laughing and having a good time. He turned back to Jonas. "You know, I think it's about time I let Alanis set me up with one of her friends."

Jonas jumped up. "Are you for real?"

Aiden smiled. "Yeah, I am."

Jonas raised his beer. "To you, Aiden Greene. May my wife have you married within a year!"

Aiden almost choked on his beer. "Hey, alright now, slow down."

Jonas motioned to the table of food. "Come on, let's go make a plate. I can't wait to tell Alanis the good news."

The party continued until around 9:30 p.m. when the kids all started to fight with one another out of pure exhaustion. Aiden thanked Jonas and Alanis for a wonderful evening and promised not to back out of the date. He waved at everyone and whistled for Samantha. She quickly got up, but then her steps were a little slow after her fun in the sun with the kids. Aiden laughed as he hooked a leash on her collar. "Let's go, my tired girl."

Aiden arrived home to his condo and enjoyed the quietness. After he settled Samantha for the night, he felt a little sad climbing into an empty bed alone. After plugging in his phone, he propped up his pillows, got comfortable, and turned on the TV. He flipped one channel after the next, but nothing seemed to hold his interest. His mind continued to return to the case.

He remembered his first interview with Cassandra. He had listened to her story about the boat accident and the car accident. Addison had collaborated her story about switching cars. He remembered Cassandra laughing as she had explained, "I can saw through a breast plate, so trust me, I can fire a gun and swim through a window." Then Aiden had asked her about swimming to shore after the boat explosion with no one seeing her. She had another witty comment: "There are so many people on the beach. When you get close enough, you just start swimming parallel. Then you blend in."

Addison hadn't questioned anything. Aiden contributed that to the fact that she had just been so happy to see her sister alive. He thought of Addison again and considered calling her, then looked at the time: 10:20 p.m. Aiden picked up the remote and turned the TV off. Then he went to set his alarm but stopped. He smiled. It was going to be hard for a while as he tried shutting his mind down for the next week. The case was successfully closed. It was indeed time to move on and relax and enjoy life for a change.

# CHAPTER 37

The next morning, Aiden woke to wet kisses on his face from Samantha. He lovingly played around with her as he got out of bed. Soon he was dressed in shorts and a T-shirt, and they were headed down the stairs to the dog park. Just as he opened the wrought iron gate to the park, he got a call. He glanced at the caller as he closed the gate behind them and threw the ball to Samantha.

"Sorry to bother you so soon, Aiden," Quincy said.

Aiden watched as Samantha retrieved the ball and ran back to him. "Not a problem, sir. What can I do for you?"

"We got a call from Tampa County Jail. It appears Juan Diego is requesting a meeting with you."

Aiden threw the ball again and said, "No kidding. Do we know why?"

"It's a mystery. He hasn't said anything to anyone except to request this meeting. Can you make it?"

Aiden looked at the time. "I can head that way in twenty minutes, sir."

"I appreciate it with your time off and all. I'll look forward to hearing from you." Quincy ended the call.

Aiden threw the ball twice more to Samantha and then told her it was time to go. She obediently followed. After getting her settled, Aiden quickly fed her, showered, dressed, and opened the door to leave. "I'm sorry, buddy. I have no clue what this is about. Stay. Guard."

The parking lot to the jail was relatively full on a Sunday morning. It wasn't surprising following a Saturday night. Lots of action happened in and around Tampa, and not all of it was good. Aiden found a spot and set the alarm to his truck. He opened the door to the police station and identified himself. Soon he was escorted to the area of the building where they held prisoners. Aiden entered a holding room and took a seat.

Soon Juan was escorted in. He took a seat across from Aiden. Once Juan's handcuffs were attached to the table, the officer who had escorted him informed Aiden he would be outside if he was needed.

Aiden sat back in his chair as if he was bored with Juan already. He had no intention of starting this conversation. He wasn't the one who had requested the meeting. He didn't have to wait long before Juan began talking.

"We have TV. I saw the news."

Aiden smiled. "I thought I looked good, didn't you?"

Juan frowned. "You're so arrogant. I'm going to enjoy this."

Aiden grabbed his pen from his jacket and held it above his pad of paper, making a show of being ready to write. "Okay, Juan. You got my attention, so let's cut to the chase and tell me why you dragged me down here on a Sunday morning. What do you want to tell me?"

"I want you to guarantee that I cooperated first."

Aiden raised his hands. "You want me to find the district attorney on a Sunday morning?"

Juan banged his fist on the table. "Don't lie to me. If I cooperate with you, will it help with my case?"

"Depends on what you have to say. As of now, I plan to testify that you broke into the Rose beach house with the intent to kill a witness and a federal agent. So what am I missing?"

"The news didn't say anything about Cassandra Rose being alive. Why not?"

Aiden studied him briefly, then stated, "Cassandra died in a boating accident along with Keith. Now stop wasting my Sunday." He stood to leave.

"Liar!" Juan shouted. "We both know she's alive. Now sit down, and I'll tell you how I know."

Aiden sighed and sat down. "Go ahead. The sooner you get whatever it is you want off your conscience, the sooner I can get back to my Sunday."

Juan demanded, "I want this recorded."

Aiden stood again, tapped on the door, and requested a tape recorder. After it was set up, Juan began talking.

"I, Juan Pedro Diego, am giving a statement with . . ." He paused. " . . . hope that my story will help play a role in my upcoming trial. Everything I say today is the truth." He looked up from the recorder and straight into Aiden's eyes before he resumed.

"Wayne Keaton and Sebastian Hawks hired me four years ago. But they didn't own me like they thought they did. Sebastian hired me to kill Keith and Cassandra Rose. I agreed. Before I made the hit, I was contacted by Isaac Mullins. Somehow, he had heard about the hit. He said he wanted me to fake their deaths and that he would pay me more. It would be our little secret. No one would be the wiser."

Aiden sat up in his chair. "Are you claiming Keith Rose is alive?"

"Yes. On the day of the accident, I grabbed Keith and Cassandra and put them on my boat. Then I set fire to their boat and created an explosion. I sailed away and met Isaac out at sea on his boat. I was paid immediately in cash, and then I handed Keith and Cassandra over to Isaac."

"You got paid twice?" Aiden asked.

Juan smiled. "Yes. Then I carried on as if it never happened and continued working for Wayne and Sebastian as needed."

"Did you kill Maria Hawks in Miami?"

"No. That was Jayden Hart. I only drove her from Tampa to Miami."

Aiden nodded for him to continue.

"Sebastian then ordered me to kill Addison Shaw. Since I got paid twice before, I decided it would work again. I reached out to Isaac and told him that I was planning to kill Addison, but I could make it look like an accident if he paid me again."

"Are you saying Addison had no knowledge that her sister was alive?"

"I don't think so. I was watching her, and she was doing weird stuff like dyeing her hair to look like Cassandra."

"What happened on the night of the car accident, when the Lexus drove into the bay?"

Juan laughed. "You never saw me. I was climbing up the ladder when you and your partner were jumping in the water."

"So Cassandra wasn't in the car?"

He shook his head. "Cassandra drove off in the car, and I met her down the road. We traded places, and she was to walk back to her sister and drive away. Once the news claimed Addison was dead, I would be paid."

Aiden shook his head in disbelief. If he was telling the truth, Cassandra had lied when she had said she had driven the car into the bay and sustained a concussion. "Where was Addison while this happened?"

"I don't know what Cassandra told her. I still needed to rig the car to make it look like an accident. Once I got that done, I called her, and she told me to leave and meet her a mile away. Then we swapped places, and I created the accident."

"Did you fire a gun?"

"Yes. To bust the windshield."

Aiden thought of his interview with the young couple, Casey and Robby Wentwood. They had been wrong about seeing two people in the car but right about hearing a backfire that could have been gunfire. "So now you were to be paid twice. What happened next?"

Juan frowned. "I was until that bitch double-crossed me."

"You mean Cassandra?"

Juan nodded. "She called me the night before I was arrested. Told me she had my cash at the beach house. I was told what time to arrive and how to enter the house. And, well, you know the rest."

"What about Addison? Did she know Cassandra's plan?"

He chuckled. "Hell if I know. Looks like you'll have to figure that one out on your own."

"Why are you telling me this now? I gave you a chance to talk to me earlier."

He frowned again. "I had some time to think. It was good when I double-crossed everyone else, but not when it happened to me."

Aiden sat back and crossed his arms. "And why should I believe all of this? Like you said, you've had a lot of time to think. You could have just made up this entire story to save your ass."

Juan slammed his fist into the table, and the recorder flipped over and stopped recording. "Because I want Keith and Isaac behind bars, and then I plan to kill them."

\*\*\*

An hour later after arriving at the jail, Aiden was jogging to his truck. He called Quincy. "We need to meet, sir. I'm heading over."

Aiden sat before his boss and relayed the whole story Juan had just shared. Quincy sat listening without interruption. Aiden concluded with, "Then, as you know, the rest was history for Juan. Cassandra set him up, and us as well. So it appears, sir, we have all been played by Keith and Cassandra, as well as Isaac."

Quincy shook his head in disbelief. "What is Addison's role in this? She collaborated the story about the car accident."

"I've been thinking a lot about that." Aiden looked at his notepad. "She only stated in her interview that Cassandra drove off in the car and they met up later. I honestly don't know for sure if she's in on this or not. I would like to think if she was, she would have never called us and told us about Cassandra being alive and having the key to the lockbox. Which, as you know, held incriminating evidence on Keith, Wayne and Sebastian."

"So you think Cassandra was able to call to Juan to set him up after Addison called you, all without her knowing?"

Aiden frowned. "I honestly don't know, sir. When Addison called and told me she was alive as well as Cassandra she stated that some-

316

one was trying to kill her, and she couldn't shake the fact that someone was still out there watching her."

Quincy sat pondering. Finally, he broke the silence. "Let me get this straight: Cassandra comes out of hiding to protect her sister and hangs everything on Juan. Then she takes the five million, enters witness protection, and keeps the lid on the fact that Keith is still alive. Well, if that's true, it's one hell of a brilliant plan. In all my years, I haven't seen anything like it."

Aiden slowly nodded. "Which means—again, if it's true—at some point, Isaac and Keith will resurface."

"And Cassandra will lead us straight to them." Quincy stood. "You did good work, Aiden. I'll get Joe Billings to start researching Isaac and Keith's connection to each other. We missed that. I'll see you in a week, and we'll start fresh with the team to check out his story."

"But sir, I can start . . ."

His boss immediately cut him off. "No, Aiden. You are off duty for one week. This case will and can wait for you." Then he nodded and gestured to the door. "Have a great week."

# CHAPTER 38

*Six Months Later*

It was cold in Great Falls, Montana, in December and set to get even colder by the new year. Cassandra was now Dr. Harper Henderson. The FBI had chosen the name Harper because it was unisex and would help Cassandra hide her identity so she could continue practicing medicine. For the most part, Cassandra loved working at Great Falls Hospital in the emergency room. Her biggest complaints were back aches and swollen feet due to her pregnancy.

She had waited till she had started showing to set the gossip trails burning that she was newly widowed and pregnant. From that point on, she had had more friends and support than she had had in a lifetime. There was a lot for Cassandra to enjoy in Great Falls. It was small but not too small, and the people were friendlier and moved at a slower pace than in Tampa.

Cassandra sat in her small office in the back of the ER, drinking tea and working on paperwork from the day's cases. At the moment, it was slow, but she knew not to get too comfortable because it could change in a blink of an eye. She liked the days when it was busier than normal; it helped count down the days till she walked out the door for good.

Cassandra looked at the time: it was nearing 2 p.m. She would have one more hour to go on her shift and only thirty minutes before Dr. Pena came in to start the transition to relieve her.

Last week, she had set the ball in motion. She had worked six consecutive fourteen-hour shifts that had included the weekend. Now she would be rewarded with three days off. If everything worked as planned, no one would miss her until Thursday at 6:30 a.m. With her being six months pregnant, that would buy her an additional hour before alarm bells started to sound. Cassandra also knew the FBI would be alerted. Hopefully by then, she would be sitting on a beach, her feet propped up with the sun's rays warming her pale body.

She heard a knock and looked up. It was Nurse Julianna French, holding a covered dish with a big smile on her face.

Cassandra smiled back and stood from her desk. "What do we have here?"

Julianna walked to her. "Homemade chicken pie casserole."

Cassandra's heart melted. She loved Julianna, and they had become good friends. "How did you know that's exactly what I needed?"

"Because you probably have nothing in your refrigerator, and you're going to be too tired to stop at the grocery store on your way home. So I cooked for you."

Cassandra took the dish and placed it on the desk and then gave her a big hug. "Thank you so much for your friendship and your kindness." She pulled away and had to wipe her eyes because tears had formed.

Julianne replied, "It was my pleasure. Oh, you're crying. You poor dear. I don't think I've ever seen you cry!"

Cassandra forced a smile. "All these pregnancy hormones and long shifts are making me soft."

"So you got big plans on your time off?" Julianna inquired.

"Oh yes! I'm going to sleep, and now with food, I can veg out on the couch and catch up on all my TV series." Cassandra reached back out and squeezed her hand. "Thank you for this. It was so very unexpected and so kind."

Their conversation was interrupted by an announcement on the intercom: "Dr. Henderson to room three, Dr. Henderson to room three."

"Okay, well, it looks like I've got to go. Thanks again." Cassandra took another look at her friend and then forced herself to turn around and walk away.

In room three sat a teenage boy, age fourteen, who had a nasty ankle break from ice hockey practice. Cassandra had called the ortho doctor and was helping with the preparation for surgery when Dr. Pena walked in and took over. Cassandra gave some encouraging words to the young man and then returned to her office. She eyed the medical license hung on the wall. With the help of the FBI, she had become a Vanderbilt graduate of internal medicine. She was tempted to grab it but shrugged off the temptation. She was determined to leave no trails.

Cassandra drove home and parked in the garage. Taking the casserole to the kitchen, she removed a plate from a cabinet and warmed up a large portion. Then she tossed the remaining casserole down her garbage disposal and placed the dish in the dishwater. Thirty minutes later, with a full stomach, Cassandra was in her car with one carry-on bag and a backpack, pulling away from her cute little townhome of the last several months with hope of never returning.

The FBI Tampa Field Office got the call from their undercover agent. Julianna French, who had been a registered nurse with the army before joining the FBI, had called to inform them that something had seemed off with Cassandra and she was set to have a three-day break. It was enough time to bolt before anyone would notice. Add that to the fact that Cassandra was six months pregnant and most likely reaching the point to limit travel, they concluded that Cassandra was finally making her move.

Cassandra already had a tail on her when she had left Great Falls

Hospital at 3:08 p.m. in her white SUV. She had gone home just a few miles away, and from there, a team had been waiting for her next move. They didn't have to wait long. At 3:50 p.m., Cassandra pulled out of her garage and left her residential area. When she passed all the local stores that she frequently shopped, they correctly predicted she was heading to the Great Falls International Airport.

After a few calls were made, the FBI determined there were three flights that were optional, all leaving at 5:30 p.m. At this time of year, there were no later flights. The FBI placed an attendant on each flight and then set a team up at the airport to monitor the area.

At 5:15 p.m., Cassandra boarded a flight to Salt Lake City, Utah, en route to Houston, Texas, under the alias Tiffany Austin. The manifest showed first-class seat 2A to Salt Lake City and first-class seat 3A to Houston. No other tickets had been purchased using that name.

Joe walked into Aiden's office. "Cassandra is on the move. She just boarded a plane headed to Salt Lake City for a quick layover. Then she's scheduled to fly to Houston."

Aiden looked at his watch. "What's her ETA?"

"If she gets on the correct plane at Salt Lake City, then she lands in Houston at 12:57 a.m." Joe read from his report. "We won't know for sure until she boards the flight to Houston. It could be a decoy and she gets in a car at Salt Lake City instead."

Aiden nodded. "Do we have someone on the flight to watch her?"

"Yes, a flight attendant."

Aiden looked at his watch. "This could be it. I'm going home and packing a bag. I'll let Jonas and Trevor know. We'll be ready to go in an hour, tops. Can you get the jet on standby?"

Joe smiled. "Already on standby."

\*\*\*

When Cassandra's plane landed at George Bush International Airport at 1 a.m., she was exhausted. Having no help from alcohol, she had slept very little on the flight. No matter how many blankets or pillows the nice attendant had brought her, she just couldn't get in a comfortable position for sleeping. Once she was able to stand and take her seat belt off, she stretched her back in many directions. The man sitting beside her offered to help retrieve her luggage from the top, and she thanked him. Soon she was disembarking from the plane. Once off the jet breeze, she read the signs to the Marriott Hotel. She only had to catch the tram to the hotel, which was on site at the airport. Tomorrow, she would be flying again, but this time under a new name. She looked around and saw no one suspicious. So far, everything had gone perfectly to plan.

She remembered the day in October when she had received a package in the mail with no return address. It had contained a passport and a postcard of Ambergris Caye, Belize. She had quickly hidden the passport and then used her work computer the next day to research Ambergris Caye. It was a beautiful island off Belize. She had been a bundle of nerves over the next two weeks, but nothing else had followed in the mail.

Cassandra had pushed it all away to another compartment deep within her brain and continued with work as if nothing had happened. Then in November, she had received a Montana license in the mail under the name Tiffany Austin with her photo. Included was a postcard showing a ferry company named Ocean Ferry. She researched the next day at work and found that it transported people to Ambergris Caye from the mainland in Belize. She had tucked the license away with the passport and tried to block it all out as she concentrated on work and her life in Montana. It was important that she carried on as if all was normal. She had been warned a long time ago that the FBI was always watching.

On Thanksgiving Day, when she returned home from working a fourteen-hour shift, she saw a package against her door. Dead tired, she walked into the house and then opened the package. Inside was a picture of two small children playing on the beach. She immediately recognized them as Demi's kids. On the back of the photo was the name of a street. Cassandra flipped the photo back over and studied the picture. The kids looked so happy. She smiled.

She closed her eyes. It was time for her to make a choice: Montana or Keith. She had slept little that night, even after fulfilling her long shift on Thanksgiving Day that she had willingly signed up for since she had no family she could spend it with and only time on her hands as she waited for her baby to arrive.

Cassandra's thoughts returned to the present when she arrived at her hotel. She checked in with record speed and was in her room at 1:35 a.m. She would make no phone calls and no credit card purchases. She set the alarm for 8 a.m. and then settled in under the covers. Within three minutes of lying down, she was fast asleep.

# CHAPTER 39

Aiden woke at 6 a.m. at a hotel just outside the George Bush Houston International Airport. He quickly packed his bag and then took the elevator downstairs and met Jonas for breakfast at 6:30 a.m. They would wait until video surveillance showed Cassandra on the move again. Tiffany Austin had only booked a one-way ticket to Houston. Yesterday, they had traded theories and concluded that she was planning on using another alias for today's flight. Why else would she stay at an on-site airport hotel unless she was catching another flight in the morning? For now, they played the waiting game, as a team was in place to continue to watch Cassandra.

Aiden sipped on his coffee and said to Jonas, "The airport will have planes fly to hundreds of destinations today as well as overseas. All we can do is wait, and I've got to tell you, this is driving me crazy."

Jonas chuckled. "I know. I couldn't sleep last night. I kept tossing and turning as different scenarios played out in my head. But this is it. Our monthslong investigation is finally paying off."

"Yeah, I still can't believe we missed the connection between Demi and Cassandra. If we would have picked that up earlier, then—"

Jonas interjected, "Seriously! There was no way of knowing that Cassandra had befriended Isaac's wife through a book club."

Aiden laughed. "Yeah, what are the odds that they would develop a yearlong friendship and then eventually introduce their husbands, who probably looked at each other in disbelief. They had to know the other existed with their dealings with Wayne Keaton."

"I would like to have been a fly on that wall the first time the wives got them together. Do you think they were like . . ." Jonas mimicked a female voice. "Hi, babe, I met this nice woman who is pretty awesome and would love to get together one weekend. We could meet at the marina and take one of our boats out."

Aiden laughed and took another sip of his coffee. After a moment, he said, "I talked to Addison last Wednesday."

Jonas nodded. The plan had been for Aiden to stay in contact with Addison and befriend her. That way, if Cassandra tried to include her in any foreseeable plan, they hoped to pick up on it. "How's she doing?"

"She said the second-graders are getting harder to handle with each day as they near Christmas break." Aiden paused. "She suggested that we have dinner sometime over the holidays if I wasn't busy."

Jonas made a face. "Sorry, I know you don't enjoy leading her on like that."

Aiden shrugged. "We'll see. Most times when we talk, I sort of forget all about the case. I enjoy our conversations. It's gotten a little complicated, to say the least."

Jonas leaned in closer and asked in a serious tone, "Are you falling for her?"

"Oh no. I mean, I can't. It's a job. It's just, you know—I enjoy our conversations."

Jonas nodded. "Uh-huh. You know, so far, she's done nothing to implicate she's guilty with conspiring with her sister. And she didn't accept any of Cassandra's five million."

Aiden smiled as Jonas continued to use logic to explain why he was falling for Addison. He said, "Like I said, it's complicated." He got a text message and read it to Jonas. "She's on the move."

\*\*\*

Cassandra gave her passport to the agent at security. He looked at her and back at the photo. He nodded. "Enjoy your trip. Next."

She pocketed her passport and then removed her liquids, computer, and shoes for screening. Soon she was through security in search of terminal D. She took the stairs that led to the tram and waited to board. After a short ride, she exited the tram and caught the escalator back downstairs to the correct terminal. Another sign pointed her in the direction of gate twenty-one. After arriving at the gate and reading on the board that the flight was on time, she glanced around for something to eat. She found a café and bar within viewing distance of her gate and headed in that direction. She was famished and ordered the largest breakfast on the menu.

Another hour passed, then Cassandra paid for her meal and walked over and stood in the line for first-class passengers. She was greeted warmly as she scanned her ticket and presented her passport. Then she walked down the jet breeze and boarded the plane and took seat 3A in first class. She watched as everyone boarded, looking for anyone whom she had seen recently or who looked suspicious. Nothing.

Finally, they closed the plane door, and she took a breath and tried to relax. She told herself, *I can do this.* She was going to become Savannah Sims. From here on out, she would be with Keith, and they would start fresh with their newborn son.

She listened as the flight attendant explained that the flight from Houston to Belize would take two hours and thirty minutes. Then she gave the safety demonstration.

Cassandra closed her eyes and thought of her future. She had been at a crossroads while living in Montana. She had been starting to like her new life, but every day, she had been reminded of her past with the ever-growing child inside her. The truth was she missed Keith, and she loved him. But there was this other tug on her heart, and that was Addison and Riley. If she chose this path, she would never see them again. Her old life would be dead to her.

Last night, she had awoken at 2 a.m. in a fright. She had flipped on the bedside lamp and looked around the empty room. Then her hands had gone to her full stomach. She felt a kick. Life. There was life kicking inside of her. Then she couldn't breathe. It was all coming to a head, and the one person in her life she wanted to talk to the most was her sister. It took an hour to get back to sleep, and then she awoke in a fog at 8 a.m.

The FASTEN SEAT BELT light appeared, and Cassandra bolted. She apologized as she ran to the first-class bathroom and vomited. The flight attendant was right behind her. She didn't even have a chance to close the door.

Cassandra sank to the floor. She looked up and found the kind eyes of the flight attendant, who offered her a cold washcloth. Cassandra took it and apologized.

The woman gave her a reassuring look and then replied, "We're number seven for takeoff. You got about ten minutes, but then you'll have to take a seat." She closed the door with a wink.

\*\*\*

Aiden and Jonas separately followed Cassandra through the Belize airport and out into the street, where she took a cab. For thirty minutes, they followed as the taxi led them to a busy marina. From there, they boarded the Ocean Ferry bound for Ambergris Caye, about ninety minutes away. They watched Cassandra closely and could tell she was anxious. She would sit and then she would stand and pace for ten minutes and then sit again. It was enough to make Jonas and Aiden anxious too.

Finally, the island of Ambergris Caye was in sight. They patiently waited as the ferry was secured and the door was opened for departure. From a distance, they followed Cassandra. She seemed quite clueless as she looked around. Finally, she motioned for a taxi. Aiden and Jonas quickly did the same. The whole time, there was a team watching Cassandra, so if Aiden or Jonas fell behind, they would be able to catch up with the surveillance team.

The cab drove down a road with four houses. They stopped out of sight and waited as the taxi did a U-turn and came back at a snail's pace. Finally, the cab stopped at the third house, and Cassandra got out with her luggage. The taxi drove away.

Cassandra looked down the street in both directions and then finally walked to the house that the cab had stopped in front of. She rolled her luggage to the front door and rang the bell. Soon the door opened, and a woman appeared. Demi Mullins reached out and hugged Cassandra. Then they disappeared inside the house.

Aiden looked at Jonas. "Looks like the gang's all here. Let's set up a perimeter."

***

At 6 p.m., a little party was taking place on the beach at 32 Lagoon Drive. Lobster and steak were being served, and Aiden's and Jonas's tastebuds were watering as they watched. Jonas commented, "So when it goes down, does anyone log the food?"

Aiden laughed. "Right?! We haven't eaten since breakfast."

"We should be entitled to hazard pay," Jonas joked.

Aiden picked up the binoculars and saw Keith Rose wrap Cassandra in his arms once more. They had been inseparable the last few hours. Aiden looked at his watch. They were going to move in when Demi and Isaac put their two children to bed. The amount of alcohol that had been consumed would help with the takedown. The agents just had to patiently wait and watch as they ate and drank, having themselves a merry time.

# CHAPTER 40

At 7:30 p.m., Cassandra offered to help Demi put the kids to bed. They each took a child and gave them a bath, took them to the room that they shared and tucked them in. After lots of hugs and kisses and promises of tomorrow's adventures, the women left the room and closed the door.

"They are so beautiful, Demi. Are they happy here?"

Demi smiled. "Yes. They have Mommy and Daddy time every day. Personally, I think we're starting to spoil them a little. At some point, we need to get back to an everyday routine where Isaac goes to work." She giggled. "Actually, I'm ready for Isaac to get a job or something. I miss having my own daily routine with him away at the office." She looked at Cassandra. "Is that awful?"

Cassandra gave her a quick hug. "No, not at all."

Demi took a good look at her. "You look amazing. When I was pregnant, I gained so much weight. What's your secret?"

Cassandra shrugged. "Twelve- and fourteen-hour shifts at the hospital will do it."

"Ouch, I can't imagine. Your poor feet." Demi grabbed her arm and led her to the living room. "Let's have some girl time and catch up."

They walked into the living room and took a seat. They could see the men sitting outside on the terrace smoking cigars with a bottle of whiskey on the table. Cassandra caught Keith's eye, and he smiled at her. She smiled back.

"So, tell me, was Montana horrible?"

Cassandra looked away from the men and faced Demi, who was sipping a glass of wine. "Actually, no. At first, it was hard, and then it sort of grew on me. The people were nice."

Demi placed her glass down and repositioned herself on the couch. "Are you having second thoughts?"

Cassandra quickly shook her head and looked outside again at the men. "No. I love Keith."

Demi relaxed and picked up her glass of wine again. She took a sip and then stated, "I'm not going to lie, it took me several months to forgive Isaac and learn to trust him again."

Cassandra nodded. "Do you ever ask yourself why they did it? We both had the perfect life and they just went and screwed it up."

Demi frowned. "Too many times to count. Some days are good and then there are some days where I miss my parents so deeply that I consider driving into town and calling them to just hear their voices. But of course, I can't so I don't."

Cassandra saw the sadness in her eyes and remembered that fateful day on the boat when Keith told her everything. At first, she thought they had been kidnapped when she saw Juan Diego with a gun pointed at Keith. Then Keith quickly hugged her and told her everything was okay and to trust him. He had promised to make it right, he just needed the world to think they were dead until he found a solution and they would be safe again. When the time came to run away forever, Cassandra refused to go. She needed more time, and she was worried about her sister.

"Hey, are you okay?" Demi asked in a caring voice.

Cassandra gave a small smile and then looked at the time. It was 8:30 p.m. "If you don't mind, I'm going to take a bath. It's been a very long day. Can you let Keith know and tell him to give me thirty minutes?"

Demi smiled and winked. "I will. I know how much he's missed you."

Cassandra reached out and gave her a hug. "You're a great friend, Demi. I missed you."

Demi squeezed her back, then broke away. "Me too. Now go and relax. I'll keep an eye on the men."

Cassandra stood and took one more look at Isaac and Keith, then walked toward the bedrooms.

***

Aiden saw the men on the back porch. The women and children were in the house. They weren't guaranteed a better opportunity. They moved in.

To say Keith and Isaac were shocked was an understatement. Demi was in the kitchen when another agent busted through the front door. Within thirty seconds, all were standing in total disbelief with their hands up in surrender. Aiden took great pride in seeing Isaac's expression. Demi started crying and Keith looked around for Cassandra in confusion.

Cassandra heard the commotion and waited in the bathroom. Two minutes later, she heard the kids crying, and her heart broke for them. Then the tap came, and she heard Aiden's voice. "Cassandra, are you alright?"

She slowly opened the door and looked at him. She nodded. "Is it over?" she asked in a frightened voice.

He nodded. "Yes. You can come out now."

She shook her head. "I can't face them."

Aiden consoled her by touching her shoulder. "You don't have too. We've already moved them."

"But I still hear crying."

"Yeah, about that, we could use some help there. The kids were woken up and they're scared. We've got someone on the way."

Cassandra pushed him aside and made her way to their bedroom. Jonas was holding Annabelle and trying to comfort Oliver at the same time. She walked his way and took the fourteen-month-old girl. The crying immediately stopped.

Cassandra looked at the agents. "Can't they just stay with me for the time being until we sort this out?"

Aiden said, "If only it was that easy. I'm sorry."

She frowned. "Okay, then what's next? I did call you, remember?"

Aiden remembered getting the call from Cassandra after she had boarded the flight to Belize. She had surprised everyone by changing her mind and calling them. She had been crying and upset and said she just couldn't do it. She had asked for forgiveness and said she would do anything to help.

"You'll fly back with us to Tampa in our jet. We'll have to take your statement and make everything official," Aiden explained.

"And the kids?"

"They'll stay here until someone from the Mullins family can come get them." He saw her expression and added, "Don't worry. They'll be with one of our agents at a hotel, not some city orphanage."

She relaxed. "And Demi? What about her? None of this is her fault."

Aiden interrupted. "Cassandra, for now, try to relax and think of yourself. The stress can't be good for the baby."

Instinctively, she reached for her stomach. "No. You're right. I . . . well, I knew the consequences for her when I called. I just . . . well, it's real now."

A female agent walked in, and quick introductions were made. Then Agent Whitney Shelton offered, "I can take them now."

Cassandra looked her over before releasing Annabelle. "She just needs her stuffed animal and blanket." Then she looked at the little boy. "Hey, Oliver, is there anything you need to take with you?"

He grabbed his stuffed shark. Cassandra could tell nothing made sense to him, but for the moment, he wasn't scared. She bent down and ruffled his hair. "This nice woman is going to take care of you, and I bet she'll find you pancakes in the morning. And then before you know it, you'll be with your family. Okay?"

He held his shark and nodded. She stood back up and looked at Whitney. "I can walk you out if that will help."

Whitney looked at Aiden and he nodded. Cassandra grabbed Oliver's hand, and they left the house. Once the kids were buckled in car seats in the back of an SUV, Cassandra gave each a kiss before closing the door. Soon they drove away.

*** 

Two days later, Cassandra was sitting at the FBI Tampa Field Office. She sipped water as she answered all the questions concerning her communication with Keith over the last six months. She said she had never talked to him and had only received the two packages. For now, the agents believed her.

It also helped Cassandra's cause that she hadn't touched a dime of the $5 million. She had left it in the overseas account and had only spent the money she made from her salary at Great Falls Hospital. The hardest part of the interview was admitting that she had lied about the car accident. She insisted, though, that Addison knew nothing and she had been tricked just like everyone else.

Cassandra was using her pregnancy hormones to her advantage. She claimed she wasn't thinking straight back in July when she had made some of her decisions. She now regretted them all. She was adamant that she had never known of Keith's wrongdoings until the day Juan Diego had shown up on their boat with a gun. At the time, she hadn't known he was trying to help, as she had collaborated Juan's story about Isaac helping them escape. Since that fateful day out on the water, she claimed she had been in much distress and depressed while trying to comprehend what her husband had done to her. Her main goal was to survive for the sake of her unborn child. After all, someone had paid to have her and Keith killed. She had chosen to stay behind and not run away with Keith.

At Cassandra's request, the FBI flew Addison in. She was set to arrive any minute, and they would give them some time before Cassandra was whisked back to a safe house.

Jonas got an alert that Addison had arrived. Aiden stood, opened the door, and waited. Soon Addison appeared, holding Riley's hand. She gave a slight smile before walking in.

Riley ran to Cassandra, and she scooped him up. Soon the room was filled with giggles. Addison hugged Cassandra and commented on her growing belly. Then she turned to Aiden. "Thank you for calling me."

He nodded. "I'll give you some privacy."

\*\*\*

An hour passed before Addison walked into Aiden's office. She looked around. "So, this is your office. It's nice." She walked around his desk and then looked at his credentials hung on the wall.

"Where's Riley?" Aiden asked.

She smiled and turned his way. "With Agent Parker. He likes him." Then she asked, "What's going to happen with Cassandra?"

"I'm not a hundred percent sure. The investigation is still ongoing." He saw her sad expression and added, "There are a lot of things in her favor, though. We'll just have to wait and see how things play out."

She nodded. "It was a lot for me to grasp as well. I still can't believe this whole time Keith has been alive and living in Belize."

Aiden didn't comment.

She picked up a baseball off his desk and examined it as she stated, "I'm not set to leave until tomorrow."

Aiden said, "Oh, I didn't know."

She gave him a look and then stood patiently, waiting for him to say something more. Finally, he walked over and placed a hand on her arm.

"Addison, I would very much like to take you and Riley out to dinner tonight."

She gave him a big smile. "Well, I was wondering if you were ever going to ask me."

He laughed. "Well, now I have."

She stood up on her tippy-toes and gave him a soft kiss on the lips. Then she pushed away and winked. "Thought I would just get that out of the way. Now we can enjoy a nice dinner."

He laughed. "Yes, we can. Yes, indeed we can."

Dear Reader,

I hope you enjoyed *In Plain Sight*. If you enjoyed my novel, kindly write me a review on Amazon Kindle or Goodreads. Currently, I'm working on a sequel to *Breathless*, another crime thriller set to release in 2024. I will take my readers back to Australia, where I had the opportunity to live for three years. Follow me on Facebook @ Tonya Sharp Hyche Author for more information.

Made in the USA
Columbia, SC
12 April 2025

56406748R00207